Okay, I'm a geek . . .

. . . but I confess I was a little giddy. I had no idea why someone had sent me a coded message, but whoever it was knew me well.

My B.S. is in math with a minor in history. That surprises most people. Apparently math majors are supposed to be surgically attached to their calculators and wear plastic pocket protectors. It's an irritating stereotype. Like saying blondes have more fun. I'm a blonde, and believe me, that's one old adage that simply doesn't hold true. I will say, though, that even when the hair falls short, the math comes in surprisingly handy. Take parties, for example. Whenever the conversation gets slow, I can amaze and astound the other revelers with fractals, Fibonacci numbers, and Smullyan's logic games. In those situations, I really am the life of the party.

The point is, the coded message on the thick brown paper was right up my alley. If the sender was a guy, I was already half in love.

> "Kenner's star is definitely on the ascent.
> She's not only skilled, but prolific as well."
> —Publishers Weekly

The Givenchy Code is also available as an eBook.

Also by Julie Kenner

NOBODY BUT YOU
THE SPY WHO LOVES ME

Available from Pocket Books

Enjoy!

THE
Givenchy
CODE

JULIE KENNER

doWn tOwn press

Naughty Girls

New York   London   Toronto   Sydney

An *Original* Publication of POCKET BOOKS

 DOWNTOWN PRESS, published by Pocket Books
1230 Avenue of the Americas
New York, NY 10020

Library of Congress Cataloging-in-Publication data is available.

ISBN: 0-7434-9613-2

First Downtown Press trade paperback edition June 2005

10 9 8 7 6 5 4 3 2

DOWNTOWN PRESS and colophon are
trademarks of Simon & Schuster, Inc.

Manufactured in the United States of America

Designed by Jaime Putorti

For information regarding special discounts for bulk purchases,
please contact Simon & Schuster Special Sales at
1-800-456-6798 or business@simonandschuster.com

To Lauren, who chose "Game" because she loved it. To Megan, who had to deal with a flurry of changing jpgs and did so without strangling me. To Lisa Litwack and the art department for a truly awesome cover. And to Kathleen "The Title Queen" O'Reilly—brilliant, dahling, just brilliant. Air kisses, chocolate, and venti nonfat lattes to you all!

acknowledgments

The author extends profuse and profound thanks to all of the wonderful people (especially my New York pals) who generously offered to answer odd questions about locations and codes and math. You all know who you are, and I'm in your debt!

Chapter 1

This was not my day.

First of all, it was drizzling. Which would have been just fine if I'd been curled up on my couch watching *Sex and the City* or *Desperate Housewives* reruns. Or buying shoes on eBay. Or even working on my thesis.

But I wasn't doing any of those things. Instead, I was being yanked down East 86th Street by six furballs eager to reach the dog run at Carl Shurz park. So far, both Poopsie (aptly named) and Precious (definitely *not* aptly named) had left little steaming presents on the sidewalk for me to retrieve with the plastic grocery bags I'd shoved into my raincoat pocket before leaving the Kirkguard Towers.

Second of all, immediately after depositing steaming package number two in a cheerfully labeled Keep Our City Clean! trash can, I ran smack into my ex, Todd. Or rather, little Daisy,

Mrs. Oppenmeir's Lhasa apso, ran smack into Todd. I managed to skirt gingerly to the right, avoiding him but hopelessly tangling him in six leashes.

"For God's sake, Melanie," he said. "What the hell are you doing?"

Now, see, that's one of the reasons Todd and I broke up. I mean, how hard is it to remember that I prefer "Mel" and hate "Melanie"? And, frankly, it was perfectly obvious what I was doing. I really didn't need to be reminded. "I'm maxing out my credit for Manolos, Todd." I shook the handful of leashes at him. "What the hell does it look like I'm doing?"

"What happened to the job with Josh?" Unperturbed by my annoyance, he looked up at me from a bent-over position, talking even as he struggled to loosen the ever-tightening leash-noose. Part of me was tempted to plant the heel of my left Prada sneaker on his gluteus maximus and give a little shove. But that would have upset the dogs, so I managed to stifle the urge.

"It didn't work out," I said stiffly. Right after we'd broken up, I'd become a victim of university budget cuts and had lost my not-so-lucrative-but-still-handy-for-rent job as a teaching assistant. In what I'm sure Todd had considered a supreme act of chivalry by the male exiting stage left in my life, he'd arranged for me to get a flex-time receptionist job at a tiny little public relations firm on Madison Avenue. What Todd had neglected to mention was that his friend Josh was a prick who, when he hadn't been talking about my tits, had filled in the conversational blanks with comments about my ass. The man clearly wasn't acquainted with Title VII, and I didn't intend to be the one who introduced him.

"You could have called and told me," Todd said, picking

Daisy up and lifting her over a crisscross of nylon leashes. He shot me a look that could have been recrimination or a request for assistance. Not sure, I just stood there and shrugged.

Once I'd discovered Josh's more endearing qualities, I wasn't about to call Todd. For one, we'd been quite broken up by then (if we hadn't been, introducing me to Josh would have been grounds, that's for sure). For another, I like to fight my own battles. So I'd called Josh a chauvinistic, Neanderthal prick, and then I'd quit. (Unfortunately, the name-calling was all in my head, but it had made me feel better.) Then I'd fallen back on my old standby of answering ads posted in the student newsletter or on the bulletin board in the grad student lounge.

I've used this method to earn extra cash on and off since my first day on the NYU campus as a wide-eyed and innocent freshman from Texas. The results have never been fabulous, but the experience has certainly been varied. In addition to the wonderful world of pet care, I've also worked as a short-order cook, a Circle Line ticket agent, and a cocktail waitress at a restaurant with food so horrible it went out of business a mere five days after it opened. To mention just a few.

Todd always looked askance at my revolving-door job situation, but so far I haven't minded (well, the dog thing *is* a bit much). With an undergraduate degree in math and a master's (soon!) in history, I figure I'm going to be spending the rest of my life behind a podium trying to get teenagers to listen to me upon threat of failing their midterms. Either that, or I'm going to be perpetually in academia, taking the degree train to Ph.D.-ville and then settling down to an assistant professorship while I try to think of something brilliant to publish so that I can snag tenure.

With all that to look forward to, is it any wonder I like a little variety in my life? Or at least that's what I told myself when I slogged outside this morning, ready, able, but not entirely willing to escort a group of little poop machines on their morning constitutional.

The sad truth is that I flat-out need the money. I'll do (almost) anything to make the rent on the tiny one bedroom I share with my roommate, Jennifer. Each month, I barely squeak by. Yet somehow, I have enough left over for shoes, cocktails, Starbucks, and food. (Yes, in that order.) Tuition, thankfully, is covered by scholarships and grants.

Beside me, Todd finally managed to extricate himself from the web of leashes, and the dogs were straining, their collars pulling tight around their little necks as they whined for the park. All except Gomer, who looked poised to produce another package. I winced. That's it for me. No more dog-walking. Even the adorable pair of hot pink Jimmy Choo wedge sandals I saw online at designerexposure.com aren't worth the indignity. Not until they're marked down by at least 20 percent, anyway.

"Well," I said brightly, tugging on Gomer's leash in the hopes of distracting him. "You probably have somewhere you have to be."

"I took the day off," he said. "I've got nowhere to be."

A finger of worry snaked up my back as I squinted at him. "Did you come here looking for me?" A stupid question, really, since what are the odds I'd just happened to bump into him? I'm a math geek. Trust me. The odds aren't good.

At least he had the good grace to look sheepish. "I called your apartment. Jennifer said you might be here, and since I wanted to talk to you . . ." He trailed off, flashing that endearing little smile that always got me in trouble.

I fisted my hands around the leashes and mentally dug in my heels. *No, no, no.* I did *not* want to date Todd Davidson again. But more than that, I didn't want him to broach the subject. If he asked me out, I knew I'd say yes. It's stupid, but it's my nature. Ask me to discuss Euclidean domains or couture shoes, and I'm all over it. But put me in a room with a man, and my fortitude dissolves. Sad, but so very true.

He rummaged in his shopping bag and brought out a brightly wrapped shoe box topped with a big pink bow. "I saw these and thought of you." He passed me the box, and I took it, exchanging my leashes for my present as my heart raced. "Go ahead," he said. "Open it."

I didn't. Opening it would be like tempting fate, sealing a pact in blood. Silently telling him that this was okay and that there was still a chance things could be good between us.

"Come on, Mel. It's a present, not a time bomb."

I could never resist him when he remembered to call me Mel. For that matter, I never could resist a pair of shoes. . . .

I used the tip of my forefinger to ease the lid off the box until I could peek inside. I saw just a hint of red, and then. . . . OHMYGOD!

"Givenchy?" I kept a tight hold on the box as I flung my arms around him. "You bought me a pair of Givenchy pumps?" I lust after all shoes (and handbags for that matter), but in my mind, Givenchy represents the pinnacle of fashion. Givenchy *is* couture. After all, back in the day, Hubert de Givenchy designed practically all of Audrey Hepburn's clothes and costumes. If that's not the most amazing endorsement, I don't know what is.

Audrey may have had breakfast at Tiffany's, but I have

breakfast, lunch and dinner at Givenchy. I'll happily go out of my way to pass by 63rd and Madison, just so I can get one more look at the window display. Someday, I'm going to walk into that store and actually buy something. Until that happy day, though, I'm going to have to settle for acquiring my prizes through eBay and various online designer outlets. And, it seems, gifts from my ex.

"Put them on."

"Are you nuts? It's drizzling."

He leaned in closer, then popped an umbrella open over our heads. How suave. "At least take a closer look. See if you like them."

He didn't have to ask me twice. I slipped my hand inside the box and stroked the smooth red leather that would, soon, cup my foot. *Heaven.* (And probably a little pathetic, but we all have our weaknesses. Mine, like my mother before me, is shoes.)

"How are they?" he asked. From the way the corner of his mouth twitched, I think he knew the answer.

My mouth itched to say *orgasmic,* but I bit back the urge. Fabulous shoes or not, Todd was still my ex . . . and I'm pretty sure that's all I wanted him to be.

"Fabulous," I said instead. "They're really great. Thank you. This is really sweet."

"You're not going to go all Emily Post on me and say you can't accept them?"

"Are you nuts?" I clutched the box tightly against my chest. "Of course I'm accepting them."

He laughed. "That's my Mel." Only, of course, I wasn't his Mel any longer. He cleared his throat. "So, um, I thought maybe we could go out later. Get a drink or something."

Aha! The other shoe drops.

How pathetic did he think I was that I'd go with him just because he'd brought me a pair of shoes? I opened my mouth to tell him off, then heard myself say, "My parents are in town for their anniversary weekend. They're doing the whole Broadway thing, and I'm supposed to meet them for dinner before the show." Hardly the resounding no I'd been aiming for. But it was true. They'd been in town for almost a full twenty-four hours, and so far our schedules just hadn't collided. Or, more accurately, my mother hadn't managed to carve out a slot for me before this evening. Since I was dying to see my dad, I really didn't want to bag.

"How about now, then? It's still early," he said in his best I'm-a-lawyer-and-argue-for-a-living voice. "Plenty of time for a martini with me and dinner with them."

I knew I should just nip this in the bud and tell him we weren't having drinks, parents or no parents. Instead, I let him down gently. "I have to finish with the dogs, and then Jennifer and I are going shopping. Besides, it's too early for drinks."

"Coffee, then. Jennifer will understand."

Actually, no, she wouldn't. Being my best friend, Jennifer would strap me to the refrigerator if I told her I was about to go out with Todd, the man who'd been the subject of so many late-night bitch sessions. At least I thought she would. I could be wrong about that. She had told the man where to find me, after all.

"I promised her," I said. That was more or less the truth. When we'd first moved in together, Jenn and I had promised that we would never ditch plans with each other just because some guy asked us out. There were a variety of exceptions to this rule—the guy resembled Johnny Depp, the guy *was* Johnny Depp, the guy had an employee discount at Bergdorf's—but Todd didn't fall within any exception.

"You're certain? What about another time?"

I opened my mouth, hoping some clever excuse would leap to mind. Nothing. In lieu of cleverness, I just waved the leashes and said I had to get on with it before the dogs mutinied.

"I'll come with you."

"Oh. Well, okay. Sure." I figured it was only polite. The guy had bought me *shoes,* after all. Besides, I was standing there in the drizzle with drenched dogs and not feeling altogether attractive. Maybe Todd was the best I could do. Maybe no one else in my whole life would go out of his way to buy me shoes.

More likely, I'm a wimp. And Todd knows how to push my buttons.

We started walking toward the park and, when we were about halfway there, he reached out, his pinkie brushing against my thumb. "I've missed you, Mel."

Oh, *man.* I should have melted at that. His tone was sincere, his expression penitent. Gifts. Soft words. The man really, truly wanted me back. And I was flattered as hell and even a little bit humbled.

What I wasn't, was interested. Which made for a rather awkward moment. The moment stretched out, finally bursting when we reached the dog run and I set the dogs free. Thank God.

I cleared my throat. "Listen, Todd—"

He held up a hand. "Just a drink. If you can't do tonight, then tomorrow." He flashed the same smile that had gotten me into his bed about fifteen months ago. "Come on, Mel. No pressure. Just alcohol."

"With us, there's no such thing as just alcohol," I said.

His grin reflected all the nights that proved my point, and I felt my resolve waver. My phone rang, and I snatched it open, grateful for the interruption. My mom. "Hi, Mom. I was just talking to a friend about meeting you guys tonight."

"Well, I hope it won't inconvenience you if we take a rain check for tomorrow." A statement, not a question, with no room for argument on my part.

"Oh." I licked my lips. "I was really hoping to see Daddy. And you."

She didn't even bother to muffle her sigh of exasperation. "For goodness' sake, Melanie. Whose vacation is this? It turns out that one of your father's old classmates lives on Long Island, and he's going to join us for dinner before the theater. Surely you wouldn't want us to miss the chance to get reacquainted with an old friend?"

Ever think about getting reacquainted with your only daughter? I wanted to say it. I really, really wanted to say it.

Instead, I said, "Sure, Mom." I plastered on a bright smile. Shrinks everywhere said that if you smiled even though you were depressed or angry, your mood would shift to match your expression. I waited a beat, testing that theory. Nope. No change.

"Good."

"So, um, what time tomorrow?"

"Good Lord, child, I don't know. We'll call you after we get up. Really, I don't know how you ever became so regimental."

"Me neither," I said, picturing the rows and rows of calen-

dars in our Houston house, each entry color coded to corre-
spond with some society function my mom had going on at any
particular moment.

"Well, that's that, then. We love you, sweetie."

Since I hadn't thrown a fit and messed up her plans, suddenly I was golden again. "Love you, too, Mom."

And the truth was, I did.

But she still drove me absolutely fucking nuts.

Todd reached out and took my hand. "*My* invitation still
stands."

Bless the man. He'd soothed me through many a parental
rough spot during the time we'd been together, so I was quite
sure he'd comprehended the entire conversation even though
he'd only heard my half.

"Thanks," I said.

"So you'll come?" His grin broadened, both devilish and
inviting, and suddenly the reasons we'd gotten together were
much more prominent in my mind than the reasons we'd broken up. I was weakening, and I knew it. I grabbed hold of the
metal fencing that marked the dog run.

"I just don't think—"

"Melanie Lynn Prescott?"

Saved by a stranger. I whirled around to face the voice behind me, then gasped and took a step backward. Todd's hand
closed on my shoulder, and I didn't shrug it off.

Books always describe men as dark and dangerous, and now
I know what that means. The man standing in front of me was
positively gorgeous in a way that made me want to touch him
and run from him, all at the same time. Total eye candy, with
coal black hair and a movie star jawline.

I almost moaned—okay, maybe I *did* moan—but I stifled the sound quickly enough. Swallowed it, actually, and then was even more grateful for Todd's hand on my shoulder. There was something about the stranger's eyes. They seemed cruel and hollow and, without any reason at all, they scared me to death.

"You *are* Miss Prescott?" he said.

"Oh, yes, me, right." The man's voice was like honey. If it hadn't been for those eyes . . .

"And who are you?" That from Todd, still behind me.

"I have a delivery for you," Mystery Man said, ignoring Todd. He took a step toward me, then held out a manila envelope.

"What is it?" I asked.

He smiled, but the gesture didn't seem to fit his face. "I couldn't say. I'd suggest you open it." He touched a finger to his brow as if tipping an imaginary hat, then turned and walked away, leaving me holding the envelope and feeling more than a little perplexed.

I frowned, my brow crinkling in a manner that really isn't my best look. Too curious to wait until I got back home, I slipped a finger under the flap and ripped the envelope open. Inside was a thick piece of brown paper that looked like it had been torn from a grocery bag. I pulled it free and immediately saw the markings. *Totally cool.*

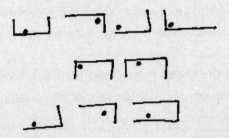

***

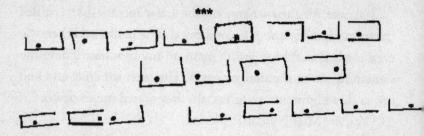

Okay, I'm a geek, but I confess I was a little giddy. I had no idea why someone had sent me a coded message, but whoever it was knew me well. My B.S. is in math with a minor in history. That surprises most people. Apparently math majors are supposed to be surgically attached to their calculators and wear plastic pocket protectors. It's an irritating stereotype. Like saying blondes have more fun. I'm a blonde, and believe me, that's one old adage that simply doesn't hold true. (I will say, though, that even when the hair falls short, the math comes in surprisingly handy. Take parties, for example. Whenever the conversation gets slow, I can amaze and astound the other revelers with fractals, Fibonacci numbers and Smullyan's logic games. In those situations, I really am the life of the party.)

Now that I'm working on my master's, I've switched the focus to history. My thesis is on the derivation and primary characteristics of codes and ciphers used by prevailing nations during wartime. (And yes, I realize that's *way* too broad. I've already had that conversation with my advisor, thank you very much.)

The point is, the coded message on the thick brown paper really was right up my alley. If the sender was a guy, I was already half in love.

"Somebody knows you well, Mata Hari," Todd said, referring to his pet name for me. He'd latched onto it after our first date, when he'd learned about my fascination with the Enigma machine, along with my rampant lust for all things footwear. I'd told him I'd rather be Sydney Bristow, but he'd never taken the hint.

Todd took the sheet from my hand and turned it over, examining it. "So who's it from?"

I examined the envelope for a return address. Nothing. "No idea. Weird, huh?" And it really *was* weird, no doubt about that. But something about the whole situation—the messenger, the coded message—seemed oddly familiar.

"Probably an invitation to a party. Like a Mensa thing. If you're clever enough to break the code, then you get the address. I bet Warren sent it. That's right up his alley, isn't it?"

I shrugged. "Maybe." Warren is both a character and my sometimes study buddy. Less so now that I've moved to the history department and he's working on his master's in mechanical engineering. Or he says he is. Sometimes I think all Warren does is sit in his apartment, listen to obscure music by bands I've never heard of and work his puzzles. "His thing is crosswords and anagrams," I said. "He was never really into codes."

"So it's someone else. Or he sent it to amuse you. Or maybe it's from some super secret spy agency and they're trying to recruit you. If you figure it out in time, you're in the agency and they'll pack you on a plane for your first mission."

I shot him a *Drop it* look. Todd is one of the few people who knows I secretly lust after a cool job doing cryptology on a day-to-day basis. But those jobs are few and far between. I've printed out the job applications for the NSA on more than one occasion, but I always seem to toss them without filling them in. It all seems so unlikely. I mean, I'm about as average as they come, and I couldn't really see me doing code-breaking for the government, even as much as I'd like to. And the thought of applying and getting rejected was downright depressing. Most likely, I'll end up teaching history to seventh graders. Oh, the joy.

"Well, I'm sticking with my invitation theory. One of your friends is having a party. And knowing you, you'll get to the bash years before anyone else."

"Thanks," I answered, looking at him with a new respect. He'd never much complimented my brains, being much more interested in the softer, rounder parts of my body. So it was a welcome surprise to learn that maybe he'd seen more in me than I'd given him credit for.

"So tonight, then?"

I nodded. Why not? He'd bought me shoes, he'd complimented my brain, and now he wanted to buy me a drink. If I didn't already know he was all wrong, I'd say he was the perfect man.

"Great." He snatched the envelope and code from my hand.

"Hey!"

"Collateral," he said with a mischievous grin. "Just so you don't change your mind and back out of our date. Come by around six."

"Todd, don't you dare . . ." But he was already gone, waving at me as he headed back the way we'd come. And what could I do? I was stuck there with the dogs, and he knew it. By the time I gathered them up, he'd be long gone.

Sometimes that man could be so infuriating.

I was still fuming when I realized the rain had stopped. I

checked the dogs, quickly seeing that they were a little muddier around the paws than I would have liked, but that was okay.

Actually, right then, pretty much everything was okay despite Todd's ridiculous posturing. I'd received an entirely cool encrypted message that might be from a secret admirer. (I can dream.) I now owned a stunning pair of this season's Givenchy shoes. And to top it off, the sun was beginning to peek out past the gray wisps of cloud fluff.

No doubt about it, the gods were smiling on me. Today, at least, I ranked as one of the chosen few.

And you know what? That felt pretty damn good.

"**D**on't kill me," Jennifer said the second I walked into the apartment. She was on the couch, wearing my favorite pair of Seven jeans and a darling Tahari top that I'd had my eye on for weeks. The *Post* was on the cushion beside her, open to "Page Six."

"For borrowing my jeans or for Todd?"

"Both," she said. She moved the paper to the coffee table and gave me her full attention. "So what happened with him? He was desperate, and he said he had something for you, or I wouldn't have told him." She held up her little finger in a symbolic pinkie swear. "So what was it, anyway?"

"Guess."

"Your denim D&G jacket?"

"No, and thank you very much for reminding me." I'd lost my favorite jacket months ago.

"Well, what?"

I held up the shoe box. "Ta-da!"

"Givenchy!" she cried, ripping the lid off the box. "Oh, Mel! They're beautiful."

"I know!" I said, still giddy. "And it's quit raining, so I can wear them. We're still going shopping, right?"

"Sure. Are we looking or buying?"

"A little bit of both, I think." My checking account was in dire need of life support, but if I ate ramen for the next two weeks and kept the dog-walking gig for the month, I could swing a new pair of jeans. And I might even lose a few pounds, too!

"So you forgive me?"

"I haven't decided," I said. I moved closer to get a better look at her blouse. "Is that the Tahari we saw at Bloomingdale's?"

Her fingers went up to graze the collar protectively. "Um, yeah. I grabbed it yesterday before work."

"It would look totally cute on me, don't you think?"

Her eyes narrowed. "You wouldn't."

"I would."

"Come on, Mel. Not my Tahari."

"Jenn! You revealed information about my whereabouts to my *ex*. I think you're getting off easy."

"You're such a bitch. But in the nicest possible way, of course."

I laughed. "Not forever. Just let me wear it today. You can still borrow the jeans. I only want the top. It'll look totally awesome with the shoes, don't you think?"

"True." She nodded, then peeled off the top. That's why we're such good friends. We both understand the important things.

She abandoned her place on the couch to go find a new shirt, and I sat down in front of the coffee table and started to untie my sneakers. Cindy Adams's column caught my eye, and I skimmed the day's gossip. Nothing too scintillating, but I have to say I love the *Post*. I skimmed the important stuff first—the gossip—then flipped back to the first page. The headline was huge—"Byte King Bites the Dust at 34"—and, in typical *Post* fashion, was splashed across the entire front page, the article taking up most of the leftover space.

> A memorial service was held yesterday for computer mogul Archibald Grimaldi at the New York office of PSW, Inc. The world-renowned computer genius made his millions writing computer code, but he made his name by applying that code to the Internet gaming community over a decade ago in a way that made multiplayer online games accessible to anyone with a computer, a modem, and a desire to play. As the popularity of such games grew, so did Grimaldi's wealth.

> His most popular game, Play.Survive.Win, has more than 3 million registered users worldwide. All players complete a detailed User Profile, which the game's operating system then utilizes to select the role to which the player will initially be assigned (Target, Assassin, or Protector), and to craft the clues which the Target must interpret in order to survive, rendering each game uniquely personal to the players involved.

> Another innovative attribute of PSW is the

cash prizes awarded to the winning players, the amount of which varies, depending on the number of players online at any particular time.

According to reliable sources within the PSW corporate structure, a new version of the popular game is currently undergoing beta testing.

I skimmed the rest of the article, which contained the usual stuff about Grimaldi's life leading up to his untimely death in a boating accident. He started out destitute, an abused child who'd grown up in foster homes. He'd run away at fifteen, he'd never gone to college, and by twenty he'd been hot and heavy in the computer industry, doing okay moneywise, but then he'd invented PSW, and it had rocked the online gaming world. Not long after, he'd become a billionaire several times over.

And here I was struggling to make my rent. I needed to seriously reconsider my chosen career path.

"Did you see this?" I asked as Jenn came back in the room. I passed her the paper, pointing to the lead article. She'd traded the Tahari for Juicy Couture and looked hot. Jenn has green eyes and coal black hair that falls perfectly into place even after she's slept on it. She's as tall as I am, and we're both a size eight, which means we each have double the wardrobe, since we can share everything.

But whereas I'm convinced I look like a gangly colt, Jenn resembles a graceful cat. She's so striking that she could be a model, but she's actually a singer. Well, a singing waitress, anyway. But she's got the most amazing voice, and I'm totally convinced that she'll be on Broadway one of these days. Actually, I suppose she technically *is* on Broadway, since she works at Ellen's Stardust Diner, a really loud, totally cheeseball restaurant at Broadway and 51st. All the waiters and waitresses have pipes to die for, and the milk shakes are just as awesome. The place is a total tourist trap, but it's also a lot of fun. Just being there makes me want to belt one out, and I've got the worst voice on the planet.

Jenn finished scanning the article and looked up. "How freaky. Didn't I play this once or twice?"

"Years ago. We both did, remember?" Back when PSW was brand-new, I'd logged in and played for weeks before getting bored with it. I'd played every role and aced them all. Grimaldi had even sent me a congratulatory email. Of course, that had been back when Grimaldi had just been rich, before he'd become Rich. Or, rather, Obscenely Rich.

Before the game had paled for me, I'd even convinced Jenn to try. She'd played one game, been killed off quickly and had decided it wasn't her thing. Jenn's idea of fun and fast is fighting over a $75 Miu Miu blouse at a sample sale. Frankly, I'm in total agreement.

"Hmm." She tossed the paper aside and looked me up and down. "So you've got the top and the shoes. What are you doing about pants? Or are you going with a skirt?"

I pulled my Gap T-shirt over my head as I considered the problem. "My black Diesel jeans?" I suggested as I grabbed the Tahari.

"Perfect. Now get changed and let's get out of here. I've got to be at the airport by seven-thirty." She checked her watch. "That only leaves us about seven hours to shop before I have to book."

Chapter

3

>>>http://www.playsurvivewin.com<<<

PLAY.SURVIVE.WIN

PLEASE LOGIN
PLAYER USER NAME: *SemperFi*
PLAYER PASSWORD: ********

> *. . . please wait*
> *. . . please wait*
> *. . . please wait*
> *>>>Password approved<<<*

>>>Read New Messages<<< >>>Create New Messages<<<

. . . please wait

WELCOME TO MESSAGE CENTER

You have one new message.

New Message:

To: SemperFi

From: Identity Blocked

Subject: Funding

Advance payment deposited your account, 09:00 hours. Amount: $20,000.

Client name: Melanie Lynn Prescott. Additional funds to be delivered upon successful completion of mission.

Game commences: 12:01 a.m.

Good luck.

>>>Player Profile Attached: MLP_Profile.doc<<<

>>>Click to Download<<<

Matthew Stryker read the message four times, but each time it stayed exactly the same. *It was starting again.*

He'd been drinking beer and eating leftover lasagna when he'd logged on, and now the food roiled in his stomach, threatening to come right back up. He stumbled to the kitchen sink and twisted the tap, letting the cold water flow. He stuck his head down and drank straight from the faucet, then tilted his head and let the stream pummel his face.

The blast of cold water got his mind off his stomach, so that was a plus. But nothing he did could make the real problem go away.

He thought of Jamie Tate, dead on the floor in a pool of her own blood. Because of him. Because he hadn't believed.

His gut clenched again, and he pressed the back of his wrist to his mouth until the nausea passed. Then, with his hands still clutching the Formica countertop, he turned his head just enough so that his laptop came into view, the blue screen seeming both ominous and uniquely important. Something that compelled and commanded him.

This time, Stryker knew, he would obey.

With trepidation, he approached the machine, like a hunter stalking a wild and dangerous beast. He bent down and put his finger on the trackball, then maneuvered over until he could click on the attachment: *MLP_Profile.doc*. He held his breath and clicked.

The computer hummed, then a Microsoft Word file opened. Innocuous enough, the document could easily have been a résumé. Name, address, phone. Educational background. Hobbies. A photo, too. A striking girl standing in front of a cage, a lion stalking in the background. The sun had caught her hair just right, and it sparkled like spun gold, vivid even on his computer screen. She was tall and poised and looked straight at the camera, her smile reflecting both confidence and joy.

Whenever that picture had been taken, it had been a good day.

Stryker focused on the name at the top of the page: Melanie Lynn Prescott. He rubbed his temples, the headache returning with full force. For Melanie Lynn, he knew, the good days were fast coming to a close.

"You're next, Melanie," he whispered. "And God help us both."

Chapter

4

"**W**ant to grab a cocktail next?" Jenn asked. We were in Bloomingdale's, perched on stools in front of the MAC Studio counter.

I made what I hoped was an affirmative sound—I couldn't actually speak because the salesgirl had her hand on my face and was concentrating on lining my lips with MAC's latest variation of burgundy liner.

So far, we'd been shopping for almost four hours. We'd started on Fifth Avenue, window-shopping our way past Tiffany's, Gucci and the like. Then we'd backtracked to 57th and headed east, rehashing the whole Todd situation as we walked—"I know you have to go there tonight to get the message, but do *not* sleep with him!"

Since I had absolutely no intention of sleeping with my ex, we'd run through that line of conversation pretty quickly, and we'd moved on to other important topics: the new waiter at Stardust that Jenn thought was cute, my prospects (or lack thereof) in the dating world, whether we had any chance in hell of finding a pair of Manolos on eBay for less than a hundred and fifty. We'd had a moment of reverential silence in front of Prada, then we'd continued our chatter all the way into Borders at 57th and Park, where we'd both bought lattes at the second-floor café (our first purchases of the day) before heading back outside.

By that time, my Visa had been itching to be used, and we'd headed to Bloomie's. I'd planned to head straight up to the second floor to see if they were having a sale on Juicy Couture, but Jenn needed some new blush for the trip, so we'd gotten way-laid on the first floor in makeup. When the MAC girl had offered me a quick mini-makeover, I hadn't been able to say no.

"You're not getting this because of Todd, are you?" Jenn asked suspiciously.

I turned my head as much as the girl, who'd moved on to my cheeks, would allow. "Are you nuts? I broke up with him, remember?"

"*I* know you broke up. I'm just hoping you remember *why* you broke up. He obviously wants you back."

I frowned and was immediately chastised by the woman for moving too much. So I sat stone-faced and considered Jenn's theory. Todd probably did want me back (which I'll admit was nice for my ego). After all, he'd gone to great lengths to find me earlier and to get me to his apartment tonight. But the feeling wasn't mutual. I'd done the right thing breaking up with him, and I had no desire to go back. Except to get my message, of course.

The girl finished my makeover and passed me a mirror. I have to say, I looked amazing. I'm no slouch at putting on makeup, but this girl had made me look like a model, all air-brushed and perfect. My eyes, under the benefit of skillfully applied mascara, eyeliner and shadow, appeared huge and more blue than usual. My cheekbones seemed high and aristocratic. And my lips . . . well, they looked pouty and kissable.

In short, I looked fantastic. And I had absolutely no one to show myself off to. Except Todd. Well, damn.

Always an optimist, I bought the whole lot of products she'd used—doing serious damage to my credit card in the process. I'd have other dates, after all. And with practice, I'd learn how to put the makeup on just as perfectly as she'd done. At the very least, I'd come close.

We made a quick run through the second floor, where Jenn talked herself out of a hot pink Betsey Johnson skirt. Jenn's willpower can be very impressive at times. Instead, we headed to the eighth floor, and she bought a stuffed bear for her soon-to-be-born niece. After that, we meandered back to the first floor and the men's department, then headed out the exit at Lexington and 60th.

The summer heat hit me like a wall, and I realized that Bloomie's icy air-conditioning must have frozen my brain. "No cocktails," I said. "The idea is great but I'm going to Todd's. I need to be sober."

"Say no more." Jenn looked around, sizing up our location, then pointed east. "We'll go to Serendipity," she announced. "You're spending the evening with an ex; you need chocolate."

Tucked into an old brownstone a few blocks from Bloomingdale's, Serendipity is a popular ice cream parlor/restaurant that's a favorite first-date location. It's past the point of trendy, having moved on to touristy, but I still love it, despite the inevitable thirty-minute wait for a table. Actually, I love the frozen hot chocolates, and as soon as Jenn and I were settled at one of the old-fashioned soda-shop-style tables, we ordered two. Since each one comes in a bowl large enough to feed a small nation, I'll admit to a certain level of gluttony. But I'd gone to the gym before walking the dogs, so I had caloric equity in my personal portfolio.

Besides, this was my lunch. And my dinner, too, unless I got lucky and Todd had food in his apartment.

"So how long are you going to be gone?" I asked after I'd made a significant dent in my lunch/dessert/whatever.

"Two weeks. They're inducing tomorrow, and I'm going to be there for that. Then I'm going to help Lisa with the baby until my mom flies out. We'll overlap for a few days, and then she's going to stay on a full month. After Mom, Katie's going to come stay for another two weeks," Jenn added, referring to her other sister. "After that, Jake's going to take paternity leave when Lisa goes back to work."

"You're going to have so much fun," I said. "In a crying-baby-tired-family kind of way, I mean."

"I know," she said with a grin. "I can't wait."

I believed her, too. Chances were she'd be stuck in the house with an exhausted sister and a crying baby, and then later a doting first-time grandmother. It would be chaos, and I totally envied her. Not only am I an only child, but I also figure that if I ever have a kid, my mom will send a gift certificate for Nannys "R" Us. Not the maternal type, my mom.

Jenn rummaged in her bags, then pulled out a sales receipt.

She scribbled a number on it, then passed it to me. "My sister's house," she said. "In case there's no cell service. Call if you want to talk after you see Todd. Or if you need anything at all."

I nodded, dutifully tucking the number in my back pocket. But I knew I wouldn't call. We'd already rehashed the Todd situation; and since I wasn't going to sleep with him, nothing was going to change on that front.

And I couldn't think of anything else that would be so important that I'd have to interrupt my best friend while her sister was having a baby. My life just wasn't that dramatic.

Chapter 5

Todd's studio apartment isn't too far from Bloomie's, so when Jenn headed for the subway, I caught a cab to 72nd and York. Todd buzzed me in, and I headed on up. Two minutes later I was in his apartment, the heavenly smell of curry, rogan josh and nan surrounding me and making my stomach rumble.

"I figured you'd want to stay in," Todd said. "So you could work on your message."

"Either that or you were afraid that if you didn't feed me I'd just grab the envelope and leave."

"That too," he said, and I had to smile. At least he was honest.

Besides, I was there and hungry, the spicy scents only making me more so. If I'd gone home, I'd only have gone back to an empty apartment. I might as well stay there. Todd might not be able to cook worth a damn, but he orders the best takeout of anyone I know. And Indian food is my absolute favorite.

"So where is it?" I asked.

He nodded toward his futon couch, which doubled as a bed. My envelope was right there, on the side with the reading lamp. On the coffee table in front, he'd put out a couple of plates and opened all the takeout boxes. He'd even poured a glass of wine. If the man was trying to win me back, he was on the right track.

"I ordered extra nan," he said, and I swear I almost kissed him. I adore the pitalike bread and always eat way more than an Atkins-friendly portion.

Todd and I settled in at the couch, and after I'd heaped my plate full, I slipped the message out of the envelope, studying it as I chowed down. To be honest, I could tell right away this wasn't going to take a lot of effort, and I experienced a sudden dissipation of respect for my secret admirer, rather akin to the flushing of a toilet. *Whoosh!* All that esteem just went spiraling down into oblivion. I mean, really. You'd think someone willing to encrypt a secret message or fantabulous invitation could have come up with something at least a *little* challenging.

"So what *is* that thing, anyway?" Todd asked, resting a hand on my thigh as he leaned closer. I didn't shrug it off; in fact, it felt kind of nice. Not sparks—the only sparks I'd ever had with Todd had been generated between the sheets—but comfortable. I'd been W.B. (without boyfriend) for over six months now, and I could feel my soul yearning to slide back into the familiar cocoon of coupledom. Where relationships are concerned, I'm weak and pathetic. I know this, but we all have our crosses to bear.

I concentrated on his question, trying to ignore his breath against my ear. "It's a pigpen code," I said.

"Of course it is." The hand lifted, and I took a breath. "Want to tell me what that means?"

I was already making notes with a felt tip on the Styrofoam container the curry came in, trying to work out exactly how this cipher was constructed. "Fences," I said. "See how each letter is like a little box?" I drew a basic pigpen.

ABCD EFGH IJKL

MNOP QRST UVWX

YZ12 3456 7890

"The letters are 'fenced,' and so that's how the code got its name."

"Uh-huh," he said, clearly not following.

"Trust me, it's cool. Confederate soldiers used codes like these during the Civil War. Just give me a sec to work it out. . . ." I tapped the pen against my teeth, thinking. I could tell from the placement of the dots within each "fence" of the message that I was dealing with a four-character pigpen, which is what I'd drawn for Todd. But I'd plugged in a few letters and come up with gibberish.

I took another bite of sag paneer as I pondered what to try next. Was I dealing with a code in a code? Or maybe I'd drawn the wrong key. Maybe this key ran vertical instead of horizontal? I tried that, creating my decryption device by writing the alphabet and first ten digits down instead of across, so that I had A, B, C where before I had had A, M, Y. Still pretty simplistic. Would it work?

Three minutes later I had my answer. It worked like a charm . . . and I didn't like the result. Not one little bit.

"What kind of a sick son of a bitch would send me a coded message like *that?*" I stood up and circled the table, and now I was standing facing Todd and pointing down at the table with an accusing finger. I'd written the decoded message across the pastel pink takeout menu:

PLAY

OR

DIE

***

PRESTIGE

PARK

39A 89225

"What do you think it means?" Todd asked.

"I don't *care,*" I said. And I didn't. I don't like scary movies, I don't like surprise parties, and I certainly didn't like strange, creepy messages . . . no matter how tall, dark and handsome the messenger might have been.

"It's probably from someone in your study group," Todd said. His voice was low, meant to soothe. Wasn't working.

"Well, screw them," I said, still fighting goose bumps. Play or *die???* What kind of a freak sends a message like that?

"Just forget about it," Todd said, getting up and coming around to me. He leaned over and grabbed the coded message off the table, crumpling it in one hand even as he pulled me closer. "Whoever sent it isn't even worth thinking about."

"But—"

"Just." He tossed the balled-up paper into the trash can. "Forget." He pulled me closer and nuzzled my neck. "About it." He snaked his hand up between my breasts, then managed (I'm not entirely sure how) to twist me around in his arms until I was facing him, and his lips were on mine, and I have to admit it felt really good.

There was something so freeing about doing exactly what he said. At the moment, he was saying that I should go with him to bed. Not in words, mind you. But in that language that we all speak. That language that doesn't have a word for *stop* or *slow down* or *this may not be the best idea right now.*

His lips slipped over mine, comforting and familiar, and as his wide palms stroked my back, I merrily beat my doubts into submission. I might have told Jenn that there was no way I'd sleep with Todd again, but right then all my reasons were forgotten, replaced by the simple fact that I was in his arms and it felt good. Besides, wouldn't not sleeping with him be a total waste of a cute outfit?

The truth was, I didn't want to go home. Normally, an

empty apartment all to myself would be good news, but right then—on a night when the downside was creepy coded messages and the upside was a familiar lover keeping me warm— well, sue me, but I picked door number two.

"The food." Not a real protest, mind you, but I had to keep up appearances. "We should put it away."

"We can always order more," he said. And then he kissed me.

And even though the smart don't-sleep-with-your-ex part of my head told me I shouldn't, I kissed him back.

After all, I was single, over twenty-one, and some creepy weirdo had ruined my formerly good day.

Really, I reasoned, what could possibly go wrong?

Chapter

6

Two mighty fine orgasms later, I was wide awake and thinking a lot more clearly. A few hours ago I might have wondered what could go wrong if I slept with Todd, but now my less-addled brain had sorted through all the possibilities and come up with quite a list.

For one thing, Todd might think that the providing of orgasms also provided him with some door back into my life for more than just this night. Second, I might slide into that girly-girl state where I think that amazingly good sex is a fine basis for a relationship. (On that score, I really should know better. I had mind-blowing sex with Todd for four months, spent another month realizing our relationship was going nowhere, and then wasted yet another month of my life working up the courage to break it off despite one killer orgasm after the other.

I finally managed the breakup, and now I own a very nice vibrator. That, however, is a different story.)

Third—and from my current perspective, the most important—what might go wrong was severe lack of sleep. I'd forgotten about the mind-numbing, rafter-shaking snoring, though how, I don't know. I certainly couldn't forget about it now. "Ignore it and it will go away" was simply not an option.

I tossed a few more times, putting extra effort into each turn so the bed bounced and shook. No effect. I pulled my pillow down over my head, doing a good impression of a woman smothering herself. I neither drowned out the noise nor passed out from lack of oxygen. Too bad for me.

With a very loud groan that did not wake Sleeping Beauty, I propped myself up on my elbow and stared at him. The shades weren't drawn, and I could see his face just fine in the haze of city lights. His mouth was open, his jaw slack, and I deserve some sort of prize for not jamming both my forefingers right up his nostrils.

Instead, I took my pillow, grabbed the quilt, and headed for the bathroom. It might not be comfortable, but at least it would be quiet.

I don't know what time I woke up. All I know is that I had a crick in just about every bone in my body. Sleeping in a bathtub will do that to a person, especially a five-feet-nine person who couldn't do yoga if her life depended on it.

I unfolded my body, moving slowly so I wouldn't lose my footing, crash backwards and bash my skull in on the porcelain side of the tub. The day was already not off to a good start; massive self-inflicted head injuries would only make it worse.

I remembered the strange encrypted note that had drawn me back to Todd's in the first place. Now, with the sun streaming through the bathroom window, making the shiny white tub gleam and the smudge-free mirror sparkle (Todd has a cleaning lady come in three times a week), the note didn't seem nearly as ominous. It probably *was* an invitation, most likely to one of those dinner-and-a-murder parties where the guests playact

some role. Clever, really, if you think about it. I mean, if I were
going to throw a party, I might just do the same thing.

The one nice thing about sleeping in the tub is that you
don't have to go very far to shower. I tossed the towels I'd
used as bedding out onto the bathroom floor, then cranked
on the water, letting the spray beat down on me until the last
of the kinks had vanished from my back and neck.

Heaven.

It wasn't until I was toweling off that I realized that Todd
hadn't barged in to use either the toilet or the shower. Considering the fact that the apartment was roughly the size of a hamster cage, I knew he didn't have a little half-bath tucked away
somewhere. Maybe he'd decided to shower at the office rather
than wake me up?

And here I'd thought chivalry was dead.

I'd left my clothes strewn on top of Todd's stereo, so now I
climbed into a pair of his sweatpants, which were hanging behind the bathroom door. The long-sleeved T-shirt hanging next
to it smelled vaguely of male sweat, but I slipped it on anyway. I
confess I was having a bit of morning-after regret, and I wasn't
about to wander out there in my altogether.

Not that it would matter, I realized about two seconds later
as I was strapping my watch to my wrist. It was already after ten
in the morning—how had I managed to sleep all night in a
bathtub?—and the living room would be perfectly empty. I
knew this because I know Todd. He's a second-year associate at
some big-deal law firm, and he considers it a mortal sin to arrive after nine.

Which is why I was so surprised to see the telltale lump on
the bed as soon as I stepped out of the bathroom. No wonder

he hadn't interrupted my beauty rest: It hadn't been chivalry, it had been exhaustion.

"Todd," I stage-whispered as I skirted around the coffee table we'd so carelessly shoved aside in our frenzy to get the bed open last night.

No movement.

"Oh, To-odd," I sang from my side of the bed.

Still nothing.

"Todd!" One loud, solid bark.

Nada.

Jesus, I'd really worn the man out. I gave myself a mental pat on the back, cheering my sexual prowess, then climbed onto the bed and leaned over him. He might need his sleep, but he'd thank me for waking him up. Todd wasn't the type to skulk into the office after lunch. Not at all.

He was lying on his side, his back to me, the covers pulled up over his head. At first I didn't notice anything remotely out of the ordinary. Then I moved closer to tap him on the shoulder, and—

Oh God, oh God, oh God.

Blood. Blood everywhere. And little clumps of stuff that had to be brains and—

I clamped my hand over my mouth, trying not to retch. I lunged for the phone, then gasped in horror when I realized the line was dead. My purse was on the table, and I snatched it up, fumbling for my cell phone as I ran for the door. My phone never had service in the building, and I had to call the police. I had to get outside.

I had to get out of there.

Once in the hall, I skirted past the elevator—I wasn't about to wait for it—then raced down the stairs, my mind going a million miles an hour. *Who? Who did this?* Did Todd have some weirdo Mafia client with a grudge? And—*oh, God, no*—was that someone still in the apartment?

My heart was pounding against my rib cage so hard that I was sure something was going to burst, and I could hear my pulse raging in my ears. I knew I should feel something for Todd, but the only emotion getting through was fear. Fight or flight, I guess.

The situation was surreal, the air seeming as thick as soup as I struggled to get to the sidewalk, where I could get a 911 call through. My mind was both blank and crystal clear. I noticed how the paint was peeling on the stairway railing, but my heart was totally empty. Some rational voice told me to dig out my keys with the little pepper spray keychain, and I did. The voice of reason in the midst of madness.

At the first floor, I yanked on the door to the lobby and experienced a minor heart attack when the door didn't budge. I could *not* be trapped in a stairwell. I tugged again with all the force I could muster, and this time the door swung open and I barreled into the lobby.

Empty.

Shit! I looked around wildly, wishing I could conjure a cop, a fireman, a delivery man, *anyone*. But nothing, and so I kept on running, right out into the bright light of the August morning, blinking furiously as I flipped my phone open and tried to dial with trembling fingers.

Come on, Mel. Come on . . .

"Hey, hey, are you all right?" A male voice, and a hand closing on my forearm, effectively preventing me from pressing the Send key. "Come on, now. It can't be that bad."

"No, you don't understand. There's been—" I swallowed the word, finally realizing who was talking to me. I scrambled backwards, fear gripping me as I tried to get away from *him*. Tall, dark Mystery Man.

The one who'd delivered a message that told me I had to play . . . or die.

T oo much of a coincidence, my mind was shouting as my head spun and my pulse pounded in my ears.

This man killed Todd. I knew it. I was certain. And I wanted nothing more than to get the hell away from him.

This wasn't about Todd's clients. It was about me. That creepy letter . . . Todd murdered . . . holy shit, what the hell was going on?

"Are you okay?" he asked, those dark eyes inspecting me.

I tried to run, but he blocked my path, his grip on my arm tightening. I felt a quick sting in my arm and realized I must have pulled a muscle, I was fighting him so hard. I gulped in air and tried to rein in my terror. I had the feeling that if I hyperventilated and passed out, I'd wake up dead.

"Miss Prescott? Please calm down. It's me." Concern flooded his face, even filling those dark eyes, and his grip didn't seem nearly as tight now. "We met yesterday, remember? Are you okay? You look scared to death."

I blinked, confused. "I . . ." More blinking. "What?"

"Yesterday," he repeated. "I delivered a package to you. You look upset. Tell me what's wrong."

I relaxed a little. He seemed genuinely surprised. Genuinely concerned. Had I been wrong about him? "A cop," I said. "I need a cop."

"Okay," he said, his ready agreement allaying my fears even more. "We'll get whatever you need. You've just had a little shock. Everything's going to be just fine now. You just need to calm down a little."

"No, no. You don't understand." I heard the high pitch of hysteria lacing my voice.

"Of course I do," he said. "You've had a fright."

He was patronizing me, and I shook my head frantically, wishing I could make him understand. He could help me. He seemed to want to help me. But he *wasn't* helping me. *"Now,"* I said, twisting to survey the street for one of New York's finest. "I need a cop now."

"No," he said, "you don't." Something in his voice made me turn back to face him. I saw the cold glint in his eyes. A shiver raced up my spine, and I knew that I'd been right all along. This was no coincidence, and I was in Big Trouble. "You've just had a shock, that's all," he said. "Must be terrifying to find your boyfriend dead."

I hadn't said one word about Todd. I opened my mouth to scream.

"Do it, and I'll kill you right now."

The bastard had played me for a fool with all that concerned talk. I'd been too frazzled to tell, but I was wising up, now. An ice-cold dose of reality will do that for a girl. I tightened my fingers around the pepper spray and waited for my chance. I also made a big show of closing my mouth tight.

"Good girl. The boy was a warning." He held me close, like he might hold a lover, then he bent down to whisper in my ear. Around us, New Yorkers plowed on down the street, heads bent, lost in their own little worlds. They weren't going to help me. I was all on my own and being held by a killer.

"You got the message, right?" he continued, his voice icy and yet eerily calm. "If I were you, I'd pay attention to it. I'd play nice. And I wouldn't get the cops involved. That's what I'd do if I were you."

Message? And then I realized—"Play or Die." I drew in a shuddering breath. I'd said I wasn't going to play. Somehow he'd heard. Somehow, he *knew.*

And now Todd was dead.

Oh, Holy Mother of God, what had I done?

"Who are you?" I spat out the words.

"Someone who's watching you. Don't disappoint me. And don't break the rules."

"Rules?" My voice was rising, taking on an hysterical pitch.

"You know the rules, Melanie. For instance, you know what will happen if you bring the police into our little game."

I had no idea what he was talking about, but I wasn't going to stick around to find out. Instead, I raised my hand, the pepper spray at the ready, and got him good in the face. I was poised to run, but I didn't get far, because the damn spray didn't even phase him. Hell, he didn't even sneeze. He just laughed. Laughed and shook his head like I was a puppy doing some cute trick.

This was bad. This was very, very bad.

"You're going to have to do better than that," he said, still holding on to my forearm.

And that, frankly, pissed me off. I mean, I'd taken a Learning Annex class. I *should* be able to do better than that. And so, without really thinking about whether it was a smart thing to do, I brought my knee up with all the force I could muster and caught him square in the balls.

His knees gave way, and as he collapsed with a whimper to the sidewalk, he finally let go of my arm.

I didn't waste any time. I ran.

Chapter 9

Memorandum

FROM: Archibald Grimaldi
TO: Thomas Reardon, Esquire

Well, Thomas, here we are. Or here *you* are. If you're reading this, I've kicked the bucket, bit the big one, gone to that great Pentium processor in the sky.

Such a tragedy, they'll say. He was so young. So brilliant. And they'll be right.

I've always known I'd die young. Just like I knew I'd clear a billion before my thirtieth birthday. I'm the man, Thomas. Remember that. I. Am. The. Man. And even death can't take that away from me. You watch. You'll see. I'm about to prove to the world that I can do something no other man can: I'm going to create reality out of fantasy. In short, I'm going to play God. I'm going to wave my wand and send my sheep to scurrying. So many little lambs running around my playing field . . . how many of them will avoid the slaughter?

I'm sure you've already figured out that this isn't part of my will. I had your secretary slip this memo into your file during our last meeting. (Great gal. Too bad about that overbite.) Who knows how long it will sit there, unopened, until you are called to probate my will. (Although, I suppose if you're reading this note, then you *do* know how long. I, of course, am oblivious.)

I've set some things in motion. Got the ball rolling. Plugged the quarter in the jukebox.

You will perhaps think me insane, but I assure you I am not. There's a fine line between genius and insanity, they say. Trust me, my friend, I have not crossed that line. Though, perhaps, I have danced upon it, preventing myself from falling into the abyss of madness by sheer will alone.

Could an insane man arrange things so beautifully? Could someone without full use of his faculties set in motion the wonders I have unleashed? I think not.

Things are going to happen, my friend. Things I couldn't do in life, I have impunity to do in death. As John Travolta said in *Broken Arrow:* "Ain't it cool?"

All the pieces are in place, my friend. All the kinks have been worked out. I even did a little test run in November of 2004. Jamie Tate. A failure, I'm afraid, as she lacked the incentive to play my little game. I've remedied that, and now the game I've set in motion will live up to my expectations. Of that I'm certain.

You see, my friend, I've done it. Brought PSW into the real world. I've pulled it from cyberspace and attached real people to it. Real life. Real death.

Didn't I tell you I was fucking brilliant?

Now here's the rub, Thomas. I've given you a part in my little drama. A small part, but so very important.

I think you will cooperate even without incentive, but in case I'm wrong, I've arranged things to ensure that you don't take steps to shut the game down, or to involve the authorities. Your daughters? Your wife? If you love them, you'll cooperate. All I require is your silence. And, really, why would you protest? What point would it serve? I'm beyond the law now. And so is my game.

This is going to be a hell of a thing. Wish I were there.

Now, Thomas, read closely, because I'm setting out for your eyes alone just what it is that I have done, and what I will continue to do from six feet under. . . .

Chapter 10

’m not a runner or a jogger—I don't even do Pilates—and yet I raced away from Todd's place with a speed that would have put an Olympic sprinter to shame. I'd fled from Todd's without my shoes, and now my bare feet flew over the cracked sidewalks until my lungs burned and icy-hot knife blades pierced my sides. Even with that magical push of adrenaline, there was no way in hell I could run all the way home.

I struggled on a few more blocks, my legs like noodles, then stumbled down into the first subway station I saw. Thankfully, the line was one that would whisk me home, and when the train arrived, I collapsed onto one of the molded plastic benches, my head tossed forward as I sucked in gallons of air.

As the train pulled away from the platform, I gathered my wits enough to look up and around, nerve endings tingling with fear. I saw a transit cop, and my first instinct was to run to him.

But I tamped it back. What if *he* was there? What if the killer saw me talking to a cop after he'd specifically told me not to? What horrible thing would happen if I broke the rules? I shuddered, then looked around, sure that I'd see those dark eyes bearing down on me.

But there was no one; at least, no one who looked dangerous to me, although I was fast learning to be cynical. Still, these folks looked innocuous enough. Men and women in business suits and business casual, Palm Pilots at the ready. Tourists with their telltale cameras and laminated maps of the city. Bohemian types who probably lived around the corner from me. Standard-issue subway folk, the kind I'd seen every morning since the day I'd arrived in Manhattan a lifetime ago.

I'd never really noticed these people before, but I was noticing them now, giving each one a thorough once-over. Was one of them working with the bastard who'd killed Todd? Was one of them following me?

I shivered, and as the train pulled into the station, the overwhelming urge to run consumed me. The doors slid open, and I burst out at a dead run. People stared, but I didn't mind. I wanted the hell out of there.

As far as I could tell, no one was following me, though a few folks did gawk at the spectacle I made careening up the stairs to that rectangle of light. I didn't slow down when I hit street level, either, just kept on sprinting, and by the time I reached my building, my feet were raw, my lungs were burning again, and death by heart attack seemed more likely than murder.

Murder.

Oh, God, Todd.

It hit me again, the pain, the memory. Like walking into an

icy wall of water. I'd been concentrating on my own hide, but now that I was home and wrapped in the false comfort my familiar foyer provided, reality sunk its nasty, brutish teeth into my hide.

Todd was dead.

He was really and truly dead, and nothing I could do or say would bring him back. There was no one I could plead with, not the cops, not the killer. He was gone, his aspirations and dreams rendered meaningless by a single bullet.

A bullet meant as a warning to me.

Why?

I had no idea. And in a day filled with terror, that scared me most of all.

Chapter

11

On a normal day, I find my building to be a little creepy—dim lighting, that musty odor that comes from too many bags of trash lingering in the hall, and greenish gray walls that, under all the mildew and dust, were purportedly white. Today, none of that bothered me. This was home—thank God—and despite the way my hands were shaking and my stomach was churning with dread, I was relieved beyond words to be in that stuffy, smelly foyer.

I stood there for a moment, the door to the outside world in front of me, both dead bolts snapped in place. A thin film of grime covered the window, and I rubbed a bit away with the ball of my thumb, then leaned up close, peering up and down the street as much as the odd angle of the doorway would let me. I didn't see the killer, and I didn't see anyone I recognized from the subway.

My relief was palpable, and my entire body relaxed, like air being let out of a balloon. For just a second, I let myself believe that this was all going to turn out okay. I'm not sure I really believed it, but I sure as hell wanted to.

My relief was short-lived, though, because the fact was, I needed to do something. My brain was just too scrambled to know what. My first thought was to knock on the super's door, but what would I say? "Hey, Mr. Abernathy, some lunatic killed my ex-boyfriend and now he says he's out to *not* kill me, but I don't really believe him. Can you help me?" *No way.* And what was poor Mr. Abernathy, with his faded gray T-shirts and Santa Claus belly, supposed to do? Wield his broom and plumber's snake in my defense, a reluctant George fighting the dragon? Somehow I didn't think Mr. Abernathy was up for playing the hero. Too bad. I was in dire need of a hero right then.

The cops. He'd said not to call them, and I'd obeyed in the subway. But I needed help. And isn't that what bad guys are supposed to say? I mean, the bastard who killed Todd certainly wasn't going to encourage me to rush to my neighborhood precinct and file a complaint. But that's exactly what I *should* do. The police would help me; they'd protect me. After all, that's what police were for.

So, right. Yes. I'd go upstairs, call the cops, and—

My parents! I just about sagged against the wall in relief as I remembered that my parents were just a few miles away instead of the usual fifteen hundred. I didn't have to go through the ordeal with the cops alone. They could be there with me.

I said a silent prayer of thanks as I flipped open my phone, thrilled beyond belief at the prospect of hearing my mom's voice. Of having my dad stroke my hair and tell me he loved me and that he'd pummel whatever asshole was harassing his lit-tle girl.

My mom might be a pain at times, but when she heard the call to action, she was a take-no-prisoners kind of gal. She'd tell me it would be okay. She'd tell me that she'd handle it. She'd tell me . . . and I'd believe her.

I pressed and held 5, my speed-dial setting for my mom's cell phone. One ring, two, then, "The cellular customer you are trying to reach is currently away—"

"Fuck." I snapped the phone shut and tried Daddy's number. Same damn message.

Shit, shit, shit.

Okay. Fine. Mom was supposed to call me about breakfast, and she obviously hadn't. Which means surely she'd call me soon about lunch.

I took a deep breath, willing myself to stay calm. I hadn't been followed, I didn't see anyone outside who looked like they wanted to kill me, and I still had a plan. It wasn't a great plan, and my parents weren't on board, but it was a start.

I took one final glance up and down the street, then headed up the stairs toward my sixth-floor flat. I'd lock myself in, dial 911, down a Diet Coke (or three) and wait for the cops. By the time New York's finest arrived, I'd be able to utter a coherent sentence again. At least, I hoped I would.

The stench of cigarettes accosted me as I reached the sixth-floor landing. My across-the-hall neighbor smokes like a chim-ney, and that hideous musty odor had permeated the cheap wall paneling and the threadbare runner that lines the hallway. Jenn and I keep a can of Lysol by the door and spray into the hall at least once a day. I think it helps a little, and I know it annoys my neighbor, which, frankly, is our primary goal.

Because this is New York, and because this is a crappy building, the door to my apartment has two dead bolts and a spring-
latch lock on the doorknob. I went through the process of
running through the locks, all the while listening for footsteps
coming up the stairs. Thankfully, the stairwell was dead silent.

As soon as the door was unbolted, I shoved it open and basically collapsed into my apartment. I've never in my life been so
glad to be home. The place was tiny, but right then, that was
perfect. I wanted to be cocooned in my quilts within my walls,
safe from everything bad outside my door.

Out of habit, I reached for the Lysol, and as my fingers
closed around the smooth, cool can, I saw the shadow of a man
moving just inside my darkened kitchen. My stomach roiled,
and I realized my mistake. I should never have come home. *He*
was here. Somehow, he'd gotten here ahead of me.

The figure moved toward me, and, once again, I screamed.

Chapter

12

"**G**oddamn son of a *bitch!*" Some sort of garden-scented toxic shit caught Stryker right in the face, and he howled, eyes burning and tears streaming down his cheeks. Whatever the stuff was, it hurt like a motherfucker.

"Jesus Christ, Melanie, what the fuck did you zap me with?"

Not that she was answering. She was already halfway down the hall. Fucking hell. He'd probably scared the girl to death.

He was out the door in two strides, but she'd already reached the end of the hall. She looked back over her shoulder, her eyes as wide as those of a deer about to get plugged and just as sad.

"Goddamn it, Melanie, *stop,*" he called, his voice not nearly as calm as he'd have liked because of the shit she'd sprayed in his face. He cringed against the pain, trying to rein in his own frustration, and forced himself to keep his voice low and reassuring.

"It's okay. For God's sake, I'm here to help you. Would you please stop?"

She didn't. Just the opposite, and somehow in speeding up she managed to snag her foot on the decrepit hallway runner. The kid was barefoot, for Christ's sake, and as she let out a pitiful little yelp, his gut twisted. He'd come here to help, and instead he was making matters worse. But he couldn't let her go back down those stairs. He needed her inside her apartment behind locked doors. Soon—very soon—someone was going to try to kill this woman, and he intended to make sure that didn't happen. If he had to drag her by the hair to get her inside, that's what he'd do.

He'd rather see her scared to death than actually dead. He'd already seen one woman dead because he'd been too much of an asshole to protect her. Stryker wasn't about to make the same mistake twice.

As he stumbled toward her, squinting, she struggled to get up, then collapsed with a piercing cry of pain as she took her weight on both feet. She fell again, rolling onto her back and scooting crablike away from him.

"For God's sake," he said. "I'm not going to hurt you. I'm here to help you."

Her expression didn't change. No trust. Just cold, hard fear.

He tried again. "I'm not a burglar, I'm not a thief, I'm not a rapist. Trust me. I'm not going to hurt you."

"Fuck you," she hissed, and although he was frustrated as hell that she didn't believe him, he couldn't help but admire her spunk. More than anything else, that kind of spirit would help keep her alive.

"Look, I know you're scared. You came home, I was in your

apartment, what else would you think? But I thought they'd already got you. I broke in because I thought you were dead."

"*What?*" Confusion played across her face. "You broke in because—*what?*"

"I thought you were hurt. I'm here to help you. I just want—"

"*No.*" She jerked away, scrambling backwards, then rolling over and trying to climb to her feet despite her bad ankle. The woman had gumption, that was for sure, but Stryker was in no mood. He lunged, and with no effort at all managed to snag the hem of her sweats, sending her crashing to the floor once again.

"Melanie, calm down. I'm here to—"

"Help! Somebody help me!"

"For God's sake, woman, be quiet." He lunged at her and clamped a hand over her mouth, undoubtedly terrifying her even more, but what the hell choice did he have? Any minute now the neighbors were going to show up, and what would he say then?

He studied her, searching her face for some clue as to how to make her understand he was one of the good guys. Her blue eyes were wide. Wide and terrified. And he saw something else, too. Resignation? He'd seen that look before in the eyes of men facing certain death. He'd never wanted to see it again, and he certainly didn't want to see it on a woman.

And that's when Stryker realized. Something more than finding a stranger in her apartment had scared her. While he'd been waiting for her to get home, she'd been somewhere in Manhattan fighting the bastard who wanted her dead.

"Something happened," he said. "Something scared you to death, and it wasn't just me."

She remained perfectly still, her eyes full of terror. His muscles strained with unreleased tension. He couldn't abide anyone terrorizing a woman, and now he'd done it himself. He'd come to protect her, but they'd gotten off to a bad start, and now those ocean blue pools were full of fear instead of hope.

He kept his hand over her mouth, and she breathed through her nose, her fast, shallow breaths tickling his palm. Her eyes never left his, and he focused on her, trying to judge the depths of the strength that had gotten her away from harm and back to her apartment. "I'm going to take my hand away, okay? Promise me you won't scream."

She just stared at him, her eyes widening ever so slightly.

"Nod your head, Melanie."

She nodded, and he gently pulled his hand away, cringing as he anticipated her screams. But she obeyed him, staying silent, cowering into herself even as he held her in his arms.

"We're going to stand up and go back inside our apartment so we can talk."

"No," A hoarse whisper. She struggled backwards, and Stryker knew he'd never get her in that apartment, not without a fight.

He drew in a long breath. He couldn't blame the girl, but damn, this was frustrating. He'd done the bodyguard gig at least a dozen times, always where there'd been a legitimate threat against the subject's life. Stryker had dealt with terror, with ego, and with outright stupidity, but never once had a subject flat-out ignored his instructions, much less cower in fear of *him*.

Goddamn it all. He needed her to work with him, not against him.

"Okay, Melanie, here's the situation. I'm not out to hurt you. In fact, I've been assigned to help you. But you don't believe me, do you?"

Her teeth grazed her lower lip, and she shook her head just once, a tiny movement, but one that confirmed his question.

"In that case, I don't think I've got any other choice," he said. He was still crouched beside her, and now he reached into his shoulder holster to pull out his gun. She drew in a strangled breath, and he clamped his hand over her mouth again before she could release it as a scream. He withdrew the gun, checked the safety, and put it in her lap. "Here," he said, then backed away. He was playing a dangerous game and he knew it, but he didn't see any other way. He needed her to trust him, and he needed it fast. And he was banking on the belief that Melanie Prescott wouldn't kill a man. Hurt him, maybe, but not kill him.

"I'm unarmed." He met her wide, confused eyes. "So what are we going to do now, Melanie? Now that you're the one holding the gun?"

Chapter

13

A damn good question.

I don't like guns, but I'm not an idiot. I hefted this one with both hands and aimed it at him, thinking vaguely that this man was either brave or stupid. The way my hands were shaking, he could have ended up with a hole in his face whether I'd meant to fire or not.

"Talk," I said.

His gaze darted toward the door. "Maybe we ought to do this inside."

"Do I *look* stupid?" I asked. "Now talk. And if I don't like what you say, I'm calling the cops." I sounded tough, but I was scared to death. I thought about calling the cops right then, but I ruled that option out almost immediately. He'd handed me a very slim advantage here, but the truth was, he didn't look stupid either, and I was betting that he had another gun tucked away somewhere, but perfectly accessible should I do something rash.

"Do you play any Internet games?"

The question was so unexpected that for a moment I could only stare at him. Then I frowned and half shrugged. "Sure. Some." The truth was, I played around a lot on the Net. Spend as much time as I do at the computer, and cyber-surfing becomes the procrastination method of choice.

"Multiplayer games? Like PSW?"

I kept the gun trained on him, but I was becoming more curious than scared. "Yeah," I said, still wary as I remembered the article in that morning's *Post*. Weird that this game I hadn't thought of in years suddenly seemed to be everywhere. "I don't play PSW, but I have in the past."

"So you remember how it works."

"Pretty much."

"How?"

"Why are you asking me this?"

"Humor me," he said.

"Players log on all over the world and are assigned to a role—a target, an assassin and a protector. They all race around a cyber version of Manhattan doing their thing and following the clues." Actually, it was more complicated than that. That was the allure of PSW. The game was both incredibly complicated and beautiful in its simplicity, but I wasn't inclined to discuss the ins and outs with this man.

"So you have a profile in the system?"

Handguns are small but heavy, and I was getting tired of twenty questions. "What's this all about?"

"Melanie—"

"Oh, for Christ's sake, what's this about?" He started to open his mouth, but I waved the gun, and he shut up. Oh, the power. "I've played a zillion of these kinds of games. Did I submit a profile? Sure. Do I remember the details? No. But I haven't logged on to PSW in years. Sorry if I'm a little fuzzy."

"That long?"

For some reason, that really seemed to bother him. "Yeah. Why is that bad?"

"I just assumed you were a regular player."

By now, confusion had totally surpassed fear, but I kept the gun aimed at him for appearances' sake. "I don't know you from Adam," I said. "Why on earth would you assume that?"

"Because you're a target, just like in the game," he said, the force of his words almost knocking me over. "And I've been assigned to protect you."

Chapter

14

>>>http://www.playsurvivewin.com<<<

PLAY.SURVIVE.WIN

WELCOME TO REPORTING CENTER

PLAYER REPORT:
REPORT NO. A-0001
Filed By: Lynx
Subject: Game commenced.
Report:

- Target approached and package delivered. Tailed
  target to non-residence location >>>database entry
  noted<<<

- Utilized eavesdropping equipment.
- Target announced refusal to participate in game.
- Persuasive tactics applied.

>>>End Report<<<

Send Report to Opponent? >>*Yes*<< >>No<<

His target was on the run.

Lynx reached across the table for his pack of Djarum cigarettes, his eyes still fixed on the glowing screen. He tapped out a
smoke, then slid it between his lips, lighting it with one quick
flick of the silver-plated lighter his grandfather had surrendered
to him so many years ago.

His first prize.

He could remember the move so clearly. He'd sacrificed his
rook and his queen in homage to the strategy played so bril-
liantly by Adolph Anderssen in 1853. *Checkmate.* He'd been
thirteen, and that had been the first time he'd beaten the old
man. He'd known he would, too. For two weeks, he'd studied
and played. He'd practiced opening with the Evans Gambit and
had tried out the Alekhine Defense. In the end, he'd beaten
every fucking little dweeb in the Delaney High School chess
club, then he'd rubbed their noses in the fact that a lousy freshman had whooped their sorry asses.

Fuckers. They hadn't taken him seriously, but he'd known.
He'd always known. He was destined to be a winner.

He'd wagered his signed Willie Mays starting lineup card
against his grandfather's lighter, and he hadn't sweated it for a
minute. He'd never give up Willie. But that just hadn't been a
risk. Lynx had known even then that he'd come into his own.
He was special. He'd been *ready.*

More than that, he'd been right. A handful of moves, and it had all been over.

And as Lynx had closed his fingers around the cool, polished silver, he'd known that he was the best. He always would be.

And he'd always win.

He'd been winning now for twelve years. Not roulette or slots or those other baby games of chance. Real games. Where skill mattered.

He'd spent his school years dividing his time between the chess club and football, not giving a damn if his pumped-up but brain-dead teammates thought he was a pussy. He'd had things on his mind past high school. He hadn't given a rat's ass about the sport—any other game would have done just as well. He'd been in training, then. Training his mind and his body. Making sure he was ready. For what, he hadn't known. Not exactly. But there was something out there. Some prize that was his.

Even then, he could feel it.

Even then, he could taste it. The sweet nectar of success.

He'd spent long weekends in the summer with his grandfather, his rifle at the ready, waiting for just the right moment, just the right shot. Hunting had been a game, too. Hunter and quarry. And he'd always won.

His grandfather's cronies used to smack him on the back after they'd returned to the lodge with their kill. They'd pound him between the shoulder blades and tell him what a fine job he'd done. Later, when he'd taken his seat at the fire with *Chess Traps, Pitfalls and Swindles* open on his lap, they'd looked curiously, but they'd never snickered. He'd proven himself already. He wasn't a sissy-boy.

Not fun, though, playing against dumb animals. They didn't know about the game, after all. And so he'd found a new thrill. In no time at all, he'd aced every single-player game that Sierra, Broderbund and all the other developers had had to offer. That had gotten old soon enough, and by his sophomore year of college, he'd graduated to multiplayer Internet gaming. Going through all the levels of Anarchy Online, EVE, Doom and dozens of others. RPGs, MMORPGs. The works. He'd done them all and started surfing again, looking for some new challenge and turning up empty. Not a damn thing out there. At least, nothing worthy of his skill. Nothing worthy of his time.

Hell, nothing worthy of *him*.

And then he'd found it. Play. Survive. Win. He'd played for over two years, relishing the challenge, thriving on the adrenaline rush of chasing or being chased.

Even that, though, had eventually gotten dull.

And then the new version had shown up in his in-box, and the anonymous package containing the message and the syringe had arrived soon after. . . .

New rules. New challenges. And a thrill like nothing he'd ever experienced before.

Suddenly the playing field was all of Manhattan, and his tools were real weapons, not merely a computerized image. As in the online version, his role in the game wouldn't start until the target successfully interpreted the qualifying clue. But once she did, then the game wouldn't be over until he killed her. Or until she finally located and nailed the final clue, which would send the signal to stop.

He wasn't worried that would happen, though. If the clues were as far-reaching and complex as those in the online game, the target would have to be constantly on her toes to success-fully interpret them. That meant he had the advantage: He didn't have to decipher codes, he simply had to hunt.

He had another advantage, too. He never lost. *Ever.* And he wasn't about to start now.

Yes, he couldn't wait for the chase to begin.

He hoped Melanie Prescott would play. He thought she probably would. Once she realized what was at stake, she'd play like her life depended on it.

And why not? Her life *did* depend on it. And the clock was ticking. . . .

I still held the gun, but we'd moved into my apartment, the open door a concession to my continued (though lessened) fear of this man. I was sitting beside him on the sleeper sofa as he manipulated Jennifer's laptop. Mine was in the shop getting a variety of upgrades, and I didn't figure she'd mind.

I was sitting at an angle, facing him, and while he concentrated on the computer, I concentrated on him. I still wasn't prepared to totally trust him, but I had to admit he had a trustworthy face. A firm chin and a strong jawline shaded by the faint stubble of a beard. He looked to be in his thirties, rugged and sexy in a Russell Crowe kind of way. I guessed that the color in his skin had come from working outdoors, and that the muscles that strained against the short sleeves of his burgundy T-shirt weren't the result of working out with a personal trainer.

This was a man who wouldn't blink at the idea of getting his hands dirty.

The hands in question looked rough, calloused even. But his fingernails were clean, and for some absurd reason, that put me at ease.

The uninvited thought alarmed me, and I tightened my grip on the gun. Mystery Man had been good-looking, too, I reminded myself. And he'd tried to kill me.

"You okay?" He turned his head to look at me, and I nodded, focusing on his gray eyes. Unlike the cruel eyes of the delivery man, this man's eyes reflected warmth and concern, with a hardness I found reassuring instead of scary. I relaxed, but only a tiny bit.

"Just get on with it," I said.

He looked like he might say something, but then he decided against it. The PSW website was up on the screen, and I watched as he entered his password, then pulled up a saved message. "SemperFi?" I asked, reading over his shoulder.

"My login. I used to be a Marine."

"Mmm." That didn't surprise me at all.

"Just read." He turned the computer so the screen faced me. I leaned closer and skimmed the info. When I finished, I realized I was a little sick to my stomach.

"Twenty grand?"

"I got it, all right," he said. He opened his wallet and flashed some bills. "Showed up in my checking account this morning. I went straight to the bank and withdrew a chunk. I'll take the rest when the hold lifts. I figure we'll need the cash."

"But how? Who sent the money?"

He shook his head. "Honestly? I don't have a clue. Online it shows up as a wire transfer. My guess is that whoever's pulling our strings hacked in and transferred the money from some-where."

"Can we find out where?"

"Possibly. With some poking around. Or if we get the authorities involved." Warning bells went off in my head as I remembered what the Mystery Man had said. But I needn't have worried. "Right now," he continued, "I'm more concerned about keeping you alive."

"Oh." The reality of the situation smashed against me, mak-ing me light-headed. I stood up and moved toward the window. I shoved the sash up and stuck my head out, suddenly desperate for air. "A target. I'm a target." I whispered the words, as if by not giving them voice, I could make this all go away.

"It looks that way."

He stepped up behind me and put a hand on my shoulder. I whipped around, aiming the gun at his chest. "Wait just a fuck-ing minute," I said.

He backed away, hands in the air, his face placid. All of which confirmed to me that this was not a stupid man.

"Calm down, Melanie."

"Calm down? I really don't think the situation calls for calm. I'm thinking it calls for abject hysteria. Too bad for me I'm not the hysterical type."

"More the sarcastic type," he said, and the tiny smile that lit his eyes made me feel a little better.

"Or the careful type." I kept the gun on him, but I nodded toward the computer screen. "For all I know, you set this up. Carried some cash you could whip out for my benefit. Sent yourself this message from a different player profile. You haven't

said one thing that makes me want to trust you." Although I
did want to trust him. At the moment, though, I'd willingly
trust Attila the Hun if I thought he could give me a moment's
peace.

Todd's murder was still hanging over me. I wanted to curl
up and cry. I wanted to grieve. Mostly, though, I didn't want to
be next. But at the same time, I would have given everything I
owned for the chance to hide under the covers and let someone
else cope for a while.

"Fair enough," he said. "But how would I have gotten your
profile?"

"What profile?"

"You didn't read the whole message."

I looked back and, sure enough, the message included a link
to a player profile. I swallowed, fighting off a wave of bile. I
didn't want to click on that link. I really, really didn't want
to. . . .

"Go on," he said. "We might as well be sure."

I drew in a breath and nodded, then moved his finger
around the touchpad and clicked. A profile came up. All my
various stats and interests. All the silly little life stuff that made
PSW such a cool game—Grimaldi had used nascent artificial
intelligence technology in such a way that the game was different depending on who the players were that filled each role.
Each of the clues, tests and game levels were constructed from
the information set forth in the player profiles.

"Is it your profile?"

I nodded, the queasiness being replaced by anger. "Yeah." A
lot of folks make up personal stats when filling out various online profiles. For PSW, I hadn't, and if the media coverage was

accurate, neither did most of the game's players. PSW's appeal was that it incorporated a person's real-life interests into the clues. What incentive would I have had to lie? None. I'd told the truth, and look what happened. There's a lesson there somewhere, I think.

"This doesn't make sense. My profile should have been deleted years ago."

"Mine should have, too," he said. "But it wasn't. And there's nothing we can do about it now. We're playing the game, Melanie. Whether we want to or not."

Chapter

16

I couldn't sit still. I paced the room, the gun still in one hand, as I tried to process everything that was going on. My head pounded with the beginnings of a hellacious headache, my eyes burned with unshed tears, and my feet ached and burned. I wouldn't let myself cry, though. I had to stay sharp, because for all I knew, I was still in danger.

I sat on the edge of the couch, then bounced back up again. I paced some more.

I opened a Diet Coke, then spit it out, too tense to swallow.

"Melanie?"

"Quiet," I snapped. His voice was soft, calm and soothing, but I reacted as if he'd just shouted at me. I drew a breath and tried to calm down. "I just need a minute."

He didn't push again, and I gave him points for that.

After a few deep breaths, I tried sitting down again—this

time at the little table in the tiny area that the real estate agent had called a dining room (with a straight face, no less). "Okay," I said, managing to stay put. "Let me get this straight. You got this message with my profile attached, and you immediately raced to my apartment looking to protect me? Forgive me if I find that more than a little curious."

I still hadn't told him about Todd, and he hadn't said anything. I'd locked my grief away to deal with later, and now Todd's death was information—a cold, hard fact that, when revealed, would hopefully reflect on my Marine companion's face. Guilt, surprise, sorrow. I didn't know. I just needed Todd as the last piece of the puzzle. I was playing off my boyfriend's death to hopefully save my ass, and I felt like shit doing it.

I didn't think I had a choice.

Marine man was at the kitchen counter, popping the top on another soda. So far he hadn't answered my question, but I wasn't inclined to prompt. Let's see what he fabricated.

When he turned around, his expression was hollow, guarded, as if he feared he might reveal too much. It wasn't an expression that encouraged me to warm to him.

"A girl named Jamie Tate," he said. "Recognize the name?"

"No. Should I?"

"I don't know. With all this . . ." He trailed off, then shrugged, leaving me to guess what "all this" was. "I just thought perhaps your paths had crossed."

"Not that I know of. I suppose she could have some classes with me, but I don't know her."

He nodded toward the computer. "Look her up."

"In the game? I can't access her profile unless we're assigned to the same game set." I frowned, something else occurring to me.

"So how did *anyone* get my profile? I mean, surely PSW didn't really send someone out to kill me." I laughed, the sound more of a cackle, which is my usual unattractive nervous laughter. I figured I had reason to be nervous. "I mean, that would be taking reality shows to the extreme. Reality computer games?"

"Snuff games at that," he said, then shook his head. "No, I don't think PSW's behind it. But maybe someone who works there is. Or maybe one of the players is just taking the game a little too seriously."

"But he has my profile."

"If he plays PSW, most likely he knows his way around computers. He could have hacked in. Or maybe he's played against you before."

I stifled a shiver as I tilted my head back to look at him. *"You* could have hacked in. I could have played against *you* before."

"But I didn't. And you haven't."

I stared at him, my mind mush. "What did you mean when you said your profile should have been deleted a long time ago?"

"I meant that I've never actually played the game. I figured the system would cull inactive profiles."

"If you never played, why are you in the system at all?"

"A buddy of mine played all the time. Convinced me to sign up. I filled out the profile but never got around to actually playing a game. Got shipped off to Iraq instead. By the time I got back, I'd had my fill of danger and intrigue in the real world. I wasn't really interested in killing or being killed on the Internet, too."

"Oh." I wasn't sure what to say. Should I ask him about the war, about what it was like and what he was doing now? I wondered if combat had given him the hardness I saw in his eyes, or if that had been there before. And I realized I was thinking way too much about this man I barely knew. I was rattled, and my mind was bouncing all over the place, trying to process every tiny piece of information simultaneously. That's my typical re-action to stress. I multitask. Great when the stress is caused by final exams. Not so great at the moment.

I drew a breath, determined to stay on track. "You seem like you know a bit about the game."

He shrugged. "Like I said. My friend played a lot, so I knew the basics. And it's no trick to go to the website and read through the FAQs."

That made some sense, but I still saw one gaping hole. "But if you aren't a player, how'd you get the message about me?"

"The system sent a message to my regular email address. Told me that there was a message waiting for me in the PSW user area. I figured it was my friend, so I clicked over. The rest you know."

I believed him. Not enough to *tell* him I believed him, though. At the moment, I wasn't exactly trusting my judgment. "Prove it."

"What? That I'm telling the truth? That I didn't set you up?"

I nodded. A tense moment passed, and I was afraid he was going to say he couldn't. Not a good answer. My scientist's mind wanted proof. Otherwise I might believe him just because he was so damn good-looking.

"All right," he finally said, and I stifled a sigh of relief. He pointed to the computer. "Jamie Tate, remember?"

"What about her?"

"Look her up."

I was tempted to argue. I didn't know the woman, and I

couldn't see what she had to do with me or Todd's death, but the Marine's expression was grave enough that I knew better than to argue. I took the gun and crossed back to the computer. About a minute later, I was looking at a list of hits pulled up from a search on the name Jamie Tate.

"Try that one," he said, leaning over me to tap the screen. I clicked on the link, and an article appeared.

> November 18, 2004
> Brooklyn, N.Y.—Thirty-eight-year-old Jamie Tate was found dead in her Brooklyn Heights apartment yesterday afternoon. Tate, a copy editor with Machismo Publishing, was discovered by former Marine Maj. Matthew Stryker. Though Stryker refused to comment, sources close to the investigation confirm that the Marine allegedly received a tip about the woman's death over the Internet. Details were unavailable at press time, but the same sources have confirmed that Stryker has been ruled out as a suspect in Tate's death.

The article went on from there, but I didn't want to read any more. I felt cold and hot all at the same time, and didn't much like the feeling.

I concentrated on breathing, and when I had that under control, I turned to look at him. "What's *your* name?" I asked, my voice barely a whisper.

"Stryker," he said. "Matthew Stryker."

"They ruled you out as a suspect," I said.

He nodded.

"They could have been wrong."

"They weren't."

I just stared at him.

"If I had killed her, would I have sent you to that article?"

Maybe. Maybe not. I wasn't sure. I cocked my head to one side and squinted at him. "Did you get money for her, too?"

From his expression, you'd think I'd kicked him in the stomach. "Yeah," he said. "Twenty large."

"And?"

"And she died anyway." He practically spat the words. "So much for money well spent."

"Dammit, Stryker. You want me to believe you? Then tell me the truth."

"The truth? I didn't do a damn thing for her. I thought it was some sick joke, some perverse scheme. And I guess it was. I just didn't realize how sick until I got a second message saying that she'd been terminated. That's when I went to find her . . . and found her too late."

I closed my eyes against his pain and forced myself to focus. "The money," I pressed.

"It's gone. I had buddies who died in combat. They left widows. Kids." The look he shot me was filled with remorse. "I figured they could use the money more than I could. And maybe I figured it was a tiny bit of retribution."

I drew in a breath and nodded. His pain was palpable, and my interrogation came to a halt. I had nothing left to say.

"You asked me why I raced over here to help you, and that's why. I *didn't* race to help Jamie. I didn't know. I was too late." He closed his eyes, and when he opened them again, his entire expression seemed steely calm. Oh yeah, I trusted this guy. More than that, I was glad he was on my side.

I reached out and took his hand, finding comfort in the fact that I'd been right. His skin was calloused and rough, his large hands strong and sure. A fighter's hands, and I needed a fighter right then. "Thank you," I whispered. And then—damn it all—I started to cry.

He knelt in front of me, pulling me over so that I was leaning against his shoulder. I slumped off the chair and let him cradle me as I cried. I cried out of fear and frustration and grief. I cried for Todd and everything he'd lost. I cried for myself and for everything I might lose. And I cried for this man, who, for whatever reason, had shown up to help me.

I'm not sure how long I cried, long enough to reach that

point where it's not easy to stop, and where your gasps for air turn into loud, painful hiccups. When I hit that point, he backed away, then returned momentarily with a glass of water. It was a nothing gesture, but to me it seemed incredibly sweet, and the damn tears almost started up all over again.

I sipped, trying to slow my breathing and get my body back under control, feeling both grateful for his comfort and mortified that I was falling apart in front of him.

"Did Jamie play PSW?" I asked, once I was pretty sure my voice would cooperate.

"Yeah. She did."

"Why was she killed?"

"I don't know, but I can guess."

"Guess," I said.

"She wouldn't play the game. *This* game."

I thought of the message Todd had thrown into the trash. "What exactly do you mean?" I asked the question slowly, carefully. I was pretty sure I knew the answer. But until I heard it out loud, I could pretend it wasn't true.

"Someone's taking the game to the streets. I don't know how. I don't know why. And I damn sure don't know who. He killed her." He half shrugged. "Or, rather, the assassin did."

"How do you know she wouldn't play?"

"The police found a message balled up in her trash. It was in code. They showed it to me—probably wanted to gauge my reaction in case I'd written it."

"What did it say?"

"I didn't know at the time. I found out later. The police investigated for a while, but the case went nowhere. And budgets being what they are, the detectives eventually turned to cases with hot leads. Since the police investigation was going nowhere, I decided to do some poking around on my own. One of the detectives in the precinct nosed around and got me a photocopy along with the interpretation."

Once again, he held me rapt. "Exactly what do you do that you have detectives running around doing your bidding? Or is that a perk enjoyed by all ex-Marines?"

A muscle in his jaw twitched, and I really didn't think he was going to answer me.

"Does it really matter what I do?"

Okay. That pissed me off even more than if he'd just stayed quiet. "Hell yes," I said. "You show up in my apartment and announce that you're there to protect me, and then you tell me that some other woman's dead because of you—"

He winced, but I was on a roll. And, no, I didn't feel guilty. This was my life I was dealing with.

"So yeah," I went on. "I think I have a right to know why you think I should listen to you. I mean, other than that you served your time for God and country. Or are you still one of the few and the proud?"

"I got my discharge papers three years ago," he said, his voice tight. "Honorable, since I'm sure you want the full résumé."

"And now?" I hadn't had the upper hand all day. I wasn't about to drop it now.

"Now I'm in the private security business. Freelance work."

I thought of the gun on the table, and the gun I assumed he'd kept hidden. "What exactly does that mean?"

He fixed me with a hard stare. "It means it's private. And that means it's none of your business."

He must have read my reaction on my face, because he held up a hand, effectively stopping me from spewing a string of invectives all over him.

"It also means that I'm more than qualified to protect you. And as for Jamie Tate . . ." As he trailed off, a shadow crossed his eyes. I, of course, felt guilty as hell.

He shook his head like someone shaking off sleep. "Let's just say that you can rest assured I won't make the same mistake twice."

A sarcastic retort flew to my lips, but I managed to hold it back with my tongue. I *did* want this man on my side. I'd be wise not to insult him. Or piss him off.

Slowly, I nodded, letting the matter drop. "All right," I finally said. "Do you still have it? The photocopy of the message, I mean."

"Burned it. But I read it first. You can guess what it said." His gaze was tight on me, and I squirmed a little under the attention.

I opened my mouth to speak, realized my throat was too dry, and took a sip of water. "'Play or Die,'" I said.

His eyes narrowed just slightly, but otherwise his expression didn't change. "Okay, Melanie," he said. "I think it's your turn to fill me in on just what happened to you today."

Melanie didn't answer right away, and Stryker didn't push her. She had to take her time. Reach her own conclusions. Learn to trust him and realize that he could help her. He couldn't help her if she didn't trust him. Or, rather, he *could*. Hell, he intended to help the girl whether she wanted him or not.

He just hoped that she wanted his help. Working together would make this whole thing so much easier.

Now she looked up at him, her eyes sharp despite fear, and once again he got a peek at that core of strength.

"All right," she said. "You want my story? Here it is." And then she told him. Running into her ex-boyfriend. The note in the park. Going back to her ex's place last night. Translating the code, then scoffing at the message. "I was pissed," she said, "and Todd calmed me down." Her cheeks colored a bit. "We had our problems, but in some ways we were good together, too."

"Go on."

She licked her lips, not meeting his eyes as she explained how she'd discovered the body, then had run straight into the killer's arms. "I was so scared. I was sure he was going to kill me. And then I ran into you—"

"And I scared you even more."

"Hell yes," she said. "You'd broken into my apartment."

He held up a hand to ward off a fresh tirade. Her being pissed at him might have calmed her fears, but neither of them had time for another dressing-down.

"You came to help," she said, her tone even.

"I was assigned to help."

"Why kill Jamie and not kill me?" she asked.

"Don't know. Different assassin, maybe."

She cringed. "Nice to know it's so easy to round up assassins to pick off innocent grad students."

"Put an ad in *Soldier of Fortune* and you'd be surprised who'll come running."

"*The Most Dangerous Game,*" she said. "I watched that movie once. Didn't like it much." She met his eyes, and he was impressed by the spark of humor he saw beneath the fear. "I can't say I like the concept any more today."

"Me either."

She frowned. "It could be the same killer, though. Maybe the police have a lead. Maybe they can find him. Track him down."

"No go," he said. "I checked. The case has gone completely cold."

"I think I've just heated things up."

"That you have. Are you going to call the police?"

Her forehead creased, and from her expression, you'd think he'd asked her if she'd like a nice glass of gasoline on ice. "I think you missed a few rules in your review," she said.

He shook his head, not following. "So tell me."

"It's what the messenger meant," she said. "Now that I know what the game is, his warning makes perfect sense." She took a deep breath, and he saw that her hands were shaking. She clasped them together, her fingers so tightly twined her knuckles turned white. "There are authorities in the game—cops, FBI, whatever. And you can ask them for help if you want, and if you do, you might even jump a level or two. But there's a price. Any target who calls in an authority for help loses their protector. Get it?"

He got it, all right. She called in the cops, and the assassin would pick him off. Or try to, anyway.

"Don't even think it," she said.

He met her eyes, careful to keep his expression bland. "Think what?"

"I'm not calling the cops. For one thing, he told me not to, and I'm beginning to think that's an order I should follow. Mostly, though, I'm not about to hang you out there like that."

"I know how to watch my back." Not entirely true. He was good, but even he couldn't stop a sniper's bullet if he didn't know when or where it was coming from.

"Maybe," she said, "but I couldn't stand the guilt. Todd's already dead. It's not my fault, I know that. But I don't want your blood on my hands, too."

She rushed on before he could get a word in. "If he kills you too, I'm on my own." Her eyes flashed with dark humor. "And if I'm stuck playing this game, I'd just as soon have company, you know?"

"I know." He took her hand, gently squeezing her fingers. "I'm sticking to you like glue, Melanie."

She managed a smile. "Call me Mel."

He nodded, then swung an arm around her shoulder and pulled her close, half expecting her to tug away, insisting on her own personal space. She didn't. Instead, she leaned against him, the soft sound of her breathing marking time in the otherwise silent apartment. He wanted to whisper comforting words, to tell her it would all be okay and that they'd get through this nightmare. But he couldn't. Melanie already knew the score, and he wasn't about to lie to her. Comfort, yes. But lie? Never.

They sat that way for a while before she spoke again, so softly that he had to strain to hear her. "I don't think Todd even played PSW. Why did they have to go and kill him?"

"I don't know."

A tear trickled down her cheek, and Stryker steeled himself against the urge to wipe it away. "I said I wasn't going to play. Todd even crumpled the note and we threw it away, just like Jamie Tate did. So why is she dead and I'm still alive?"

"Maybe he didn't have any fun with Jamie."

She pulled out of his embrace then and turned to face him, her brow furrowed in concentration. "What do you mean?"

"The chase," he said. "That's got to be why he signed on. That and the money." How the killer knew Melanie wasn't going to play remained a question Stryker couldn't yet answer.

"So he killed her and then realized that it was all over. With me, he thought he'd try a little persuasion?"

"It's only a guess."

"We need that message." She closed her eyes, then sighed

deeply before adding, "There was more to it. Nonsense stuff. The next clue, I guess."

"So we go get it," he said.

"Todd's place." Her voice was flat, leaving no doubt that she didn't want to go back to that apartment.

He took her hand, surprised when she didn't jerk it away. "I know you don't want to, but we don't have a choice."

"I know. Like the note said—'Play or Die.'" She met his eyes, hers cold and full of determination. "Looks like I'm going to play."

Chapter

19

Stryker got us into Todd's apartment—I didn't ask how—but I couldn't bring myself to follow him in. I also couldn't handle waiting in the hall by myself, so I ended up just inside the door, my back pressed against the wall, as Stryker crossed the short distance to the sofabed.

I realized that something was wrong about the time Stryker lifted the sheet, and when he turned back to look at me, I already knew what he was going to say.

"The sheets are clean. Someone's done a number on this apartment."

I checked the trash can and the table, but the crumpled message wasn't there. Neither was the menu with my decoded message.

The situation was surreal, and part of me expected Todd to walk in at any moment and ask what the hell we were up to.

Please, please, please let him walk in. . . .

He wasn't going to, though. I knew that. And reality tugged at me like the tide. I held on tight to the back of the kitchen chair and just breathed, waiting for my equilibrium to return.

"You doing okay?"

"I've been better."

"Let's get out of here."

I liked that idea. Liked it a lot, actually, but first I had to do one thing. I took a deep breath and circled the bed. Sure enough, my clothes and my new red Givenchy shoes were still in the tangled mess I'd left before falling into bed with Todd last night. I grabbed them up, then followed Stryker back out onto the street. I eyed the passersby while he hailed a cab. No sign of the messenger, though, and I wasn't certain if that made me feel better or worse.

I *did* know that I was exhausted. I collapsed gratefully into the cab, and when Stryker put an arm around me and told me to lean back and relax, I didn't argue. I liked the feel of him next to me, and I liked that he was there to protect me. I didn't know him—not really—but I was grateful not to have to go this alone.

He smelled like safety, all soap and fabric softener, and for the first time since I'd seen Todd on the bed, I relaxed. I closed my eyes and faded into that familiar half-sleep that comes from riding in one too many unair-conditioned taxicabs.

All too quickly the lulling bounce of the shock-absorber-less cab ended, and we screeched to a halt in front of my building. I knew we were there even without Stryker nudging me. That's the sign of a true Manhattanite—knowing the cab's arrived at your apartment even from the depths of a catnap.

Stryker paid the driver, and we headed into the building. As we were about to step into the stairwell, I noticed an envelope shoved into the space between my mailbox and the mailbox for 4E, the same place where Mr. Abernathy leaves the overdue rent notices.

"Stryker . . ."

He turned in the direction I was looking, then crossed to the row of mailboxes and plucked up the envelope. Even from that distance, I could see that my name was printed across it in neat block letters. He handed me the envelope, and I slipped my finger under the flap, breaking the seal. I peered inside. The note. "Play or Die."

"He's giving you a second chance," Stryker said.

I nodded, not sure how I felt about that. Angry. Bewildered. Grateful. Not to mention incredibly confused.

Right then I was sure about only two things: that I wanted to nail the son of a bitch who'd done this to me, and that I was glad Stryker was there. Maybe I was being stupid and naïve and he was going to blow a hole through my head, too. But I didn't believe it. There was too much comfort in his touch, and when I pushed away, my skin was hot and my movements awkward.

"Looks like we're back to square one," I said, holding up the envelope. "Let's go figure out what this message means."

PLAY

OR

DIE

***

PRESTIGE

PARK

39A 89225

Stryker and I stared at the paper now lying on my kitchen table. "The 'Play or Die' part I think we've figured out," I said. "I'm not sure about the rest of it."

"Well, it's a park, right?"

I shrugged. "I've never heard of it." Jenn and I have a tourist map of New York pinned to the back of the front door, and I marched over to it, my eye drifting first to Central Park and then to all the other little dots of green across the map. I frowned. "There's a lot of them. And we don't even know if it's in Manhattan."

He moved to stand beside me. "It probably is. PSW is set here. I'd bet we're playing the game here, too."

"Shouldn't there be a list of parks? I don't see a list." I started poking at the tape that held the map down, trying to slide my fingernail underneath. "Maybe there's a list on the other side." I gave up on the tape and just yanked the damn thing down. It ripped at the bottom corner, leaving a tiny bit of lower Manhattan taped to the back of the door.

Stryker took the map from me and spread it on the table. We both leaned over, concentrating on the tiny printed lists. Hotels, Restaurants, Museums, *Parks*. I ran my finger down the column, squinting as the letters seemed to swim in front of my eyes. I didn't see Prestige Park, but I wasn't trusting myself at the moment. I scanned the list again. "I don't see it."

"Me either," he said, then pushed back from the table. "Got a phone book?"

I shrugged. I rarely know if there's food in the apartment. The odds that I'd know where to find a phone book were slim. "I can look."

The place isn't overflowing with space or storage capabilities, so it didn't take me long to check all the various nooks and crannies. "No luck," I said. "Why would it be in the phone book, anyway?"

"Maybe it's not a park," he said. "Maybe it's a parking garage."

"Well, duh," I said. "We should have figured that right off the bat."

He tilted his head and smiled—he had a really nice smile.

"It's been a rather unusual day. I think we can cut ourselves some slack for not thinking completely clearly."

He had a point. "Okay. So, should I go ask my neighbor for a phone book?"

"Let's try the Internet first."

He tugged Jennifer's laptop over and hit the power switch. While the machine booted up, I pulled my feet up on the chair and hooked my arms around my legs. I propped my chin on my knees and voiced something that had been bugging me. "Why clean Todd's apartment?"

"Maybe it's like you said. Keep the police out of it. Even if you had decided to run to the police, think what it would look like if there's no body, no sign of a struggle . . ."

"They'd just think I'm a kooky ex-girlfriend."

"Maybe."

I didn't like this (okay, that's pretty much a given, but I *really* didn't like this). I snatched up my phone and called Todd's direct dial at the office. His secretary picked up.

"Hi, Jan. It's Mel. Can I talk to Todd?"

"Well, a blast from the past. How've you been?" I closed my eyes, fighting frustration. Jan is a few years past sixty and has mentally adopted Todd. I think she was more distressed than either Todd or me when I pulled the plug on the relationship.

"I'm fine," I said. "But I'm in a bit of a rush. Is he available?"

"Oh, sweetie, I'm afraid he's not in today."

"Oh." I realized then that I'd really expected to hear his voice. Jan hadn't spouted gloom and doom, and I'd immediately latched onto that as good news. "Do you know when he'll be back?"

"Actually, I don't. He was very vague. Frankly," she said, low-ering her voice. "I'm a little concerned. It's not like him to just take off like that."

"He was vague?" I repeated, hope swelling. "You *talked* to him? When?" I'd seen Todd myself, all bloody in the bed. But I'd been freaking out, too. Had I seen someone else? Had it all been some horrible joke?

"This morning," she said, and just as I was about to fall to my knees and thank God, she added, "Well, I didn't actually speak to him. He sent an email."

"An email?" I closed my eyes, certain I knew the end to this story. Stryker reached out and touched my arm. He was only getting my side of the conversation, but I was pretty sure he'd clued in to the more salient points.

"Apparently he was heading off to catch a plane. Some sort of family emergency. Douglas was *not* happy," she added, referring to the firm's senior partner.

"No," I said. "I bet he wasn't."

Jan chattered on a bit more, but I'd quit listening. When she paused for breath, I made the appropriate good-bye noises, then hung up the phone.

"He's gone home," I said, my voice tight. "Family emergency."

"I'm sorry, Mel."

I felt hollow as I crossed to the sink. I turned on the cold water, then shoved my wrists under the stream. I don't know when I'd first picked up that habit, but it never failed to calm me. And right then, I felt remarkably calm, all things considered.

As I stood there, another thought occurred to me, and I turned around, my hip pressed against the countertop as I faced him. "Have you checked your message log?"

"That's how I knew about the money, remember?"

"I meant recently. In the game, sometimes the assassin will send a message. At least, that's how it was set up when I played." Actually, all the players communicated by sending messages among themselves. Getting a message from your assassin psyched some players out. And if you were playing the assassin's role, getting a message from your target could be just as unnerving.

"Shit," he said. "We should have looked hours ago."

"Sorry."

He held out a hand, urging me toward him. "Not your fault," he said. "Like I said, I'm not totally ignorant about how the game is played, and I didn't think of it, either."

"You wouldn't have. It's not a rule, or even anything that you'd find in the FAQs. It's one of those things you have to actually play to learn."

I'd moved beside him, but I hadn't taken his hand. Now he took mine, his expression serious. "I may not know the ins and outs of PSW, but I do know the real world. More important, I know how to fight. And how to kill if it comes to that. Don't doubt me, Mel. I promise I won't let you down."

"I believe you," I said. And it was true. I might not know him, but I didn't doubt him.

He'd said his piece, and now he concentrated on the computer. I pulled one of the chairs over beside him so that I could see the screen, too. As he typed, his arm brushed against mine. He was solid and warm, a man's man kind of guy. The kind of man I'd pretty much avoided in my dating life, tending more toward the guys I could talk numbers with. The jocks always bored me to tears. Now, though, I wasn't interested in brains. I wanted brawn, and lots of it. What can I say? I'm adaptable.

He typed in his login information, then entered the site and navigated to the message center. Two messages. Stryker looked at me, then clicked the icon to open the first one. The sender was someone named Lynx—and it didn't take long to realize that Lynx was the assassin, and that he'd started the game by killing Todd.

And that he'd been watching me.

"Eavesdropping equipment," I said with a shudder. I remembered making love to Todd, sickened at the thought of someone listening in on our private moments. "Bastard."

To say I didn't like being a victim was putting it mildly. I'd been in control my whole life—graduating as my high school valedictorian, organizing the first-ever science fair at my school, finding my own tuition help for college since the high school counselor was such a twit, making my own way in New York since my parents refused to toss any cash my way, and on and on and on. The only possible exception was my relationships with men. There my confidence lapses. But even so, I've never been a *victim*. Any asshole creep of a guy treats me badly, and I'm out of there in a heartbeat.

With this asshole, there wasn't any place to go.

"I hate this," I said.

"I know," Stryker said. He moved to the television and turned it on. Loud. Then he came back and leaned in close to my ear. "It gets worse, too. If he eavesdropped on you and Todd, who knows what he's doing now."

Well, hell. Stryker was right. The killer could be listening to us right then. The idea gave me the shivers.

"He definitely knows we're together," Stryker said. "The message came to me, not you."

"What's the other message say?" I asked, over the din.

Stryker clicked on it, and a new screen popped up showing nothing but a hyperlink.

Stryker clicked on the link. The page came up, and I gasped as I saw the image. . . .

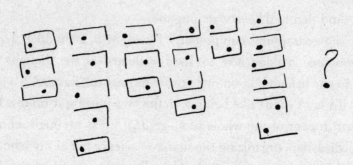

MEL—NO COPS
PLAY THE GAME
24 HOURS FROM OUR SWEET MEET.
OR DIE.

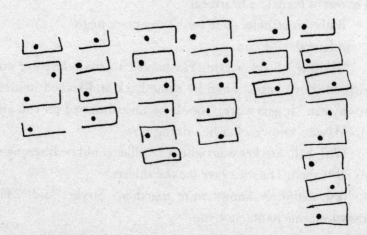

"I've never wanted to kill anyone in my life," I whispered. *"But I want him dead.* I want to find him, and I want him dead."

"So do I, kid," Stryker said.

I leaned over him and grabbed a piece of paper, then started drawing out the pigpen again. I might be pissed, but I wasn't stupid. I had twenty-four hours to figure out this Prestige Park bullshit. (I didn't know what would happen in twenty-four hours, but I really didn't want to learn the hard way.)

I started with the symbol at the very top of the screen and dutifully wrote *N* on my pad. Not very illuminating, but it was a start.

Beside me, Stryker was staring at the screen, a finger tapping against his jaw.

"What?" I asked him.

He looked up at me, a question in his eyes.

I made a production of tapping my own finger against my jaw. "You were thinking. What?"

"The website. I'm wondering if we can track him. Figure out who our enemy is."

"But if he realizes, that will just piss him off." I glanced around, nervous. We were speaking softly and the television was loud, but I was still afraid he could hear. I lowered my voice even more. "If he gets pissed off, he'll just kill me straight away."

"Won't happen," he said. "Qualifying round, remember?"

"Oh, that makes me feel better."

"If we want to win, we need to get the advantage here." He nodded toward the computer. "We need to figure out how he posted that message. It could lead us to him."

"If we want to win," I countered, "we need to play the game. I can do that. I can win." I hadn't lost this game yet, and I didn't intend to start now. Not with the stakes so high. And how did Stryker plan to find the guy, anyway? He was a ghost. No, playing was my only option. I was certain.

"I'm not saying don't play. All I'm saying is that you need every advantage you can get. You can't afford to lose this game."

"No shit," I said. "Rebooting isn't an option." And then, because I knew that I was talking from somewhere in hysterical-land, "*I know.* Really. I just . . ." I let it go.

"What?"

I shook my head, tightening my arms around my frame.

"Mel." His voice was gentle this time. "What?"

I closed my eyes. "I'm scared, okay? And I don't like it. I started college when I was sixteen. I've won math tournaments where I have to stand up on a stage and solve equations in my head. The pressure is intense, and I thrive on that shit. I don't get scared. But I'm scared now. I know how to play PSW. But what if I don't know how to play *this?*"

"Then let's try to end it. Let's track down the bastard. Let's get him first."

"What if it doesn't end it? What if it only escalates it?"

"He won't know we're looking. Not until it's too late."

"He could be listening right now," I said. "Even over the TV."

"I know." Frustration flashed in his eyes. "I think we're okay for the moment, but we need to move soon."

I nodded. I didn't like the idea of leaving. My apartment might be tiny, but at the moment, it was the only place in all of Manhattan that I felt safe. We had to go, though. We couldn't risk having the killer listening to our every word. "Where?"

"Not sure. Right now I just want to find the next clue. We'll worry about the other details after we know you're safe."

I licked my lips, realizing what had been bugging me. "But I won't be safe. Not if we're really playing the game. If you're right about the qualifying round, then as soon as I solve the clue, I'm a walking target."

Once the target solved the qualifying round clue, the game was truly under way. The assassin could pick a target off at any time after that. Of course, in the cyberworld, certain actions could provide you with a level of security. You could trade the clothes on your back for money and then buy a bulletproof vest, for example. I presumed the same applied in the real world. But since I had no idea where to buy a bulletproof vest—and since Stryker hadn't suggested it—I wasn't even worrying about that yet.

"The first clue," he said. "That's the Prestige Park one?"

I shook my head. "I don't think so. Let me see if I remember how this works." I might not have played in a while, but the idiosyncrasies of the game were coming back to me. "When the game starts, all players get a message letting them know. The target also gets a coded message telling her what to do."

"That's the Prestige Park message."

"Right," I said. "That message will lead somewhere in the cyberworld where the target will find *another* clue. That's the qualifying clue. As soon as the target solves that qualifying clue, then the assassin is free to cut her down."

"So what's our second message? The one in my inbox about twenty-four hours? Could it be the qualifying clue?"

"I don't think so. The intro message always *leads* to the clue. That message just came out of nowhere."

"Any ideas?"

"One," I said. But I didn't much like it. "The bit about twenty-four hours makes me think it's a warning."

"I'm listening."

"PSW's whole shtick depends on people getting in there and really playing the games, right? Finish one game, start another. That kind of thing."

"So?"

"So Grimaldi wanted to guard against people who log in, get assigned the role of target, and then spend weeks and weeks trying to figure out the first clue. Speed is the name of the game."

"What did he do?"

"He put in a twenty-four-hour kill switch."

"Right. I remember now. If the target doesn't solve the introductory code in twenty-four hours, the target is terminated and the players can move on to a new game." He met my eyes. "So much for my theory that you're safe until we hit the end of the qualifying round."

I pointed to the message still on the laptop screen. "I think that message is telling us that the twenty-four-hour kill switch applies in the real world."

"Translate the rest of the message and maybe we'll know for sure."

"I will." I sat in front of the computer and grabbed my pen. "The thing is, it's already been well over a day since he gave me the envelope. Do you think the time is running from when I ran into him in front of Todd's apartment?"

"Probably," Stryker said. "But we're not taking any chances. We need to get out of here. Go work somewhere where he can't eavesdrop, and then make sure he doesn't follow us once we've solved the clue."

"We'll go as soon as I do this," I said, tapping the screen. "We shouldn't wait."

"We shouldn't leave without knowing exactly what we're dealing with. Five minutes. That's all I need."

I thought he was going to argue more, but he didn't. Instead, he eased into the bedroom, his cell phone at his ear. I could hear the low timbre of his voice blending into the background as I worked the code, the deep rumble providing a soothing counterpart to the frightening message I was slowly revealing. *Antidote. Ricin. Deadly.*

I swallowed, staring down at the message I'd uncovered. Not a difficult code, but it hadn't been meant to be. Whoever had sent this had wanted me to uncover the message, and fast. This was a message meant to keep me alive. At least for a little while.

"Stryker." The word barely slipped past my lips. I cleared my throat and tried again. *"Stryker."*

He burst back into the room, his hand on his gun. I'd scared him, but I didn't bother to apologize. I was pretty terrorized myself.

"Here," I said. I pushed the paper with my translation toward him.

I watched as his gaze drifted to the paper, then he looked up, meeting my eyes. "Shit," he said.

I nodded. The man sure had a way with words.

Chapter 21

NOT RICIN BUT JUST AS DEADLY?
PLAY GAME FOLLOW CLUES GET ANTIDOTE.

Stryker read the words twice, looking for a hidden message. He didn't find one. Everything the killer wanted to say was laid out with stunning simplicity.

Mel had moved to the couch, and now he joined her, pressing his palm against her forehead. She didn't pull away, and for some reason that scared the hell out of him.

"Why didn't you tell me you felt bad?"

"I *don't* feel bad. But I guess now we know how the kill switch works. Some poison that'll kick in after twenty-four hours. *Fuck.*" With the last, she hurled a pillow across the room. It hit the television and bounced ineffectually to the ground. "Is that even possible?"

He nodded. "Yeah. It is." He'd worked in counterterrorism long enough to know that there were all kinds of nasty bugs being developed in labs all over the world. A Ricin-like toxin with a twenty-four-hour antidote window wasn't outlandish at all. Still, that intense a poison would be hard to get hold of, and hard to deliver. "It could be a bluff," he said. "Designed to psych you out."

She raised an eyebrow. "You think?"

"Poison has to be administered," he said. "It couldn't be airborne, because there's no way to regulate who gets infected. Something in your food? Maybe. But I don't think you've eaten anything since last night."

"It could have been in the Indian food," she said, leaning forward, her forehead creased in concentration. Even scared, she was analytical and engaged.

"That may be the most logical answer," he confirmed. "Especially since the only other way I can think of to infect you would be to inject you."

"Oh, shit." Her eyes widened, and she rubbed her tricep with her opposite hand.

He watched her, a bad feeling building in his gut. "What?"

"On the street, I tried to pull away and I felt a sharp pain in my arm. I thought I'd pulled a muscle, but—"

"Let me see."

She complied silently, pulling the long sleeve of her T-shirt up so that half her tricep was bare. He ran his finger over every inch of her bare arm but found nothing. "Let me see the rest of it."

She turned her head to face him. "Excuse me?"

He pressed his hand against her shoulder, which, along with

a good portion of her upper arm, was covered under the now-bundled-up sleeve. "I need to check the rest of your arm, Mel. We need to be sure. Take off your shirt."

"I . . . It's not my shirt." Her teeth grazed her lower lip. "It's Todd's. And I'm not wearing a bra or anything."

"Oh." He swallowed, his mind filling suddenly with an image of Mel peeling off the T-shirt and standing before him, half naked and ready for his intimate inspection. He shoved the image away; now really wasn't the time. "Go change," he said, his voice more gruff than he wanted. "A few minutes won't make a difference."

"No. I want to know." As he watched, she tugged the sleeve back down, then pulled her arm out so that her arm was inside the shirt. Then she pressed her other arm and hand against her chest, keeping the thin cotton pressed against her breasts. "Go ahead," she said. "Look."

He peeled up her shirt, revealing her naked arm and back. Her skin was white and creamy, and as his fingers explored her upper arm, he had to fight an almost overwhelming urge to stroke her back as well, to slide his hand underneath the T-shirt and to cup her breast in his palm.

Goose bumps appeared on her skin, and she shivered under his touch. "I'm sorry," he said. "Are you cold?"

She shook her head, a slow blush easing up the back of her neck. "I'm fine," she whispered. "Did you find it?"

"Not yet. I— Shit." And there it was. A tiny red prick. Not even noticeable unless you were looking for it. "Goddamn it all to hell," he said.

She drew in a loud, shaky breath, then eased out from under his touch. Her arm snaked back up, and when she turned back to face him, she was dressed again. "It happened this morning," she said. "Ten-thirty. Maybe eleven."

"It's almost one now."

"Should I go to a hospital?"

"I don't think so," he said. "If the doctors think you've been infected with that kind of a toxin, they'll raise the alarm. Call in Homeland Security and get all sorts of authorities involved. You'll be quarantined. And by the time we get it straightened out, twenty-four hours will be long gone."

"We don't have to mention the comparison to Ricin. We could just say poison."

"There's no guarantee the toxin will be isolated in time even if we *do* mention Ricin. And if we don't, we can pretty much guarantee they won't find anything out in time. In the meantime, the antidote will be out there waiting for us. But if we don't find it in time—"

"You're right," she said. "No hospital." She squared her shoulders and looked him in the eyes. "We follow the clue."

Chapter

22

I felt fine, and I couldn't quite get my head around the idea that I'd been poisoned and had less than twenty-four hours to find the antidote. If this were a movie—or even an episode of *24*— I'd find the antidote in the last possible second, then I'd turn around and kick the shit out of the bad guy.

Would be nice, but I wasn't going to bank on it.

I shoved Kiefer out of my mind and focused instead on the man who was with me. The man who'd promised to help get me through this. I believed him, too, and already I'd come to rely on his strength, to anticipate his thoughts and suggestions. I'd only known him for a few hours, but my life was running in fast forward now, and Stryker was running right alongside me.

At the moment, though, he wasn't running anywhere. Instead, he'd parked himself back at the computer, and now he pulled up Google and typed in a search.

>>>*New York Prestige Park*<<<

About a million hits came up, all of them raving about the *prestigious* apartments/offices/restaurants on *Park* Avenue. So much for an easy answer.

We were running out of ideas. If we couldn't figure out Prestige Park, we couldn't find the next clue. And if we couldn't find the next clue, I was dead.

"Let me try," I said. I didn't care if there were two thousand pages of hits. We were going to look at every single one of them.

"Hold on," he said, then typed in a new search.

>>> *"New York" "Prestige Park"*<<<

He hit Enter, and *bingo.* A car park. "Well, hello," Stryker said. And I actually almost smiled.

We'd decided to stay in my apartment until we figured out the clue, since moving to some other location would take too much time. But we'd also decided to be quiet, just in case there were other eyes and ears watching us. I'd changed out of Todd's clothes and pulled on my Miss Sixty jeans and a Goretti tank top I'd scored off eBay.

Beside me, Stryker had his cell phone open and was dialing information. "Turn up the radio," he said.

I rushed to the stereo and complied, turning the volume higher and higher until he finally nodded, satisfied. How he'd hear his conversation, I didn't know. Didn't care, either, so long as he got it done. I knew he would, too. The man had it together, that was for sure. He'd told me that his earlier phone call was to a computer geek friend to try and figure out who posted that Web message. Nice to know he was on top of that. And now he'd solved the Prestige Park mystery. And the best part? He was on my side.

Behind me, Stryker muttered into his phone, then snapped it shut. He leaned onto the table, brushing my shoulder as he picked up the pen I'd been using earlier. He scribbled a note, then inched it toward me. *Prestige Car Park—downtown & Bronx.*

"Looks like we're going downtown," he said.

I nodded, trying to remember if the online version of the game extended to the boroughs. I didn't think it did. A plus for me, since, like so many Manhattanites, I was entirely clueless about life outside the island.

He snapped the screen shut on Jenn's laptop, then slid it into the case, balling the cords up and shoving them in, too. I thought about protesting—it was Jenn's computer, after all— but I didn't. Jenn would understand, and we might need the thing. Finally, he grabbed the original message and my notes interpreting it. "Let's go."

I stood up, then took the papers from him. I dumped them and my pocketbook-sized purse into a tote bag that I regularly schlepped to class with me. "Are we coming back?"

"Not if I can help it."

I nodded, shifting my weight on the balls of my feet, now snugly encased in my Prada sneakers as I stalled in the doorway. What can I say? It was hard to leave. I hated the idea of abandoning all my shoes. Not to mention my handbags, clothes, photo albums, books, and favorite CDs.

"I'll buy you a change of underwear," Stryker said, since my thoughts were apparently transparent. "But we need to get moving. We've already wasted enough time, and—"

"Fine. You're right. Let's go." I told myself that this wasn't good-bye forever—just until we'd won the game.

I tugged the door closed and locked it, my worldly possessions now measured by the width and breadth of the Kate Spade tote I'd snagged last fall in a seventy-five-percent-off sale. "I'll be back soon," I said to the door. I hoped I was telling the truth.

Twenty minutes later, the taxi dropped us off in front of the entrance to Prestige Car Park. "What now?" I asked. "Can we just go in and look for spot 39A?"

"Not likely," Stryker said, taking my elbow and pulling me aside. "The attendant's going to be well tipped and very protective."

"So what are we going to tell him?"

"Not a damn thing," Stryker said, nailing me with a sideways glance. "We're sneaking in."

I was on the verge of asking how when a car pulled into the drive. Stryker held up a finger, signaling for me to be quiet. I wasn't thrilled about being kept in the dark about his plan, but at the moment I had no choice.

The car—a Lincoln—stopped just inside the garage. Stryker and I watched, waiting for the attendant to show up. Apparently the driver was just as impatient, because he tapped the horn twice. I heard a door slam from somewhere toward my left, then a young kid in a blue blazer with *Prestige* embroidered on the breast pocket hurried over.

As the attendant bent down to speak to the driver, Stryker's hand pressed against my back. "Come on," he whispered. He took my hand, and we scurried inside, keeping toward the walls as we hoofed it toward a marked stairwell near the back. Stryker tried the door, then gave me a triumphant smile when he realized it was unlocked. He ushered me inside, following right on my heels.

"What are we doing in here?" I asked as the door closed behind us.

"The first floor is probably short-term parking. People shopping or going to lunch. Since whoever's behind this bullshit must have taken some time to put the pieces in place, I figure the car we're looking for must have been left in a long-term space."

He was right, and I lifted myself up on my tiptoes and gave him a quick kiss on the cheek. I didn't think about it; I just planted the kiss impulsively. And as I pulled away, I was relieved to see that he looked pleased. Surprised, but pleased.

"What was that for?"

Since I wasn't entirely certain, I said the first thing that came into my head. "For helping me."

That won me a quick smile before he took my hand and led me up the stairs. We emerged on the next level and started checking space numbers. The cars were stacked three deep in the spaces, with C being closest to the wall, B trapped in the middle, and A free to pull out into the driveway.

We'd split up when we emerged on this level, and I was having no luck. My side was all teens and twenties. I was circling back toward Stryker when I heard him call me, his voice low in case the attendant was in earshot.

"Here," he said.

I hurried over and found him tugging a cream-colored cover off what turned out to be a navy blue Mercedes. The top-of-the-line kind with a keypad entry system and everything.

"What do you think?"

He walked the perimeter, his eyes on the vehicle. "I think the answer's inside somewhere." When he made it back to the driver's side door, he scowled at the door, then started to reach for the handle.

"Wait! It's probably got a car alarm. You need the key."

"Thanks for that bit of insight," he said, "but in case you forgot, we don't have a key."

I dug in my tote and came up with the Prestige Park message, then waved it at him. "I think we do," I said.

I read the numbers off to him, and he dutifully punched them into the door's keypad: 89225.

I smiled as he gave a tug, certain we were golden.

Since this day was *not* going well, of course I was wrong. As soon as Stryker gave the door a yank, the alarm system started blaring.

"Damn it!" Stryker yelled over the din. The thing screeched at an ear-piercing level, and I gritted my teeth against the noise, afraid someone was going to come see what we were up to.

"Shut it off," I said. "Make it stop!"

He looked around, as baffled as I felt, then he reared sideways, lifted his leg and struck out, smashing his heel against the window.

Nothing happened, and the car continued to squawk.

"Find me something metal!" Stryker called. "A crowbar or something."

I turned in a circle but didn't see a thing. "Where's your gun?"

"I'd rather not use it," he said. "Ballistics."

"Oh, for crying out loud . . ." At the moment, I was much more concerned with my antidote than with the crime tech analysis of some random bullet in a Mercedes. "Just blast the thing."

He reached toward his jacket. "Stand back." He aimed, and then, just as he was about to fire, the alarm shut off. Silence had never sounded so good. "Well, that's one thing going our way," he said, slipping the gun back into his jacket. "Any bright ideas how we can get in without setting off the alarm?"

"The keys?" I said brightly.

"Unfortunately, I think you're right." He slid Jenn's laptop case off his shoulder and passed it to me. "Wait here."

"Wait here?" I repeated. "Where are you going?"

"To get the keys," he said. "Where else?"

I couldn't really argue with that, so instead I just watched him leave, my fingers crossed tight beside me. I would have liked to believe he could simply ask the attendant for the keys and the request would be granted, but I knew better.

Stryker was going to steal them.

Feeling suddenly extraneous in my own dilemma, I started to lean against the car, then stopped myself before I triggered the alarm again. I could believe that we were supposed to steal the keys—considering the game as a whole, what was a little larceny, after all? But what I couldn't believe was that those numbers—89225—had no meaning. I just hadn't figured it out yet.

I leaned against a cement pillar and ran the digits through my head, looking for a pattern. They weren't prime numbers. Some other relationship, maybe?

Probably, but I couldn't think of anything.

Stryker might not be a math aficionado, but I still wanted to bounce ideas off him, and I wished he'd hurry up and get back with the keys.

The keys.

Of course. Could it really be that simple?

I dug in my tote and found a pen and a scrap of paper. I'd created the pigpen translation key by putting a 1 after the Z. But there wasn't any real reason for doing that except habit. It made just as much sense to start a string of ten digits with 0. And so that's what I did now. And when I translated the original message using my new key with a different number sequence, I got an entirely different last line:

28A 78114

I looked around, wondering where 28A was. I knew I should wait for Stryker, but I had to know if I was right. So I rummaged some more until I found my brand-new MAC lipstick. I said a little apology to the fashion industry, then used the lipstick to write "S—MP @ 28A" on the cement pillar. Then I headed off, hoping like hell I was right.

It didn't take me long to find the car, a late-model Jaguar two-seater, sleek and silver. And, I noticed right off, with a keyless entry system. At least my tormentor had good taste in cars.

I took a deep breath and punched in the new numbers. *Click.*

I said a silent prayer and opened the door. The heady scent of new leather accosted me, and I breathed in deep as I slid inside. I love new car smell. But I didn't have time to enjoy. If there was a clue inside this car, it wasn't immediately apparent. I put my hands on the steering wheel and tried to think. *If I were a clue, where would I be?*

"Nice car, lady. Care to give a soldier a lift?"

I yelped and jumped so high I almost hit my head on the roof. My heart was pounding, and I turned to glare at Stryker, but it was for show only. I was too impressed with myself—and too thrilled by his wide smile of approval—to truly be angry he'd snuck up on me.

"Found your message," he said.

"I started with zero instead of one," I explained.

"If you say so," he said. He dangled a set of keys. "I'm guessing we don't need these after all?"

"I don't think so." My eyes drifted out of habit to the ignition, then widened as I saw what was already there—one shiny silver key. "Looks like this car comes fully equipped."

He tossed the Mercedes keys in the air and caught them. "Guess it wasn't an entirely wasted venture. It can't hurt to keep my burglary skills sharp."

"You never know when you'll need to break and enter," I agreed. "So do you think the key means we're supposed to take the car?"

"Possibly," Stryker said. He moved around to the passenger

side, then checked the empty glove compartment. "At the very least, we should write down the license plate number."

"Here you go," I said, then fumbled in my bag for paper and a pen for him.

While he did that, I flipped down both visors. Nothing. Ditto the ashtray, the cup holders and the little repository for loose coins. "I'm out of ideas," I said. "The clue should be someplace pretty obvious, I'd think. The first level's always easy. Relatively speaking, I mean."

Stryker signaled for me to pop the trunk, then he circled the car. "Nothing here," he said after a few minutes. He slammed the trunk closed.

My heart lurched, but I wasn't yet ready to voice defeat. "It's got to be here," I said. "We just have to figure out how to think like we were in the real game."

"Right," he said. Then, after a moment, "Any ideas?"

Not one, a little fact that irritated the hell out of me. How many times had I sat in class, imagining a tall, dark stranger passing me an encoded message, absolutely critical to national defense? I'd crack the code, even while being chased by vile counteragents out to kill me. They wouldn't succeed, though. I'd do whatever it took to survive, whether that meant a night of lipstick and Manolos or slogging across enemy lines in camo pants and military issue moon boots. In the end, it would be my quick mind and sharp wit that saved the day. Jennifer Garner might be famous, but she had nothing on me.

I stifled a snort, disgusted with myself. Fantasy was one thing. Survival was another. So far, I might be surviving, but I'd hardly pulled out all the stops. I hadn't turned the tables on this guy, I hadn't even made an effort to get the upper hand. Instead,

I was wandering around stunned, letting someone else call the shots—whoever was orchestrating this game, my assassin-opponent, and yes, even Stryker. Well, no more. . . .

He might be on my side, but there wasn't anyone on the planet more loyal to my cause than me. That was simply a fact. My three loves are shoes and math and history—believe me when I say I know all about fashion and facts. I live and die by them. Yesterday, that had been metaphorical. Today, I feared, I was being entirely literal.

What I needed to be, though, was analytical. That's what I was good at, right? That's why I'd gotten sucked into this freak show, wasn't it? Someone out there knew I could play this game. And in the end, this was all about playing a stupid computer game in the real world.

And that, I realized with a start, was the answer. Aloud, I asked, "Know anything about Jaguars?"

He shot me an unreadable look. "I've got a Triumph Trident. Sweet little bike. I know her inside and out, but that's it."

"Do you know if they're computerized?"

His forehead creased as he frowned, but I wasn't sure if he was confused by my question or unsure of the answer.

"Computer diagnostics," I said. "This whole thing started with a computer game. So maybe . . . ?"

He stared at me, and I began to feel a little uncomfortable under the scrutiny.

"What? It's not *that* dumb an idea."

"Are you kidding?" he asked, and I was just about to defend myself some more when he added, "It's brilliant."

That was more like it. I couldn't help my grin.

"Let's go," he said.

I blinked, not feeling like such a brainiac after all. "Go where?"

"That explains why we have a key. We need to find a garage if we're going to plug the system into diagnostics. And if that comes up flat, we can scour the car again."

"So I'm right? They can really do that? Stick a message in a car's computer system?"

He shrugged. "Beats the hell out of me. I guess we'll find out."

I slid to the passenger side. "Ready."

He got in and turned the key. The engine purred to life, and the CD player clicked on. A low hum came from the speakers, followed by a series of clicks. Then a computer-generated voice spoke: " 'I know *something* interesting is sure to happen,' she said to herself, 'whenever I eat or drink anything.' "

"What the fuck?" Stryker asked, but I was already pushing the Eject button and carefully taking the CD out.

"Alice in Wonderland," I said, referring to the quote from Alice before she swallowed the Drink Me juice. "I don't know how exactly, but I'm sure this CD is our clue."

Chapter

24

I held the disc up, examining it in the dim light. "It's just a CD-R," I said. "Someone burned this disc for us."

"So our clue is about eating and drinking?"

"Maybe," I said. "But I don't think so."

"I'm listening," he said.

"I think I'm supposed to be Alice. And the voice on the disc was just to get my attention."

"To let you know that the CD was the clue," Stryker said. "OK. So we have to see what else is burned on that disc."

"Exactly."

"No time like the present." He opened the computer case and slid the laptop out, then drummed his fingers on the armrest as we waited for it to boot up. As soon as it did, we slid the CD in and shut the drive door.

At first, nothing happened, then the familiar hourglass icon appeared on the screen, telling us the computer was busy. When the hourglass disappeared, Stryker slid his finger on the touch-pad, clicked on the My Computer folder, then navigated to drive D.

"Here goes nothing," he said as he double-clicked on the icon. The display for the drive pulled up, revealing two files. One was a .wav file, which we assumed was the Alice message. The other was a .doc file. I itched to take the computer from Stryker's hands, but he was moving just as fast as I could have. He clicked, and the file opened—a Microsoft Word document with one line of text: http://www.playsurvivewin-message.com/, complete with hyperlink.

"Do we have Internet access here?" he asked.

"We should. Jenn's got an aircard. She's supposed to be able to get on the Net from anywhere." As a rule, Jenn is as broke as I always am. Her parents, though, are a lot more generous, and they'd set her up with the wireless system last Christmas. I coveted the technology myself. Like a cell phone, the wireless air-card let Jenn connect from pretty much anywhere. I knew it would be handy to have something like that, but aircards were expensive, and my need wasn't as strong as, say, my desire for new shoes.

Sure enough, Stryker clicked on the link, and a Web browser opened. It took a second to pull the webpage down, and then there it was, just as I'd both hoped and dreaded. A message. Meant entirely for me.

Close, my dear, but not quite yet. . . .
How long has it been since you felt my assassin's kiss?
Like Dorothy, the sand slips away. . . .

$$x^2 + y^2 = r^2$$
$$y = mx + b$$

Like starlight in your pocket, a touch of the familiar
before your lights
go out
and you're lost . . . alone . . . in the dark . . . never
again to be found.

Chapter

25

Stryker thought seriously of smashing his fist through the monitor. He was supposed to be protecting her, not slogging through the goddamn *Da Vinci Code*. "This is crap," he said. "What the hell are we supposed to do with this nonsense?"

"We'll be fine." Mel's hand pressed lightly against his wrist. "It's okay."

"The hell it is." He'd served twelve years in the Marine Corps, protecting his country and the citizens of a whole slew of countries under the thumb of despots. But this damn game had thrust him into battle with unknown enemies. He was chasing ghosts—the assassin Lynx, some toxin hidden in Mel's own blood. All unseen enemies, and each one ready to do her in at any time.

Ruefully, he glanced again at the computer screen. He couldn't even make sense of the clue. How the hell was he supposed to protect her?

Beside him, Mel was pushing her door open. "Let's go."

"Go? Go where?"

"Where the message is sending us," she said. "Circle Line Tours. The Harbor Lights Cruise."

"Of course," he said. "You want to tell me how you know that?"

She leaned close, brushing against him as she pointed to the x-y-r equation. "This is the standard form equation for a circle. And this is one equation for a straight line," she added, pointing to y = mx + b.

"Sure it is," he said.

She laughed, the first genuine laugh he'd heard since they'd first met. It was a wonderful sound, and he realized suddenly how much he wanted to hear it again. "Trust me," she said. "That wasn't even really a code. More like a riddle."

"So that's how you got Circle Line. The Harbor Lights Cruise came from the starlight reference."

"Exactly." She flashed an impish grin. "If this whole thing weren't such a nightmare, it might actually be fun."

"You're probably the type who works the Sunday crossword puzzle."

"Oh no," she said, but the corner of her mouth twitched. "But I do play chess in the park on Sundays."

"So do a lot of folks," he said. "The question is, do you win?"

She looked at him as if he'd just asked if she needed air to breathe. "Of course I win. What's the point of playing if you don't win?"

And that, he thought, pretty much summed up the whole damn day.

"**W**e have to hurry," I said, jogging along Broadway with Stryker at my side. I was looking for an available taxi, but of course there were none. "The boat leaves at seven."

I was right about the clue. I knew I was. But if that boat left without us . . . *shit.* I needed that antidote. Twenty-four hours, the message had said. And time was ticking away.

A taxi turned onto the street half a block ahead of us. I jumped into the roadway and held out my hand, but some bastard in a suit stepped out ahead of me, and the taxi pulled over. "No!"

Naturally, he didn't pay a bit of attention to me. Stryker, though, grabbed my hand and pulled me into a dead run (a hell of a lot faster than I ever thought I could move). "I'll give you fifty bucks to take the next taxi," he yelled at the suit as we tumbled to a halt beside the cab. Stryker let go of my hand to fumble for his wallet even as he ushered me into the backseat.

"Hey!" the guy said, glaring at me. "Get your ass out of my taxi."

"A hundred bucks," Stryker said, peeling off bills and pressing them into the guy's hand.

"I got a meeting," the guy said, but most of the oomph had left his voice.

Stryker elbowed the guy aside and squeezed in next to me, passing another fifty to the driver. "He can wait for the next one."

The driver didn't answer, but he did accelerate, leaving Stryker to tug the door closed to the sound of the man's curses echoing after us.

Now we had a chance of making it in time.

My optimism lasted all the way to Broadway and 38th before it came to a screeching halt along with the traffic.

I exchanged a frustrated glance with Stryker. "Twelve minutes," he said. "From here we go on foot." He checked the meter, passed the fare plus some over the partition, and opened the door. "It's about ten blocks total, at least five of them crosstown. You okay with that?"

"Believe me, I have incentive."

He nodded and took the computer case from me, slinging it over his shoulder before he grabbed my hand and turned left, hauling ass down 38th Street and right into the heart of the garment district.

It was a testament to how frantic I was to get to the pier on time that I didn't even slow my pace to gawk in the windows. Instead, I just ran.

I never in a million years thought I could keep up with a Marine where anything remotely related to exercise was concerned, but I didn't do half bad keeping up with Stryker. Of course, by the time we reached Pier 83, I was thoroughly winded and had a stitch in my side. On the upside, I was glad I'd chosen my Prada sneakers over the Givenchy pumps. Score one on the side of practical fashion.

"Time?" I yelled, breathless, as I hunched over, my hands propped on my knees while I sucked in air. At least I didn't have to feel guilty about not making it to the gym that morning; I was getting one hell of a workout.

"Six-fifty-eight."

"Thank God."

The Circle Line building loomed in front of us. A massive structure, it takes up the width of the pier and rises several stories. The top resembles a whitewashed water tower, with red letters spelling out Circle Line, a logo featuring Lady Liberty taking up the space between the two words. The main floor is not much more than in and out driveways flanked on either side by ticket windows, which I knew very well. I'd done a very brief stint behind one of those windows when I'd first moved to New York.

Now Stryker raced to the window on the left, his wallet already open. I was right beside him, terrified that his watch was slow and that the boat had already left the dock.

We were in luck, though. We really had made it with two minutes to spare, and we rushed down the pier toward the sleek white yacht that would take us on the two-hour cruise around lower Manhattan.

As soon as we were on the boat, I burst out laughing. Stryker shot me a curious glance, but I couldn't help it. I was giddy with relief. It had been a hell of a day. Exhausting, terrifying and a whole lot of other *-ings* I couldn't think of at the moment. But we'd made it! We'd solved the clue, we'd made it onto the boat, and damn it all, that was a victory I intended to revel in.

Stryker indulged me for a few minutes, the corner of his mouth twitching in amusement. Then he put a firm hand on my arm and steered me across the deck and into the cabin. I'd worked at the ticket window, but I'd never actually taken one of the cruises before, and now I drew in a breath, impressed by the polished and gleaming interior. The crew member who'd welcomed us aboard had mentioned that the ship was new to Circle Line's fleet, and I could tell. Everything seemed shiny and snazzy, much more like a hotel ballroom than the dingy, damp interior I'd always imagined.

We crossed a parquet dance floor, the various shades of wood tiles set to form a star pattern. Now, tourists holding drinks mingled there, but I could imagine ballroom dancing if the yacht was rented out for black-tie extravaganzas.

"This way," Stryker said, leading me past rows of royal blue upholstered benches and snazzy chrome and wood tables. The walls were almost entirely windows, slanting up to give some view of the sky. I heard the low, mournful cry of the yacht's horn and realized we were starting to pull away from the dock. Lower Manhattan filled the view, and I paused for just a second, staring at the magnificence of my city, before Stryker urged me on. We passed a mahogany bar, behind which two busy bartenders filled glasses with wine for the gathering crowd. I looked longingly but didn't ask Stryker to pause. We both needed to stay sharp, after all.

"Look at every face," Stryker said. "If Lynx is here, I want to see him before he finds us."

I nodded, suddenly less interested in Circle Line's interior decorating skills and much more concerned with my companions. We continued on up the stairs to the mid-deck, this level less formal than the first. We walked the length of it, examining every face, then moved outside. A walkway ran the length of the boat, the interior side lined with padded benches and the ocean side protected by a chest-high rail. We covered the entire deck, didn't see Lynx, then moved back into the cabin.

I noticed a ladies' room and told Stryker to wait up. For a second I didn't think he was going to leave my side, but fortunately we didn't have to have that argument. He silently conceded my privacy, turning to lean against a wall as I pushed open the door and entered the less plush but sparkling clean ladies' room.

I'd been desperate for a bathroom, and as I was washing my hands, I realized I was also desperate for a touch-up. I looked totally bedraggled. Not too surprising, I supposed. In the short span of a day, I'd been poisoned, chased, terrified and threatened. I still looked better than I did after a long night of drinking, though. I suppose that counted for something.

I dug in my tote until I found my brush, then tried to do something with my hair. The summer heat and humidity from the boat had hit it hard, and somehow it was managing to be both limp and frizzy at the same time. In my own bathroom— which Jenn and I keep stocked better than Frederic Fekkai's warehouse—this would be fixable. On this boat, with no product except a sample size of TIGI hairspray, I had no options. I brushed my hair back from my face, gathered it with a barrette at the base of my neck, then sprayed the flyaway ends into place.

Not bad, except that now my pasty skin couldn't hide beneath my hair. Time for drastic measures. I dumped my tote on the counter, then put everything back in, one item at a time, except for my makeup. I did a quick touch-up with foundation, used a light shade of eyeshadow to make my eyes seem wider, brushed on a hint of blush so that I looked alive, then dabbed the shiny spots with powder. I did my lips last, lining them first, then using the same MAC lipstick I'd used to leave Stryker a message in the parking garage. I had to smooth the lipstick with the tip of my finger to get rid of the dust and dirt, but once it was cleaned up, it worked just fine. See? That's why I spend a fortune on quality cosmetics. They can take the abuse.

Once I was done, I took a step back from the mirror and inspected the results. Not bad, especially when you considered that what I really needed was a shower and a nap. But I did feel better, and just knowing I didn't look like a vagrant gave me a boost. Considering my life was on the line, I figured I needed all the help I could get.

Stryker was waiting right where I'd left him, and as I stepped out of the restroom, his gaze skimmed over me. I expected to hear a sarcastic comment about females and primping and wasting valuable time. It didn't come. Instead, I saw a flicker of heat in his eyes, and for just one moment, that reaction made me forget the direness of my situation.

"Feel better?"

"Loads."

"Good. You look great."

I smiled, feeling pretty and feminine as he took my arm and led me up the stairs to the sundeck.

Smaller than the previous two, this deck was my favorite simply because it placed us out in the open with a grand view of the skyline and the sky. We were high above the river now, and the cool breeze from the water felt fabulous after the heat of the summer day. Benches were lined up one behind the other, and we walked to the back of the boat, taking a seat on the very last bench. The yacht's wake churned just below us, and that, coupled with the steady pulse of the water beating against the sides of the boat, created a cacophony of sounds that enveloped and soothed. I turned sideways in my seat, relaxing just a little as I took in the stunning skyline passing beside us.

"Keep a lookout," Stryker said. "But I don't think he's here."

"Me either." Reluctantly, I turned away from the view, the game sucking me back to reality. "I don't think I'm fair game yet, anyway."

That obviously surprised him. "Why not? The clue on the CD is the qualifying clue, right? I thought you said that in PSW once the target solves the qualifying clue, then the assassin can start doing his thing."

"That's right. But I don't think we've solved it yet."

He held his hands out, indicating the boat. "Not that this isn't a lovely way to spend an evening, Mel, but if the solution wasn't Circle Line Harbor Lights Cruise, then why are we here?"

"Maybe I just wanted to spend some quality time with you?" I retorted. My intention had been to tease, but there was too much truth in the words, and I felt my face heat. Spending time alone with Stryker *was* appealing, and under other circumstances, a slow cruise around lower Manhattan with him would be the perfect way to spend an evening.

Too bad the specter of possible death had to step in and ruin my good time.

"Sorry," I said, before he could answer. "I'm just a little punchy." I shifted again on the bench and prepared to explain. "We solved the Circle Line part, but so what? We haven't found any other clue or noticed anything relevant to the game at all. If we were online, we'd probably be maneuvering through a digitized version of this ship, clicking on various items around us until we found the solution. *That* would trigger the assassin."

"The solution," he repeated. "You mean it would be over? The whole thing just turns into a race for your life?"

"No, I just meant that particular solution. It would be another clue, actually. And then we'd have to solve it in order to find the next clue. And so on and so on until we get to the end or the assassin makes a kill. Whichever comes first." I said the words blandly, as if I were simply stating a geometric proof. But there was nothing bland about these facts, and I shivered.

Beside me, Stryker slipped off his jacket and put it over my shoulders. Before he did, I saw him take the gun and slip it into the waistband of his jeans, using the tail of his shirt to hide the butt.

"I'm not really cold," I said.

He met my eyes, and I saw understanding there. "I know." He took my hand, his fingers twining with mine. I hesitated, then leaned against him, relief pouring over me when he curled his arm around my shoulder. Beside us, the skyline seemed to float by, the lights of the buildings starting to twinkle in the growing dusk.

134 JULIE KENNER

We sat in comfortable silence for a few minutes before
Stryker spoke again. "You're probably right. But I still want you
to be careful. Don't drop your guard."

"I won't." I turned in his arms. "Too bad we can't just stay
on this boat forever. If we never solve the clue, he can never
start hunting me."

There were a lot of reasons why that plan was unworkable,
but we both knew the biggest one. It was Stryker who finally
voiced it. "If we don't solve the clue, we'll never find the antidote. And the clock is ticking. Any ideas what to do now?"

I wanted Stryker to hold me and make it all better. But that
wasn't an option. I was the one with the skill to interpret clues.
And I was the one whose ass was on the line. I sat up straight,
shifting out from under his arm as I leaned across him for the
laptop case. "We go back to the clue," I said. "And we figure out
what we missed."

Chapter

27

While the computer booted up, Stryker watched Mel with undisguised fascination. She'd put on makeup in the restroom, and in doing so, she'd also put on a layer of confidence. He wasn't surprised by the result—even when his mother had been the most ill, she'd religiously applied her makeup. At first he'd protested, telling her she looked great and needn't bother, but she'd insisted. And it hadn't taken long to see that the woman had had more energy and concentration on the days when she'd gotten dressed and made up. Even on her last days, he'd made sure the nurses had listened when his mom insisted on showing the world the face she'd wanted it to see.

He thought about her now, watching Mel, and he realized just how alike the two women were. They were both fighters. Both strong women who weren't afraid to speak their minds and think for themselves. He wondered briefly what kind of a woman Jamie Tate had been, and once again he felt the familiar tug of regret and guilt that he hadn't been able to save her.

He hadn't been able to save his mother, either. Cancer had been too elusive an assassin, even for a Marine. He'd told himself it wasn't his failure; her body had broken down, and there'd been no way he could have fought that. Time would heal the loss.

When Jamie Tate had died, though, the failure had been his alone, a wound that would scar him forever, even though he'd never even met the woman.

Everything was different this time. He knew Mel. She was healthy. She was alive. And the thought of seeing her cut down—seeing that vibrant, sarcastic, beautiful light destroyed—was simply too much to bear. It wouldn't happen because Stryker wouldn't let it happen.

He'd worked as a bodyguard enough times to know that, as her protector, he shouldn't even think about letting this get personal. Get personal, and you open the door to the possibility of making a mistake.

Too late, though, because this *was* personal. Personal for Mel and personal for him. And it was for that very reason that he'd make sure Mel stayed safe. And in the end, he'd find the son of a bitch who'd done this to them, and he'd nail his sorry ass.

"Hey," she said, her smile just a tad too knowing. "You with me?"

"Absolutely." He shoved his rambling thoughts from his head and focused on the computer. She'd opened the clue again, and now Stryker tried to coax some flash of brilliance from the nonsensical words.

Close, my dear, but not quite yet. . . .
How long has it been since you felt my assassin's kiss?
Like Dorothy, the sand slips away. . . .

$$x^2 + y^2 = r^2$$
$$y = mx + b$$

Like starlight in your pocket, a touch of the familiar
before your lights
go out
and you're lost . . . alone . . . in the dark . . . never
again to be found.

"'Assassin's kiss' has to mean when he stuck you," Stryker said, thinking out loud.

"Right. That's what I think, too. And we already know what the equations mean. Circle. Line."

"And starlight, lights and dark probably refers to the Harbor Lights cruise," he continued.

"Except here we are and no new clue has hit us on the head."

"That's why we're sitting here now," he said. He squeezed her hand. "We'll figure it out. I'm not going to let anything happen to you."

She lifted a brow. "Can you suck the poison out of my blood?"

"Want me to try?"

Her cheeks flushed red even under the makeup she'd applied, and he stifled a chuckle. "Thanks for the offer," she said, her eyes twinkling. "Maybe I'll take a rain check if I get really desperate."

"You really know how to hurt a guy."

"There are all kinds of desperate," she said, her voice husky but her eyes amused.

"Is that so?"

"Absolutely." She kept the smile, but the amusement soon faded, replaced by an expression he couldn't quite read. She reached out and stroked his cheek, the velvety touch both tempting and tender. "Thank you again," she said. "For being here. And for watching out for me."

"Mel, I—"

"Come on," she interrupted, nodding at the screen. "We need to get back to it."

"Right. Okay." He sucked in a deep breath, hoping the oxygen would help him focus.

" 'Close, my dear, but not quite yet,' " she read.

"Probably just a commentary about finding the message on the CD," he suggested.

She nodded. "That's my thought, too. Patting us on the head and telling us, 'Good job, now go jump through some more hoops.' "

"Keep going. What about this next line: 'How long has it been since you felt my assassin's kiss?' Telling you there's a ticking clock. A time bomb."

She grimaced, and he regretted his choice of words. "Okay," she said. "I'll buy that. Next?"

"The Dorothy line," he said. "That one just sounds like a warning. 'The sand slips away.' Dorothy had that hourglass, right? So he's telling us that you're running out of time."

She scowled. "I'll second that."

"I think you're right about the equations," he said without pausing. "They probably simply mean what they mean. But these last two lines. Could they mean more than just the Harbor Lights Cruise?"

"Familiar. Lost. Alone. Dark. Found." She stressed each word, and then shrugged. "Dammit. I just don't know." She got up and started pacing. "Think. We can do this. 'Familiar.' That has to be the Circle Line, right? I mean, I did work here once."

"You did?"

"For a week. Temping. Sold tickets."

"That was on your profile?"

"I don't remember, but probably. There was a space to list all your jobs, right? I probably put it down."

"It's progress," he said, "but we still don't know why we're here. And we're running out of time." He spat the words like a curse, then realized what he'd said. From the surprised expression in her eyes, she'd realized the same thing.

"Time," she whispered. "Almost every line has some temporal reference. 'Not quite *yet.*' 'How *long since.*' Dorothy's hourglass. *'Before.'*"

"That has to be it," he said.

"But what?" She looked around, scanning the walls. "Do we find a clock? Not a clock!" she said, her eyes suddenly wide with inspiration. "A watch. A *lost* watch."

"The lost and found," he said, getting it. "And it'll be a *pocket* watch. 'Starlight in your pocket,' right?"

"We're brilliant," she said, throwing her arms around him. "That has to be it."

He gave her a quick squeeze, thrilled as much by her enthusiasm as by the crush of her breasts against his chest. They couldn't stay like that, though. They might have figured out the clue, but now the work began. "Come on," he said, releasing her body but taking her hand as they moved through the crowd toward the stairs.

They headed down to the main deck and ended up talking to one of the bartenders. "Lost and Found?" he repeated. "We've got a box we put things in. What are you looking for?"

"A pocket watch," Mel said.

The bartender nodded, then picked up a small phone—an intercom most likely—and had a one-sided conversation. After a minute, he hung up and turned his attention back to them. "Sorry. One pair of sunglasses, and that's it. No one's turned in anything else during this cruise."

"Oh, did you think we meant *this* cruise?" Mel asked, her eyes wide and her expression totally innocent. "I'm so sorry. We actually lost it a while back. We'd brought some out-of-town guests on board, you know."

"In that case, you'll need to check the Lost and Found we keep in the office."

"Will it be open when the boat docks?" Stryker asked.

"Doubtful."

"Oh, dear," Mel said to Stryker. "Daddy's going to be so disappointed." She turned to the bartender, as if to explain. "He's checking into the hospital tomorrow. Heart surgery. It's pretty serious. The watch was his good luck charm."

The bartender, a kid of about twenty-two, cursed under his breath, then held up a finger. "Hang on a sec." He went back to the phone, and this time when he spoke he turned his back to them. Stryker tried to eavesdrop, but the kid's voice was too low and the din of the crowd too loud.

"Good news," he said as he turned back. "I caught our manager on his way out, and he promised that he'd have the assistant manager stay late so that you can check the Lost and Found. Her name's Kathy."

"Thanks," Mel said. She leaned against the bar and squinted at his nametag. "Doug. You've been a big help."

"What now?" Mel asked as they headed back up to the observation deck, both holding club soda courtesy of Doug.

"Now," he said, "we wait."

We reached the UN, and the boat started its slow turn in the East River. Halfway through the cruise. One hour left before we reached the office and I could check the Lost and Found. I wasn't thrilled with the idea of wasting an hour, but since I didn't have a choice, I figured I might as well enjoy the surroundings. Not to mention the company.

I have to confess, though, I wasn't really sure what the etiquette of the situation was. I mean, Stryker had paid for our tickets, but this was hardly your traditional date, no matter how much I'd seen him looking me over earlier. The attraction was there—I wasn't about to deny it, and I was certain it was mutual—but as far as I knew, *Cosmo* had never commented on the ins and outs of dating your bodyguard, particularly if you'd been poisoned and an assassin was hot on your heels.

Oh, God.

My light mood evaporated with a *poof.* For brief moments, I seemed to be able to forget my situation, but then it would all come crashing back over me. *I might never date again.* Worse, I might never shop again.

I gripped the metal railing and looked toward the city, taking in but not really seeing the spectacular way the setting sun framed the skyline. My ultra-normal life had taken a right turn toward horrific, and my head was having a hard time keeping up.

Stryker's hand closed over my shoulder, firm and supportive. "You okay?"

"Yeah. No." I shook my head. "I don't know." I turned around, leaning against the railing as I talked to him. "I'm scared," I said. "And I don't like the feeling."

"No one does," he said. "But fear is a good thing. It keeps the adrenaline flowing. Keeps us on our toes."

I frowned.

"Not good?" he asked.

"The thing is . . ." I shifted, turning words over in my head as I tried to figure out what I wanted to say. "The thing is, I don't think I'm scared enough. I feel like I'm standing outside myself and looking in. It doesn't seem real. Does that make sense?"

"Absolutely."

"I know in my head that all this is real—and that it's deadly. But none of it *feels* real. I mean, I'm about as average as it gets. Things like this don't happen to girls like me. My personal horror should max out with the power going out while I'm in the subway, or a purse snatcher, or Starbucks going out of business. It shouldn't be actual life-or-death stuff."

"Sometimes life just bites you in the ass," he said, taking my hand in his. "Believe me, I've seen some horrible things happen to really good kids. Kids barely out of high school without any preparation for the real world at all. Normal Midwestern Dairy Queen–eating kids. And then *blammo,* it's all shot to hell."

He'd started outlining my fingers with the tip of his forefinger. I'm not even certain he realized he was doing it, but I was totally mesmerized. Both by his touch and by his words.

"Trust me, sweetheart. Bad shit happens to normal people all the time. Drunk driving. Cancer. You name it, and somebody out there's had it happen to them."

"Great," I said. "Now I feel guilty, too."

He laughed. "That wasn't what I meant. I just meant that this life shit comes out of the blue for everyone, and for most people it doesn't feel real." He grinned. "I've got to say, though, of all the weird shit I've seen thrown people's way, nothing is quite as fucked as this game you and I are mired in."

"*Yes.* Thank you. It's very important to excel at something."

"I have a feeling you excel at a lot of things."

He was still holding my hand when he said that, and I felt a little frisson ripple through me. I mean, Lynx or no Lynx, this was still the Harbor Lights Cruise, wasn't it? Stars and the city lights and the sunset just over my shoulder. Romance was in the air. Or, at the very least, adrenaline-fueled lust.

I wasn't certain which. I *was* certain that Stryker was hot.

I pulled my hand away, suddenly self-conscious. "I do," I said. "Excel, I mean. I always have. Straight A's. The whole nine yards." I caught his eye. "Pretty dull, huh?"

"Not at all. You're studying math and history, right? Cryptology. That's exciting stuff."

"It is," I said. "I love it." I frowned, then amended, "Well, I love it in theory. In the real-life interpret-the-clue-or-die scenario, I'll have to admit, it loses a bit of appeal."

"I can see how that might be," he said dryly. "So how much longer in school?"

"About a year."

"And then where? Washington?"

I laughed. "Not hardly. I'm hoping to stay in New York. Maybe go after a Ph.D., maybe teach in a private school. I've got some options."

He stared at me, his expression slightly baffled.

"What?" I demanded, suddenly feeling under the microscope.

"Nothing, I'm just surprised. I assumed you'd—"

"Try for NSA or something like that?"

"Well, yeah."

I shrugged. "I used to think I'd like to do that, but I don't see the point. I mean, there are so few jobs in my field, and, really, it probably sounds a lot more glamorous than it is."

"So why not apply and then make the decision?"

"Because I won't get picked," I said. "There won't be a decision to make."

Those gray eyes seemed to look right into me. "You've never failed at anything in your life, have you?"

"Excuse me?" The man was starting to cross lines that didn't need to be crossed.

"I'm serious. You're competent, strong, smart. I bet you've nailed everything you've ever done. Am I right?"

I consistently failed at relationships with men, but I decided not to tell him that. "What's your point?"

"You're afraid of failing."

"I *so* am not." But even as I said the words, I remembered eighth grade. All my friends had taken typing as an elective. I'd taken a computer programming class. Lines of code I could control and understand. Making sure my fingers moved the way the teacher wanted on a keyboard wasn't a sure thing. And I wasn't about to tolerate anything lower than an A.

"Admit it," Stryker said. "You're afraid of failing. Afraid you'll submit the application and, for whatever reason, you won't get picked." He shook his head. "Hell of a reason to walk away from a career that's obviously in your blood. I mean, the worst that could happen is they say no. The best? Well, the sky's the limit."

I was not liking the direction of this conversation. "You want me to admit I have a fear of failure? Fine. I'll admit it. I'm afraid of failing this game. Fail, and I die. *Those* consequences are the kind I'm afraid of. Getting a rejection on a stupid job application is nothing compared to that."

"I'm sorry. I shouldn't have pushed." He took my hand and squeezed my fingers. "But you won't fail. Not this. Failing isn't in your nature."

Absurdly, that made me feel better.

The boat was gliding under a bridge, and the sound of traffic moving above us harmonized with the steady thrum of the waves. "Wow," I said, wanting to change the subject. "I don't even know where we are."

"I do." He leaned against the rail beside me. "That's the Williamsburg Bridge above us. And that's Brooklyn," he said, pointing to the land in front of us and to our left. Since Brooklyn is hard to miss, I probably would have figured that one out on my own, but it felt nice being catered to.

THE Givenchy CODE

"I've never actually been to Brooklyn," I said. I frowned, suddenly wondering if I'd ever have the chance.

"You haven't missed much," Stryker said. "And if you really feel left out, I'll take you when all this is over."

He'd read my mind, and I couldn't help but smile, even though there was no way we were ever going over to Brooklyn. (Trust me. I'll never feel *that* left out.)

The yacht glided on, cutting through the still summer water as it hugged the Manhattan coastline. In quick succession, we passed under the Manhattan Bridge and then the Brooklyn Bridge. And even though I'd seen it on a million postcards, the grandeur of that famous suspension bridge still impressed me.

His offer to take me to Brooklyn played over again in my head, and as we passed the downtown heliport, I asked one question that had been bugging me. "Do you think the poison could just be a bluff?"

"Are there bluffs in the computer version of PSW?"

I shook my head.

"Then we can't risk that this is a bluff either."

"I wasn't suggesting that," I rushed to assure him. Believe me, I wanted to get to the next clue—and, I hoped, the antidote—more than he could imagine. "I was just tossing out random thoughts."

"I'm glad you did," he said. "I may be better trained in combat than you are, but you know the game and I don't. Not intimately, anyway. You might not think your random thoughts are useful, but I need to pick up all the tidbits I can. You never know when something might matter."

"Like now you know PSW isn't poker. Very little bluffing."

"Exactly."

I stared at him for a moment, not bothering to hide my scrutiny. He really did exude strength. That he seemed smart, too, was a bonus, as was the fact that the man was hotter than hell. He stayed quiet under my examination, the only hint of his amusement a tiny twitch of a muscle in his left cheek.

"You're good at what you do, aren't you?" I asked.

"Yes."

Short, sweet and to the point. And not the least bit modest. What can I say? I really liked the guy.

"What exactly *do* you do?" I prodded. "You got my entire profile. I hardly know anything about you."

"You know the important stuff," he said.

"I do not," I countered. "What's your favorite movie?"

"Monty Python and the Holy Grail."

Not bad, I conceded. It showed a sense of humor. "TV show?"

"The Shield."

Bent, but engaging. "Food?"

"Steak."

Boring, but at least it was an Atkins-friendly answer. "Book?"

"Clear and Present Danger."

"That's a movie," I countered.

"It's both. The book's better."

Fair enough. "What did you do in the Marines?"

"I could tell you, but then I'd have to kill you."

I lifted an eyebrow and tried to look suitably bored. "Old joke, Stryker. Come on. Tell me. I should know what you did to acquire this wealth of skill that's going to keep me alive. Right?"

"I did a lot of things," he said. "Participated in a lot of security-related missions. Fought in combat. Ran intelligence. And that really *is* all that I can tell you."

"Fair enough." That was enough. It had certainly bumped up my confidence in him by at least another notch.

We were rounding the Battery now, leaving the East River for the bay, and I drew in an awed breath when I saw the Statue of Liberty rising before us. It was completely dark now, the lights of the city on our starboard side, and the statue coming up on our left. She rose victorious from the water, her torch held high, bright from the illumination of spotlights, the haze in the air seeming to give her an ethereal aura.

I felt a lump in my throat. I might be trapped in this game right now, but so help me, I was going to fight for my freedom, too.

"You okay?"

"It just gets to me."

He nodded, and we stood in silence, watching Liberty slip behind us as we cruised up the Hudson, the lights of the World Financial Center rising to our right. The center, a collection of four tall buildings with geometric roofs, was interesting not so much because of the four towers that stood there but for the Twin Towers that had fallen.

Beside me, Stryker stiffened.

"Stryker?" I asked, my voice soft.

"I was doing counterterrorism when I left the service," he said, his voice soft and his gaze never leaving Ground Zero.

I wanted to say something but couldn't find the words, so I took his hand and held it. He squeezed once, then let go and moved behind me. He wrapped his arms around me and pulled me back. I melted against him, his heartbeat echoing through my body as we stood that way, his chin just grazing the top of my head.

We were silent for a moment, and when he spoke again, the timbre of his voice tickled and his breath was hot against my ear. "The work was worthwhile," he said. "Something I really believed in. Part of me really hated leaving."

"Why did you?"

For a moment, I didn't think he'd answer. Then he turned us so that we were facing the opposite shore. He pointed toward New Jersey. "My mom," he said. "She lived right over there in Jersey City. A crappy house, but it was all hers. Now it's all mine."

"I'm sorry," I said.

He brushed off the platitude. "I left the service because my mom needed me. She had lymphoma, and it had turned aggressive. She'd raised a son all on her own. The least I could do was be there for her at the end." He took a breath, his eyes far away with his thoughts in Jersey. "But that wasn't the only reason. I'd been thinking about it for a while. I'm not the regimental type. Not unless I'm the one setting the regimen. And I'd realized that military life wasn't for me."

"And that's when you started doing the private security stuff?"

"Right. I was lucky a buddy of mine was starting a firm. I could set my own hours, pick my own projects, and work from Jersey." He shrugged. "So I left the Marines and became a civilian."

"Sounds like you made the right decision. Your mom needed you."

"I never doubted that. But I do have the occasional regret. I want to nail the bastards."

"There're a lot of bastards out there, Stryker. The son of a bitch chasing me is testament to that."

"You're right."

"And that's what you do now, right? Protect people? That's what you meant by a security company?"

"People and things," he said. "Plus I do assessments. Investigate white-collar theft. Essentially, I'm a cross between a PI and a security guard. It's not a bad job, but not exactly my dream career."

"Maybe you should do something else."

"I'm considering it. I had an offer recently to work for Homeland Security. I'd have to move to D.C., but it's intelligence work, and that's where I'd like to end up."

"Sounds perfect," I said, unreasonably depressed at the thought of him moving to Washington. What was the matter with me? I hadn't even known the guy for a full day. And once this nightmare was over, I fully intended to return to my regularly scheduled life. So, I'm certain, did Stryker.

"I think it is," he said. "I was just about to accept, actually, when something else came along."

Something else . . .

As the boat glided north along the river, Stryker led me back to the starboard side. And as we leaned against the railing, our shoulders brushed and I felt the zing of electricity shoot through my body. No doubt about it, this man had grabbed hold of my libido, and I wasn't certain he'd ever let go. Adrenaline fueled, maybe. But it felt just as real as the flashes of desire I'd felt for other hotties.

The boat lurched, and our bodies brushed again. That's when I suddenly realized: *I* was the something else.

The realization was both startling and humbling. I'd already thanked him for sticking with me, but in doing so, I'd only considered the impact on me. I hadn't yet grasped the impact this damn game had on lives other than mine.

That thought triggered a new one.

What if Stryker and I weren't the only ones out there playing the game? After all, in the cyberspace version of PSW an infinite number of games could be going at any one time. And in the real world, I knew of at least one other player. *Jamie Tate.* One who hadn't won.

I shivered and reached out for Stryker's hand. He looked at me, curiosity in his eyes. I just smiled and watched the skyline pass in front of me. My mind was spinning, though, as I wondered how many targets were hidden in that maze of lights. Targets who hadn't been assigned a protector like Stryker.

And for just a moment, despite all the horror, I actually felt lucky.

Chapter

29

Kathy was waiting for us by the employees' locker room, just like Doug had promised. She'd changed out of her work clothes and was now decked out in tight black pants and a knockoff Marc Jacobs blouse. I know it was a knockoff because I'd almost bought the same top two weeks ago at Daffy's. Her lacy bra was completely visible, and not in a cool, Sarah Jessica Parker way. I said a silent thanks to whatever little elf had talked me out of *that* shirt. Photo op for *Vogue,* yes. Daily wear for the non-celebrity crowd? A big rousing *no.*

"I hope this doesn't take too long," she said. "I'm already late for a party."

"We'll only take a minute." Stryker was practically dripping sugar, and I wondered if it was an act, or if the sheer blouse had worked a number on him.

Kathy flashed him a supermodel smile, and I decided I

didn't like the girl. Right after that, I decided that whatever toxin was in my blood must be making me loopy, because I shouldn't care what or who flirted with Stryker so long as we ended up with the next clue.

Kathy flipped her tiny little purse over her shoulder and headed back toward the rear entrance to the office. She had us wait behind a counter, then pulled out a nondescript cardboard box from a closet.

I held my breath, thinking she'd shove the box in our direction and tell us to hurry up about it.

No such luck. Instead, those green eyes landed on Stryker, and her eyebrows rose into the sky. "So. What exactly did you lose?"

I cleared my throat, and she turned, the eyebrows arching even higher as she examined me, as if for the first time noticing I was there. "*I* misplaced it," I said forcefully. Stupid, perhaps, but I had no more intention of turning invisible than I had of dying.

"Whoever," she said, appropriately bored. "But do you want to give me some clue as to what I'm looking for?"

"Could we just take a quick look in the box?"

She crossed her arms over her chest. "No, you could not take a quick look in the box," she said in an irritatingly patronizing voice. "What kind of scam are you two running, and just how stupid do you think I am?"

"Fine," I said. "You're right, of course. It's just that I feel so silly, I hate even admitting out loud that I lost it."

"Oh, Lord, if you say your diaphragm," Kathy said, "I'm just going to have to puke my guts up right here and now."

Nice. "My grandfather's pocket watch," I said, my eyes fixed on her. I knew she wasn't the killer. I even knew (or I was pretty sure, anyway) that she wasn't really involved in the game. But right at that moment, I think I hated her as much as I hated Lynx. Unreasonable and unfair, but I wasn't exactly at my best, and I make no apologies.

"Oh." She actually looked a little mollified, and I crossed my arms over my chest, feeling smug. Which was, in fact, an utterly ridiculous reaction.

I held my breath and hoped our interpretation of the clue was right. What if *pocket* wasn't relevant at all? I could think of lots of other time-related items: stopwatch, train schedule, calendar, alarm clock. *Shit.*

It wasn't as if we could keep tossing out random options and Kathy would keep looking in the box for us.

If we were wrong about this, we were done, unless Stryker could work some sort of macho Marine charm action on the girl. Actually, I had a feeling that would probably work. Trouble is, I hated the possibility, and I crossed my fingers behind me, silently hoping my ploy played out.

After a second, she popped up behind the counter, her hand closed tightly around something. A bit of gold chain peeped out from the circle formed by her thumb and forefinger, and my breath hitched in my throat.

"You found it."

"Maybe," she said. "Describe it for me and it's yours."

"Why the twenty questions?" Stryker demanded. "She already told you it's a pocket watch."

"Look," Kathy said. "If it's really yours, you can have it. But I'm not here to pass out free stuff to any freak who comes along with a wild guess about what's in our Lost and Found box. I get too many assholes every day pretending they lost a camera or designer sunglasses or portable CD players. So don't aggravate me, just tell me what the monogram says and we'll both get on with our lives."

Stryker turned to me. "Mel? You want to tell her?"

"Sure," I said, certain my face reflected my utter cluelessness. I tried to concentrate. *Monogram,* she'd said. That meant initials. But what initials? Mine? Maybe. I just didn't know . . .

"Mel?"

"*PSW!*" I cried, triumphant, then immediately held my breath.

"Right you are," Kathy said, not looking the least bit apologetic that she'd held back what was clearly (if not truly) my property. "Here you go."

I took the watch that she held out, cupping it gently in my hand, afraid that if I touched it wrong, or treated it too roughly, it would freeze up and refuse to share its secrets. "We've got you now," I whispered to it as we stepped through the front doors and back into the night. "Tell us where to go from here."

Chapter

30

"Lucky guess," Stryker said as we walked down 42nd Street toward Times Square. We were still blocks away and hadn't yet encountered a mass of tourists. Instead, the pedestrians we passed were typical New Yorkers, ultrachic and in a hurry, and they flowed around us like a current. I barely noticed. I was too focused on the gold pocket watch I held in my hand.

"Not luck," I said, still giddy with victory. "Skill. I told you I was good at this game."

I met his eyes and saw that he was grinning down at me. "Touché," he said. "As soon as you said it, the answer was obvious. Before, though . . ."

"Don't tell me you didn't know the answer." My tone lifted in mock horror.

"Not a clue," he admitted.

I gave him points. Where battles of wits are concerned, most men think they know it all, even if they don't. And if they can fake it, they will. Stryker was different, though. He'd proven that more than once already, and that fact was finally starting to force its way into my brain.

"What now?" Stryker said.

All my self-congratulations faded with that one simple question. I'd found the clue, but so far I had no inkling what to do with it.

"No idea," I said ruefully. "I was hoping for a watch fob. Something like a pill case that we could open, and there would be a note inside with a pill for me to take, or a tiny syringe with the antitoxin. No such luck."

He slanted a look in my direction. "How are you feeling?"

Not something I wanted to think about. I just shrugged. "A little tired. A little queasy now and then. But—"

"I know. You'd feel that way even without the drug." He sighed, and I could almost read his emotions: there was no way we could be certain I'd been poisoned. We might be running blind, but we had to run.

After a moment, he held out a hand. "Let me see."

I passed him the watch, and he popped open the face cover, revealing an obviously inaccurate time of :15.

"The hour hand is missing," I said.

He held it up to his ear. "Not ticking, either. I wonder if the mechanism's intact."

"Does it even have all the little gears and things?"

"Let's take a look. Maybe someone pulled out the parts and put your antidote inside."

I tried not to get my hopes up as he flipped the watch over, then pulled a pocketknife out of his jeans pocket. He flipped out the blade, then slid it into a tiny groove I hadn't previously noticed on the watch. I held my breath as he gave a tiny little twist, and then—*poof!* Suddenly I was staring at a tangle of gears. The watch innards were intact.

"Well, damn," Stryker breathed.

I seconded the thought. We'd solved the last clue and found the watch. But it hadn't given me an antidote. What now?

I held out my hand to take the watch back. "There must be another clue." With Stryker looking over my shoulder, we inspected the watch. The dial said "Hampden Watch Company" and the casing said "Oneida." On the back we saw a faded etching with dates (1880 and 1906!) and railroad inspector marks.

"A clue?" Stryker asked.

"Maybe." Or it could mean nothing. "But what does it mean?"

"I don't know."

"Me either," I admitted, then sighed.

We were missing something. Something big.

And my time was running out.

>>>http://www.playsurvivewin.com<<<

PLAY.SURVIVE.WIN

PLEASE LOGIN
PLAYER USER NAME: *Lynx*
PLAYER PASSWORD: ********

. . . *please wait*
. . . *please wait*
. . . *please wait*
>>>*Password approved*<<<

>>>Read New Messages<<< >>>**Read Saved Messages**<<<

. . . please wait

WELCOME TO MESSAGE CENTER

New Message:

To: Lynx

From: Identity Blocked

Subject: Patience

Your cloudy vision will become clear when the target solves the qualifying clue, only to waver from time to time. Watch. Wait. Play the game.

>>>Software Attached: TRK_TGT.exe<<<

>>>Click to Download<<<

Lynx sat at the battered motel desk, his laptop open in front of him. He'd downloaded and installed the tracking software that the game had sent him hours ago. The program, called Track Target, was currently running in the background on his laptop, flashing a single pinpoint of light on a map image of Manhattan. So far, the blip hadn't moved. From the moment he'd installed the program, it had flashed in the vicinity of 42nd Street and the Hudson River. Sometimes the blip would disappear for hours at a time, then reappear in exactly the same place.

Of course he didn't know for certain the nature of the tracking device. But he wasn't a stupid man, and it was easy enough to guess. A GPS tracking chip was hidden in one of the clues Melanie was hunting for. She'd locate the clue and, without suspecting a thing, would carry it away, sending a signal to Lynx's computer as she did so.

The stagnant blip would begin to move, and the hunt would begin in earnest.

He could hardly wait.

He'd played every role in PSW numerous times, and while he'd enjoyed the role of target because of the intellectual challenge of interpreting the clues and trying to outrun the killer, he had to admit that his current role of assassin was his favorite. Particularly now that the game was being played in the real world.

Even with the aid of the tracking device, he was thrown back to a primitive state. For one thing, the device was hardly precise, narrowing the field only to an area about the size of half a city block. Moreover, as the email stated, the tracking device disengaged sporadically, leaving him blind. Nor did he have the benefit of seeing the clues when she did, of knowing where she was going or where the clues would lead. Instead, he had to use cunning and skill. He had to *hunt*. Possibly find the clues after the fact and try to solve them even before she did. Beat her to the punch, as it were.

Mostly, though, he was hunting blind. Relying on the tracking device and his own abilities.

Heady stuff. And he loved it.

This game was worthy of his skill.

With his eyes fixed to the computer, Lynx drew in one breath, and then another. He flexed his fingers, imagining the cold steel of gunmetal in his hand. Soon. . . . Soon. . . .

And then there it was: a single beep. One tiny sound conquering the silence in the apartment. And along with the beep, a flash of eastward movement on the screen.

She'd done it.

With the trill of anticipation humming in his blood, he hefted his gun and checked the magazine. A full clip and one in the chamber. Always one in the chamber.

He took his time gathering his things. There was no reason to hurry, after all. She might be on the move, but he had her in his sights. She could run, but she could never, ever hide.

Not anymore.

And the beautiful irony of it was that she'd brought this on herself. She'd solved the clue, after all. She'd opened up this window to her life.

It was, he thought, absolutely fucking brilliant.

Whoever their benefactor was . . . whoever the genius was who'd brought the game into the real world and had had the wherewithal to invite Lynx in . . . well, Lynx wanted to grab him by the cheeks and smack a big fat kiss on his forehead.

He loved the game.

He loved the hunt.

Most of all, he loved to win.

Stryker paused at a corner to get his bearings, then noticed a subway station across the street. The sign above the entrance noted that the line was for the F train. *Perfect.* He grabbed Mel's hand and tugged her in that direction.

"Where are we going?" Mel asked, hurrying down the steps beside him.

"Plaza," he said. "We need to regroup. We need to eat. We need someplace quiet to sit and think."

"The Plaza?" Mel repeated. "Wow, I would've thought we could do all that at Starbucks."

They'd reached the platform and eased in among the throng. "Full alert," he said. "Don't forget. You're the only one who knows what this asshole looks like."

She nodded, then turned a slow circle, scanning all the faces.

"Hardly seems fair he could be out to kill me even before we've found the antidote."

"Agreed. But we solved the qualifying clue, right? That was the watch."

She nodded. "Yeah. I think so, anyway." She drew in a long breath. "What a nightmare."

"You ever stayed at the Plaza?" he asked after a beat, wanting to lighten her mood.

She flashed him a quick grin, clearly aware of what he was doing. "The bar, yes. A room? No way. A little too tony for my wallet."

"Everyone should stay there once in their life."

She met his eyes then. "And this is my last chance before my twenty-four hours are up?"

"No." He shook his head. "No, I'm not saying that. I'm saying that you've had a hell of a day and we need to hole up somewhere so we can think. And you deserve a treat. Yes or no?"

"You paying?"

"Blood money," he said. "Who better to spend it on than you?"

"The Plaza it is," she said, as the train rumbled into the station. "Hell, I might even order room service."

A short ride later, they emerged at 57th Street, then walked the short distance to the famous hotel.

As good as her word, as soon as they reached the room, Mel snatched up the phone and ordered pretty much everything on the room service menu. "I'm starved," she said, by way of explanation as he took the handset from her.

"I know," he said to her. To the attendant, he said, "Throw in a pitcher of orange juice."

She raised her eyebrows. He shrugged. "I'm supposed to be protecting you. I figure that includes pumping you full of vitamin C."

"Vitamins and clean living aren't going to do it for me, Stryker." She dangled the watch. "This is the only thing that can keep me healthy now. Maybe I should just eat it."

"Needs sauce," he said, taking it gently from her hand. "Besides, you've got quite a spread coming."

"I splurged a bit," she said with a shrug. "I figure you're probably hungry, too."

What she didn't say was that this might be her last meal and that a condemned woman was entitled to go all out.

He had a feeling, though, that they were both thinking the same thing.

"So," she said, a little too brightly, "this room is even more amazing than I'd imagined."

Stryker looked around and shrugged. Lots of muted colors, heavy fabrics and fresh flowers. The robe he'd noticed in the bathroom was a nice touch, but the bidet was just damned silly. To him, a room was a room was a room. Mel, though, was obviously enchanted. "Yeah, it is," he said. "It's amazing."

She laughed. "You're so full of shit."

"You wound me. You think I've got no hotel taste? Have you looked in that bathroom? You could swim relays in that tub. Trust me. This is an amazing place."

She smiled, but her eyes were sad. "Thanks for bringing me here."

"I didn't do it so you could lounge about living a life of luxury, you know. You're supposed to be working."

"I'm stumped." She puffed up her cheeks and blew out air,

then closed her eyes. "The watch has to be the clue—the missing hour hand is just too unusual—but I have no idea what it means."

"Fifteen minutes of fame?" Stryker suggested. "Some sort of Andy Warhol exhibit?"

"Maybe. But I don't know a thing about art, and the clues are supposed to be at least a little personal."

"Quarter after the hour? A famous code that used fifteen as the key? A famous cryptologist who was missing a hand?"

"Good suggestions, but I don't know what to do with them."

"What about the numbers themselves?" Stryker asked.

"The numbers one and five are prime."

"Prime hour," Stryker suggested. "But I don't know what that would mean."

"It means we're stumped," she said, coming back full circle. "I don't know if I'm just too tired or he's just too smart, but I don't have any idea what to do or where to look."

She slumped back on one of the double beds and hugged a pillow to her chest. "All the more reason to appreciate you bringing me here. At least I'm going out in style."

Stryker's gut clenched. He'd known Mel now for less than twenty-four hours, but he'd witnessed so much strength and inventiveness in the woman that he might as well have known her for years.

The one thing he hadn't yet seen was fatalism. He didn't like it.

One long step and he was at the bed. He took her by the wrists and pulled her off. "We're going to figure out the clue and find the antidote," he said.

"Too bad that won't solve my problems."

"No kidding. Here." He held her arms up, his fingers tight around her wrist. He wanted her ready if she encountered Lynx. "Try and get away," he said.

Her eyes widened. "Excuse me?"

"Just give me thirty minutes. So long as we're stuck here waiting for inspiration, I want to make sure you've got a fighting chance at staying alive." More than that, the thought of anyone hurting her made him burn with fury. "Concentrate on this for a while and give your subconscious a chance to work on the watch. You'll figure it out." He shook her wrists. "Now get away."

"Stryker—"

"Get. Away."

"I guess we've moved on to the self-defense portion of today's program," she said wryly. She gave a little tug, supposedly trying to jerk her wrists free. He didn't even have to work to keep a hold on her.

"Dammit, Mel. You need to at least try."

"Why?" She yanked down hard, surprising him, but still he held on. "Stryker, he put a bullet in Todd's head. Nifty self-defense tricks aren't going to save me. This is stupid." She tugged against his hold one more time, and this time he let go.

"It's not stupid," he said. "You need to be prepared."

"I've got *you,*" she said. "I'll be okay."

"It's not enough, Mel. You need to have every advantage. I'm not willing to take any chances with you." The words hung between them, and he wondered if she could tell how much he meant them.

Their eyes met, and he saw the same heat he felt reflected in her clear blue eyes.

"All right," she finally said, her voice low. She licked her lips, a surprisingly provocative gesture, and desire cut through him like a knife.

"Good," he said, moving closer and putting his hands on her shoulders. He leaned in, his mouth close to her ear. Her hair smelled fresh, like the wind on the river mixed with the lingering floral scent of her shampoo. He took a breath and forced himself to focus. "First lesson: a bullet can miss. And if you're in close quarters, you need to fight. In a survival situation, anything can be a weapon. A rock, a telephone handset, your fingers. Anything."

"All right." She looked around the room. "The alarm clock. I could clunk him on the head with it or get him around the neck with the cord."

"Good," he said. "That's exactly what I'm talking about. You're smart and resourceful. Use that to your advantage."

He slid his arm around her, moving from her shoulder to encircle her throat, brushing the swell of her breasts in the process. She'd tossed his jacket on the bed earlier, and her tank top revealed more than it covered.

Her skin was soft against him, and she shivered slightly in his arms, sighing softly and pretty much driving him to distraction.

"You know any self-defense moves?" he asked, telling himself now really wasn't the time to get horny. He needed to stay with the program.

"I took a class," she said. "I wouldn't say I'm good."

"You only have to be good enough," he countered. "I'm Lynx. What do you do?"

She tugged against his arm, but he just pulled her closer,

drawing his other arm around her waist to thwart her, and, in the process, bringing her into full body contact with him. Her soft body fit perfectly against him, and her rear thrust against his groin in a way that made him ache.

"I can't do this," she said, trying ineffectually to wrench herself from his grasp and rubbing provocatively in the process. He sucked in air and fought his own battle to keep from getting hard. "You won't get free that way," he said. "Smash your foot down on his. If you're lucky, you'll surprise him enough to give you a chance to get away."

She did exactly what he said—he'd give her points for that—and pain exploded in his foot as the heel of her sneaker smashed into his toes. "Shit!" he howled as he loosened his grip. Immediately, she pushed at his arms, twisting free from his embrace. She turned back to look at him, a wide grin lighting her face. "I did it!"

"Not bad," he said, the pleasure he saw in her face making him grin, too. "I'll have a limp for the next hour. If you'd been wearing heels, I'd probably be crippled."

"There's another reason that my shoe collection comes in handy. Each and every one of my stilettos is a damn good weapon."

"Trust me, Mel, I'd never argue with a woman about the value of her shoes."

"You're my kind of man, Stryker."

Her words hung in the charged air, and she met his eyes, her lips slightly parted.

"Mel . . ."

"I . . . I'm going to go take a quick shower," she said. "Clear my head, like you said. Maybe I'll be inspired." She reached up and freed her hair from the ponytail as she walked, letting her hair fall free around her shoulders. She disappeared into the bathroom, and he watched her go, his mind filled suddenly with the image of her peeling off her shirt, her thick hair brushing over her bare shoulders. Then shimmying out of her jeans and underwear before stepping naked into the shower. He imagined rivulets of water cascading down those perfect curves and her soft, soap-slicked body.

He reached out and grabbed the back of an overstuffed armchair. He wouldn't do it, he told himself. He wouldn't follow her in there.

He paused, his gaze drifting once again to the closed bathroom door.

Then again, maybe he would.

Chapter

33

I closed the door, then leaned back against it, my body all tight and tingly. I wanted a shower, but I didn't want to shower alone. I wanted Stryker. I wanted him to walk through that door and press my back against the wall and fuck my brains out. And I didn't feel the slightest bit guilty about wanting that. I had about twelve hours to find some mysterious antidote, and I'd hit a wall. I had no idea where to go or what to do next. All I knew was that this might be my last night on earth, and for just a few minutes I wanted to lose myself to pleasure. Pure hedonistic, wild pleasure.

If I was going out, I wanted to go out with a bang.

I turned on the water and let it run, letting steam fill the room. I unlaced my sneakers and then took off my socks, finally peeling off my shirt and jeans and hanging them on the back of the door underneath the complimentary robe. Then I took the

THE Givenchy CODE

towel and wrapped myself in it. I put my hand on the door-knob and drew in a breath for courage. I wasn't usually this bold, but I didn't have time to be coy.

Beneath the towel, my nipples peaked with awareness. He was right there, separated from me by nothing more than a single piece of wood. I opened the door and—

He was standing right there. His taut, lean body all naked and hard and ready. I swallowed but couldn't manage to form words.

Fortunately, I didn't need them. He moved toward me, and I melted into his arms.

"Mel," he whispered, his voice hot with a passion that made me go weak in the knees.

"Stryker . . . Matthew . . ." I breathed in his scent, almost overdosed on it, as I urged him back into the shower with me. "I know we don't have much time, but I want . . . I need—"

He pressed a finger to my lips. Water pounded around us, the heat of the shower nothing compared to the inferno that burned between us. "I know," he said, as he cupped my breast. "I'll be quick. But believe me, Mel, I'll be thorough, too. Now come closer."

With a soft sigh of pleasure, I pressed my body against his greedily. And why wouldn't I? This was what I wanted, after all. And, really, what woman could resist?

Chapter

34

Oh. My. God.

I lay on the bed, enveloped in the soft cotton terry of the Plaza's robe. My entire body was limp, sated. But at the same time, an electrical current seemed to shoot through me, filling me up and making every nerve ending tingle.

Wow.

Afterward, he'd rinsed me off thoroughly, guiding the removable showerhead over my entire body. He'd been slow and methodical, and I'd been in heaven.

And the bonus? My mind was now clear as a bell. I'd had a shower and the most intimate of massages. My confidence was renewed, and, more important, I felt completely alive.

In a nutshell, I was a walking advertisement for the joys of sex. Most important, I was primed and ready to crack this code.

Stryker was at the desk, wearing nothing but his jeans, the

watch and Jenn's laptop on the blotter in front of him. When I stood up, he lifted his head and smiled at me, and I swear I almost melted all over again.

No, no, no. Time to get back to work.

"Okay," I said, pacing in front of the desk. "Let's go over what we know." I didn't wait for him to answer, my thoughts were churning too fast. "A pocket watch set for fifteen after the hour and the initials PSW etched into the cover."

"In other words, we don't know much," he said.

"Bingo."

"The website?" he suggested. "Maybe we missed something the first time. A clue in the riddle that we missed?"

I ran my fingers though my still-damp hair. "Maybe. I don't know."

"What about the car? Could we have missed something? Maybe there was a clue other than the CD?"

"Maybe. But if we're playing the game—and we certainly seem to be—then the watch should lead somewhere or tell us something."

"Fair enough," he said. "I'm still going to run the license plate."

"Okay by me."

He drummed his fingers on the desk, then held the watch up and stared at it as if it had been a hypnotist's prop. "Let's say we were online. What would you do if you were stumped?"

"Cheat," I said, the word passing my lips without thought. And that's when I realized. "Of course!" I said, moving around the desk and urging him out of the chair with my hip so that I could get to the laptop. "How incredibly stupid. A cheat, Stryker. We just need to call in a cheat."

"A what?"

"Watch," I said. "I bet I'm right. I've got to be right."

As the laptop booted up, he rested his hands on my shoulders, looking at the screen over my head. It was a nice, intimate moment. If it hadn't been for the fact that I was running out of time, I would have even called it perfect.

The computer finished booting up, and I pulled up a browser, then clicked over to the PSW website. Then I stopped, my fingers poised over the keys.

"What?"

"I haven't played in years. I don't even think my user name's any good."

"I'm betting someone's reinstated you."

I grimaced. "Reinstated me just long enough to kill me. There's a not-so-subtle irony working there."

To be honest, I had absolutely no recollection what user name I'd picked all those years ago, so when the login screen popped up, I punched in the user name and password I use for pretty much everything: GivenchyGirl and Math4me. Completely geeky, I know, but since you're supposed to keep your password secret, it didn't cause me too much embarrassment.

The machine whirred and clicked, the little hourglass making quite clear that the website was deciding whether or not it would deign to admit me.

And then, without further ado, I was in.

"Upper left," he said, leaning in so close that his breath moved my hair. "Isn't that the icon for the help menu?"

I moved the cursor over to the icon but didn't click. A cheat is a bit of online help to get you through a particular level of the game. Were I actually playing the game, the computer would

know where I was in the game and provide cheats for that particular scenario. Usually, I try to avoid cheats, much preferring
to manage on my own. Now that my life was on the line,
though, I wasn't nearly as proud.

For some games, you had to buy a book or search message
boards in order to locate various ways to cheat. In PSW, cheats
were right there on the site. For a price, of course.

That was the online version, though. I had no idea what
would happen here, in the real world. I desperately wanted
something to tell me what to do with the pocket watch clue,
but at the same time, I feared that very thing. If my online request for help actually yielded something useful, then what did
that mean?

It wasn't something I could worry about right then, though.
My finger hovered on the touchpad, and I sucked in a breath.

"Go," Stryker said.

"I am," I protested. *Now or never.* I clicked before I could
talk myself out of it. The hourglass icon appeared, and then—

Welcome GivenchyGirl.
The watch holds the answers.
You have everything you need.
Solve the puzzle.

I sat back, staring at the screen, not sure if I should laugh or
cry.

Stryker's arms closed around me, and he kissed the top of
my head. "We'll figure it out."

I squeezed my eyes shut. Not only did I have absolutely no
clue how to interpret the message (much less the watch itself),

but the fact that this cybermessage existed at all only raised more questions about who was behind this and why it was happening to me. And how. But I couldn't think about any of those things. Not now. Because right then I had to interpret an uninterpretable clue. I had to solve a puzzle and save my own life.

Mata Hari my ass.

"Let me see the watch again," I said irritably, holding out my hand.

He pressed it into my hand, and I turned it over in my palm, trying to relax so that my subconscious could take over and I could be brilliant.

Okay. Fifteen. Hour hand. Quarter hour. Time. Minutes. Pocket watch. Pocket. Clothes. Pocket. Pick pocket. Pants pocket. Watch.

Fuck.

This was getting me nowhere.

I held the watch between my palms, pressing them together as if praying, hoping desperately that the answer would seep through my skin by osmosis.

As I sat there trying to will brilliant thoughts into my head, I heard Stryker say something, his voice low. I opened my eyes and saw him pacing the far side of the room, his cell phone pressed to his ear. I tried to hear more, but he had turned toward the window, and I couldn't pick out any more words.

Fine. I didn't need to be worrying about that anyway.

I opened my hands and looked at the watch. My grandfather had had a pocket watch. He'd worked for a railroad for forty years, and when he'd retired, he'd gotten a watch and a pension.

I held the watch up by its chain and scowled at it, getting more frustrated by the minute. After a moment, I flung it onto the desk and grabbed a piece of hotel stationery. This is what I wrote:

The watch "holds" the answers.
Watch facts:
Found on Circle Line Harbor Lights Cruise
Hampden watch.
Real Railroad watch??
Grandpa
Back opens. Gears and stuff.
Doesn't keep time.
No ticking?
:15
15
fifteen what?????
PSW inscription inside cover
Two old dates hand-etched on back. Very faded. Probably original.
Dates: Oct. 14, 1880 (!!!!), and January 15, 1906 (meaning???), each marked with C.P.R.R. - JWC
Other inscriptions: Oneida (jeweler?), serial numbers (looks preprinted),
Fuck, fuck, fuck.

I resisted the urge to ball the paper up and toss it across the room. Instead, I spread it out on the desk and dragged my finger down each item, whispering each out loud, hoping that somehow one would strike some chord.

I felt a bit silly and jumped about a mile when someone rapped on the door. "Room service."

Thank goodness. Maybe with some food my brain would start working again.

Apparently I really had ordered everything on the menu, because it took two guys to roll in all our food. They lined the carts up against the wall and took the warming lids off. Everything looked scrumptious. I had no appetite whatsoever.

"C.P.R.R." I said to Stryker as he clicked his phone off and shoved it in his pocket. "JWC? Still no ideas?"

"Those are probably just an inspector's marks, and they've been there for decades. Railroad watches were meant to keep perfect time, and they were inspected regularly and marked each time. Do you really think they're part of the clue?"

I didn't know what to think. I just don't know. I moved back to the computer and stared at the screen, willing a flash of brilliance. Nothing. I stared at the watch. Again, nothing. Finally, I turned to Stryker in defeat. "How about you? You were calling about the car?"

"I've got a friend at the DMV. I'll owe her a big favor, but she's going to go into the office now. She'll give me a call back as soon as she runs the plate."

I sighed, not really caring. At the moment, I was totally focused on the watch, though it wasn't doing me much good. I'd thought that the shower—not to mention the extracurricular shower activities—had given me a fresh perspective. Apparently not, though, because I seemed to be sorely lacking in inspiration.

"Mel?" His hand slipped inside the robe to rest on my shoulder. He had an uncanny knack for reading my mind. His

THE Givenchy CODE

other hand slipped onto the back of my neck, and he stroked gently.

I closed my eyes and sighed, the gentle rhythm of his palms against the bare skin soothing me.

"Are you okay?"

I almost didn't answer. I didn't want questions. I wanted answers. But wanting wasn't enough, and so I sat up again, determined to get my thoughts on track. "I'm fine. Really, I'm fine."

He stared at me as if he didn't quite believe me, then he nodded. "All right, if you say so."

"Don't worry about me. We'll figure this out."

He moved around to face me, then cupped my cheek in his palm. He leaned in to press his lips against mine, and I almost melted under his touch, fighting the urge to beg him to make love to me again so I could just forget this whole nightmare. Forgetting, unfortunately, wouldn't make it any less real. And we had work to do.

As if on cue, my cell phone rang, and I broke the kiss, hurrying to the dresser and scooping it up just as it rolled over into voice mail. Well, damn. I checked the caller ID and saw that it said "Unknown Number," so I pushed the speed dial to retrieve my voice mails and waited.

My mother. And from the background noise, I could tell that my parents were out painting the town . . . or at least drinking their way through it. "Melanie? Well, damn it, I didn't want to talk to your machine. . . . Ah, well, darling, so sorry we didn't call earlier. Time got away from us. Right now, we're going out to Long Island for the night, but let's do brunch tomorrow after we get back in town. Eleven sharp. We're in room 3618 at The Carlyle. Oh, darling, wait. Your father suggests we just meet in the bar. Okay, then. Love you, darling. Bye now."

And then she clicked off and I was left staring at my phone, cursing my mother's passive-aggressive tendencies. Typical of her to issue an executive command. I wished that just once she'd ask my opinion, or give any credence at all to the fact that I might want to have some say in the way my life went.

I tossed the phone onto the desk and filled Stryker in. "Call back," he said. "Tell her to get out of New York."

I blanched, realizing he was right. As long as Lynx was playing the game, they were in danger. Maybe not right away, but if I survived—and I fully intended to—Lynx might try to use them to draw me out. That wasn't technically within the parameters of the game, but it wasn't verboten either. The cyberspace version simply didn't speak to using parents as leverage. Using a target's online friends as bait, however, was totally copacetic. If Lynx was in this game to win, I had to assume he wouldn't hesitate to push the envelope where parents were concerned.

I snatched my phone back up and dialed my mom's cell phone, followed by my dad's. I left them each the same message. Get out of town; I'd explain later. "But I'm not sure they'll get the message," I said. "Mom said they forgot their phone chargers, and I don't think either of them knows how to check their messages from another phone."

"Can you call their friend?"

"I don't have a clue who they're staying with."

"We'll just have to tell them in person. They're out of town now, right? So they should be safe."

I nodded, thinking that what he said made sense. "So we'll go to brunch and we'll tell them to leave. Some sort of excuse. Something."

Honestly, I didn't have a clue, but I was at least happy to have a plan. I had to do something to make sure my parents were safe.

The thing is, I really do love my parents. Despite all their weirdness, I love them because of our history and because they're basically good and, well, because I'm supposed to. And when we saw them tomorrow, I was going to tell them. No matter how insane my mom made me every freaking second of the day, I'd give her a hug and tell her that I loved her with all my heart and soul.

"Agreed," Stryker said.

"But we'll need to be careful tomorrow," I added. "I don't want my parents in danger simply because I decided to have one last conversation with them."

"We'll get there early and scope the place out," Stryker promised. "And we'll make sure we don't have a tail." He slid onto the bed and sat beside me, then took my hand. "We'll make sure your parents are safe, Mel. I promise."

I nodded, but without enthusiasm. I suddenly felt bone tired, the weight of the day pressing down on me. A madman chasing me. Todd dead because of me. And my parents in danger because of me.

And don't forget some sort of toxic shit flowing through my veins. "This whole thing is fucked," I whispered.

"I know." Stryker hooked his arm around my shoulder. I leaned into him, grateful once again for the contact. "We're not giving up, Mel. This isn't over."

"It'll be over soon," I said. "One way or the other." I hate to admit it, but it felt perversely good to be morose. I was tired, so damn tired. I didn't know if it was exhaustion or the toxin, but

I deserved a breakdown, and if I couldn't have a full-fledged one, at least I could whine about it. "This whole thing is like a train barreling down on us. On me. And I can't outrun it. Nobody could."

"You can," Stryker said. He hooked a finger under my chin and tilted my head up. His expression was so warm and tender, and I wanted to lose myself in his eyes. "If anyone has the strength to fight this, you do. For that matter, so do I. We're going to win. We're going to show this asshole he picked the wrong two people to fuck with."

I smiled a little at that, but I couldn't speak. I just nodded and tried to look confident and on top of things. In other words, I tried to look like the woman Stryker saw instead of the woman I knew he was looking at.

"Maybe it is a train," he said, continuing, "but why does it have to run us over? What's stopping us from jumping on board and riding it all the way to the end? Catching this son of a bitch and ending this thing?"

This time, I didn't even try to smile. I was too busy turning his words over in my head. Over and over. A train, I'd called it. It hadn't clicked then, not until Stryker had repeated the words back to me. It *was* a train. A train station, to be more exact.

My pulse picked up tempo as excitement surged through my veins. I was right. I knew I was right.

I damn well better be right.

"Come on," I said, taking Stryker's hand and tugging him toward me. "We have to hurry."

*T*rains. That was the answer. It had to be. We'd been staring right at it, but we'd still managed to miss it.

With Stryker looking on curiously, I clambered off the bed and parked myself in front of the computer. We were still logged on, so it took me no time at all to find what I was looking for. All I had to do was type *C.P.R.R. inscription* into a Google search, and there it was—the confirmation that I was right.

"Central Pacific Rail Road," Stryker said, reading over my shoulder. "So?"

"Railroad," I spelled out. "Central. *Grand* Central." I looked at him hopefully, but he wasn't catching on. "Oh, come on, Stryker. The clue has to be referring to Grand Central Station. And fifteen's a locker number."

"I doubt it," Stryker said, totally raining on my parade. "Surely they took the lockers out after nine-eleven."

"But I've seen lockers there. I'm almost positive. And even if there aren't lockers, maybe they have a bag check service, like some of the train stations in Europe."

"Or it could be a train number or a platform number or a dozen other things."

I had to admit he was right. For that matter, I had to admit my whole theory sounded more thin now that I'd actually put it into words. But at the moment it was the only theory I had, and I intended to stick to it like glue. At the very least, I was going to scour Grand Central.

We got dressed in a flash. I grabbed my tote, and Stryker grabbed the laptop—just in case—and we raced into the hall. As soon as we reached the elevator, the doors conveniently opened. I automatically examined each face, looking for Lynx.

The second the elevator doors slid open on the first floor, Stryker grabbed my elbow, tugging me to the side and letting the others emerge first. Then he stepped off, glancing around before getting off, his body shielding me from harm. For just a moment, I had an inkling of how celebrities and uber-politicians must feel. The kind with stalkers and bodyguards. There'd been a brief period in my life when I'd fantasized about being Britney Spears. I can't sing, so that option really wasn't open to me (some, I suppose would argue that Britney can't sing either). At the moment, I was absurdly grateful for my lack of talent. If this was how celebrities lived, I wanted no part of it.

The elevators at the Plaza open into the reception area, the elevator banks standing perpendicular to the reception desk across the room. We stepped off, and I turned left.

He was there. Right there. Standing at the counter and talking to the clerk. I couldn't see his face, but I knew that voice.

The voice that had threatened me outside Todd's building. The voice that—at this very moment—was asking the desk clerk what room I was registered in.

"Melanie Lynn Prescott," he was saying. "She's expecting me." I froze.

"I'm sorry, sir. I've checked. She's not registered."

"What about Matthew Stryker?"

Stryker's hand tightened around my upper arm, and he tugged me sideways, effectively pulling me out of Lynx's view. We ducked around, coming out on the far side by the Palm Court and a jewelry store with diamonds in the window blinking like a beacon to the rich and famous.

Right about then, Lynx stepped into view, looking royally pissed off.

Stryker must have realized what I saw, because he leaned over, closing the gap and blocking my view. "We're newlyweds," he said. "We can't keep our hands off each other. Kiss me."

I didn't hesitate. It wasn't the best disguise, but at the moment, we had no place else to go. Maybe I trusted Stryker to protect me. Maybe I just figured that if I was going to die, I might as well die happy. I didn't know and I didn't analyze. All I did was lean forward and let him capture my mouth in his kiss.

I'd like to report that the warmth of his mouth filled me with such joy that I forgot all my problems. Forgot that I was marked for death. Forgot that I was living a nightmare.

Nope.

He might have given me the ultimate Calgon moment upstairs in the shower, seducing my problems out of my head for a few heavenly moments, but down here, with danger lurking, I was hardly even conscious of the fact that our lips were touching. I'm sure it was a lovely kiss, but I barely noticed. It took every ounce of strength in my body not to break free from Stryker's strong hands and run like hell in the opposite direction, moving as far and as fast from Lynx as possible.

I didn't, of course, but I had no idea how long the kiss went on. Interminably, it felt like. And while I'd barely been aware of the contact during our kiss, now that it was over, I was desperately aware of the absence of his touch. Stryker was safety, and though he hadn't even moved a full two inches away, I suddenly felt exposed.

"Come on," he said.

I nodded, allowing him to tug me down the wide hallway, the Palm Court—now dark, yet still elegant—on our right and the brilliant displays from the various Plaza merchants built into glass cases on our left. We rounded a corner, and Stryker stopped short. I realized why half a second later. Lynx was in the foyer, an unlit cigarette in his hand and a scowl on his face. He didn't see us, but as he passed, I got a look at those eyes. My first impression had been right. These were dangerous eyes. Dangerous and excited. He was getting off on the hunt. He wasn't just playing the game, he was reveling in it. He wanted this freak show. For him, it was power. And why not? He was the one doing the hunting. It wasn't he whose forehead was tattoed with a big red target.

For my man Lynx, this was one big jerk-off-a-thon. But was that it? Was he playing just for the thrill? Or was there something else, too?

What did he get if he won?

For that matter, what did I get if *I* won?

Survival, of course. But I had a feeling that in the mind of whoever was pulling our strings, survival wasn't a prize, it was simply a condition. Something was waiting for me at the end of the rainbow. In the cyberworld, it would be cash. Here, too? I didn't know. But I damn sure intended to last long enough to find out.

"**D**id he see us?" I asked as Stryker aimed us into the wonderfully atmospheric bar inside the Plaza, which just happened to be a convenient distance from our friendly neighborhood stalker.

"I don't think so," Stryker said, guiding us through the late-night crowd toward the long wooden bar that was the focal point of the large room.

"How did he find us?" I asked. "You didn't register under your name, did you?"

"No, Mrs. Johnson, I didn't." A muscle in his jaw ticked. "We may be playing this game in a vacuum, but he isn't. Whoever is behind this has been watching us. Probably picking up our scent at each clue. The car. The cruise line."

"They followed us here and then got word to Lynx," I said, filling in the blanks.

"I think so."

"Son of a *bitch,*" I said. "That is so unfair."

"Stay here," he said. "Try to look inconspicuous. And watch your back."

"You're leaving me?"

"Not for long." He kissed my forehead. "He hasn't seen us, which means the advantage is ours. And I know one sure way to end this." He reached under his jacket, and I caught a quick glint of metal as he checked his gun.

I looked around, frantic, sure his movement had just set off alarm bells all over the hotel. "You're not going to—"

"Damn straight I am," he said.

I wanted to argue, but I kept my mouth shut. I had no qualms at all about blowing Lynx's kneecaps off and demanding information. Hell, I had no qualms about blowing his entire head off. At that particular moment, I would have done it my-self if I hadn't been sure I'd miss and instead blow a hole in the Plaza's nicely painted wall. What I did have qualms about was seeing Stryker dead. And Lynx had already proven that he was a dangerous character.

Stryker, though, was dangerous, too. And I had a feeling that I'd insult him down to the core if I begged him not to go or even told him I was worried.

I did neither. Instead, I just said, "Hurry."

He nodded, his face tight as he passed me the laptop case. "Don't go anywhere," he added with a wry grin.

And then he was gone. I glanced around the room, trying to decide where to settle myself. I ended up on a stool near the end of the bar, my body angled just enough that I could see almost all of the seating area and the main entrance into the hotel. To

my left, there was another entrance that opened onto 59th
Street, and I had a decent view of that area, too. My only blind
spot was behind me, where tables filled the far corner of the bar.
I spent a moment examining every face and didn't settle into
my perch until I was certain the people behind me were simply
there for drinks, not my blood.

"You okay?"

I jumped about a foot at the decidedly male voice. "Shit," I
said, turning to face the bartender. "You scared me."

"Sweetie," he said, "you look like the Easter bunny could
scare you."

I grimaced, fearing that what he said was true. I didn't want
to get sucked into a conversation, but I didn't want to leave, either. I'd told Stryker I'd wait for him, and that was a promise I
intended to keep. I might be arrogant about a lot of things, but
about going this alone I had no ego at all. I wanted help. All the
help I could get.

"So you wanna tell me your sob story?"

"No," I said.

"You sure? You look like you could use an ear."

"What is this?" I asked. "A bad sitcom? Don't you have
drinks to make?"

He swept his hand in a wide arcing gesture, indicating the
crowded bar. "They've already got drinks. And I can always
spare a moment for a beautiful woman."

"Shit," I said. Somehow, it just seemed appropriate. The guy
was either gay and chatty, or straight and hitting on me. It was a
testament to my exhaustion that I had no clue which.

"Uma Thurman," he said, and it was such a non sequitur
that it sucked me right back into the conversation.

"What?"

"You look like Uma Thurman."

I've been called a lot of names in my life, but "Uma Thurman" was never one of them. And, frankly, I have a feeling ol' Uma would be a little less than thrilled by the comparison.

"It's the hair," the bartender said.

Obviously, he was straight, and this was his idea of a pickup line. I'm tall and thin. Uma's taller and thinner. My hair is blond and straight. Uma's hair is blond and straight. My eyes are blue. Uma's eyes are blue. And there the similarities end. A gay man would know that. A straight man would be clueless.

"You've never actually met Uma in person, have you?" I tossed the question to him over my shoulder as I once again circled the room with my gaze, my fingers crossed tight that I wouldn't lock eyes with Lynx.

"She came in here once," he said.

"Did you wait on her?"

"Not exactly." He jerked his head toward the wall of bottles behind him. "What can I get you?"

"Tequila," I said. "Straight up." What the hell? I'd avoided drinking all damn day. Being dead sober wasn't helping me. Maybe a buzz would.

He poured out a shot and presented me with the check. I signed it to the room, then passed him the slip.

I was still pondering the Uma mystery. "Did you see *Kill Bill?*"

"Sure thing. Why?"

I just smiled. Maybe I could take a lesson from Uma after all. Ruthless. That's what I needed to be to survive.

I needed to be ruthless. And I needed to start thinking that way now.

Stryker rushed down the hall toward the main foyer, icy calm flowing through his veins. This time, he was the stalker. And he was going to end this thing. Right here. Right now.

He kept his right hand under the left side of his jacket, effectively shielding his gun, as he moved around the corner. Nine o'clock, twelve, three. His eyes scanned the area. *Nothing.*

The bastard was gone.

The foyer opened onto the street. If Lynx had gone out that way, then he could have hopped a taxi and been halfway down Fifth Avenue by now. *Damn.*

He hurried through the doors and down to the street, scouring the view in all directions, but there was no sign of Lynx. Stryker stood stock-still, assessing the situation, every muscle in his body tensed and ready to pounce. In front of him, well-dressed couples were getting into and out of limos and taxis, some casting him uneasy glances, others not even noticing his presence. None, however, included Lynx.

He took the steps back inside two by two, stopping in front of the doorman as one horrible thought occurred to him. "The bar," he said. "Is there another way in?"

"Certainly, sir," the doorman said. He turned, his manner formal and deferential, and pointed toward Central Park. "The entrance on Fifty-ninth," he said. "It opens right onto the bar."

Stryker barely caught the last words, though. He was already flinging open the door and racing through the foyer. The hall was crowded, and he elbowed his way past women in sequins and men in tuxedos, a terrible fear rising in his chest as his feet pounded on the floor.

No, God, please, no.

He saw her then, sitting at the bar, just chatting with the bartender, perfectly casual, while a dozen or so people milled around. *Safe.* Thank God.

He took one step forward, and everything changed.

A telltale red dot on her chest. A laser site. An automatic weapon. And it was aimed right at her heart.

He didn't think. He just pulled out his gun and fired high, shattering the mirror behind the bar and sending Mel and the bartender sprawling to the ground, along with the other patrons.

Screams filled the air as Stryker raced in, then tugged Mel to her feet by her elbow. "Run," he hissed as he grabbed the laptop case and her tote bag. She didn't argue, and together they raced back out the way Stryker had come in, hooking through the foyer and down the front steps.

A woman in black sequins was about to hop into a taxi, but Stryker shoved Mel inside ahead of the woman, then muttered a terse apology as he climbed in after her. "Go!" he shouted.

The driver went, heading out and onto Fifth Avenue with only a questioning glance into the rearview mirror. Stryker ignored him, instead turning to Mel and grabbing her roughly by the shoulders as he looked her up and down.

He'd been sloppy back there, and he'd almost lost her. Goddammit! *He'd almost lost her!* "From now on," he said, "we stick together."

"What the hell happened?" she asked. She was breathing hard, her chest rising and falling.

"He had you. He had a gun aimed right at you."

Every drop of color drained from her face, and he wanted nothing more than to just pull her close and tell her it would be all right. He couldn't say that, though. As much as he wanted to believe otherwise, he'd seen how fragile his hold on "all right" was.

"He shot at me? That was him?" Her voice was a mere wisp, and he had to lean in close to hear her.

"That was me," he said. "I needed you to duck."

"Oh." A whisper of a smile touched her face. "It worked."

The cabbie looked at them over his shoulder. "So where are we going, folks?"

"Grand Central Station," Mel said. She turned her attention back to Stryker. "I hope I'm right."

He took her hand, squeezing tight. "We'll find it."

"We'd better. He's close on our heels."

"I hope you didn't leave anything important in the room,

though," he said, turning to look back toward the hotel. "We won't be going back."

"Persona non grata after your shoot-out?"

"Something like that. Sorry."

"I guess that makes us even," she said with a grimace. "I signed the check to the room. If he didn't know our room number before, he does now."

Chapter 38

We were approaching Grand Central when Stryker's phone rang. He unclipped it from his belt, then answered with a curt hello. I couldn't tell who was on the line, and Stryker's side of the conversation gave no clues.

"Girlfriend calling to check up on you?" I asked when he hung up.

He didn't smile back, and I immediately became concerned. "What?"

"That was Talia, my friend at the DMV."

I frowned, unsettled by his tone. "And?"

"She ran the plates. The car was registered to Todd."

He was looking at me as if he expected some sort of reaction. But I couldn't react. For that matter, I couldn't even get my head around his words.

"Todd," I finally repeated. "My Todd?"

"That's right."

"But . . ."

"I don't like this," he said.

I didn't either. I wasn't entirely sure what "this" was, but I didn't like it one bit.

I didn't have time to ask about it, though, because Stryker was passing the cabbie his money and climbing out of the taxi.

The cab had dropped us at the entrance on 42nd Street, near the clock surrounded by statues of Hercules, Minerva and Mercury. I made a silent entreaty, begging help from the gods as Stryker pulled me inside, out of the warm wash of the golden flood lights bathing the façade.

We passed under the celestial map and clambered down the stairs. The station's been in a lot of movies, but nothing really does it justice. Considering it's just a train station, it really shouldn't be such an awe-inspiring building. But it is.

Not only is it beautiful, but it's also all-inclusive. I swear you could live there if you really wanted to make the effort. There are shops around every corner, along with an endless variety of food kiosks on the lower level for when you just want to have a relaxing quick meal.

For fancier cuisine, you need to visit the area above the con-course. On the east end, you can reach the mezzanine from a fabulous staircase that was modeled after one at the Paris Opera House. Once up there, the opulence—not to mention the price—ratchets up even more. Todd took me to dinner once at Michael Jordan's The Steak House N.Y.C. (fabulous), and during my freshman year, I worked as a waitress for a private party in The Campbell Apartment, a fabulous bar fashioned from the former stationmaster's old office. The bar had been closed then, and my view of the place had been from the serving side of a silver appetizer tray, but the space had been one of the most spectacular I'd ever seen. I'd wanted to go back for years but had somehow never gotten around to it. Maybe when all this was over, Stryker could take me and we could toast our success.

It was late, already past one, and the station was beginning to empty out, but the last trains had yet to run, and the late-night crowd stumbled around us—teenagers, drunks, and more than a few people who really needed to discover the joys of bathing.

We'd been moving so fast that I hadn't had time to think, but now my mind latched onto Stryker's news. *Todd?* What would my clue be doing in his CD player? For that matter, what was he doing with a Jag? I had a bad feeling but no time to think about it.

"Where are they?" Stryker asked.

"What?"

"The lockers you remember seeing here," Stryker said.

"Right." I shoved thoughts of Todd out of my head; I could deal with that later. I made a circle, examining my surroundings. "Um . . ." I trailed off with a shrug. I'd never used the lockers here, and I couldn't remember where (or when) I'd last seen them.

"No problem," Stryker said. "We'll ask."

I followed him to the Information desk, then waited as the attendant finished with an elderly tourist who'd apparently never read a train schedule. Finally, it was our turn.

"Lockers?" the attendant repeated. "I'm afraid we don't have any."

I leaned forward, elbowing in closer to Stryker. "I've seen them here. I know I have."

"Recently?" The clerk looked genuinely baffled.

"Well, I don't actually remember that part."

"We took them out after nine-eleven," the clerk explained.

I glanced at Stryker, feeling stupid. The man had tried to warn me.

"What about some sort of package-checking service?" Stryker asked.

"Sorry. No. Security concerns, you know."

"Of course. Thanks anyway."

Stryker moved away, his hand loose on my elbow. I followed, my legs feeling numb. *No lockers.* No clue.

No chance.

What the hell was I going to do now?

Chapter

39

Since we didn't have a better plan, we followed the signs to track 15, which had one more departure before shutting down for the evening. The train was already there, and a few people milled about. The platform was totally nondescript. A big empty area. Nothing that looked like a clue. No graffiti that was meant only for my eyes. No geometric patterns laid into the tile floor we walked on, cleverly planted by the assassin. Nothing. Not one thing.

"Any other ideas?"

I tried to think. There were subway stations all over the island, but the only actual railway stations I was aware of were Penn and Grand Central. "We're fucked," I said. "We interpreted the clue wrong, we've been following a wild-goose chase. And to make it worse, we're the ones who made the whole chase up."

"No." He shook his head. "We're right. This feels right."

I turned in a circle, my arm outswept to encompass the entire platform, the entire station. "Feels right?" I repeated, incredulous. "Stryker, nothing about this feels right."

He frowned, but he didn't contradict me. Which was too bad. I was hoping he'd had something brilliant tucked up his sleeve. We could use a dose of brilliance right then. MENSA membership notwithstanding, at the moment, I was fresh out.

"I'm not giving up," he said, taking my elbow. "And neither are you. Come on."

I let him lead me back into the station. We followed the long hallway past the various stores that catered mostly to tourists and harried commuters. They were closed now, and I looked longingly at the drugstore, wishing for a soda.

"C.P.R.R.," Stryker said as we paused in the walkway. "Central Pacific Rail Road. We've got 'Central' and 'Rail Road,' but no 'Pacific.' Any ideas?"

"None," I admitted. "How about JWC? Mean anything to you?"

"Not a thing. Let's go back to the Information desk. Maybe if we flip through the brochures, we'll have a spark of inspiration."

I nodded agreement, and we headed that way. A man passed by, a woman glued to his arm. They'd been drinking, if their wavering walk and overloud voices were any indication, and I slowed, something about the woman's stumbling gait catching my attention.

"Mel?"

"Sorry," I said, letting Stryker lead me. But I was walking slower now, trying to force free a thought that was rolling around in the back of my mind. Something familiar. Something important that I just needed to remember. . . .

We'd reached the Information desk, and Stryker grabbed a tourist brochure and started tossing out random facts about the station. But suddenly I wasn't hearing him anymore. Because my synapses had finally clicked. And if I was right, this wasn't about Grand Central Station. Not exactly, anyway.

"What does it say about The Campbell Apartment?" I asked, interrupting Stryker's review.

He scanned the brochure, finally finding the entry on an interior page. "Here we go. One-of-a-kind space, old-world elegance, used to be the stationmaster's office and salon and—"

He looked up sharply. "The stationmaster's name was John W. Campbell."

"That's it," I said.

"I'd think so. And listen to this," he added. "In case we have any doubt, the address for The Campbell Apartment is *15* Vanderbilt Avenue."

"Well, hallelujah," I said, holding out my arm for him to take. "Let's go have a cocktail."

"The bar closes at one," Stryker said as our footsteps echoed on the ornate staircase.

"Maybe we'll get lucky and someone will still be inside closing up."

"Let's hope."

We reached the landing, then found the understated entrance to the bar hidden in one of the station's many nooks and crannies. A simple black banner with The Campbell Apartment printed in white marked the stairs leading up to the entrance. The walls were stone, the stairs decked out in red carpeting. I took them two at a time and tugged on the brass handle.

Nothing.

"Too late," I said. I pounded on the door, then pressed my face to the glass and tried to see through the etched panes. I could make out light, but no movement. I pounded again, hoping someone would come to investigate. Again, nothing. "What time does it open in the morning?" I asked.

"Not until three."

I met Stryker's eyes. We both knew that three was too late for me.

"I think I can break in," he said, not missing a beat.

"*What?*"

"The restaurant," he said. "I think I can break in."

For half a second, the word *felony* flashed in my head, but I snuffed that little thought right out. Instead of making a protest, I said, "Good. Because I sure can't, and we need to get inside. If you can get us in there, then go for it."

Less than three minutes later, I was feeling pretty foolish in my choice of words. *If* he could get us in? There was no *if.* There was simply Stryker and some thin metal tools and a faster-than-you-can-say-*felony* moment.

Stryker opened the door, the movement of his arm hustling me inside. He closed it silently behind us.

"What about alarms?" I asked.

"Didn't see any wiring, didn't see a control panel."

"So does that mean there is no alarm system? Or you just couldn't find it?"

He stopped and turned, and I could see his face in the slight illumination of the emergency exit light over the door through which we'd just entered.

"If there's an alarm," he said, "we'll know soon enough." And then he eased forward into the room. I followed. What else could I do?

The place was just as glamorous as I'd remembered. The

entrance opened onto the main room, which was worthy of royalty. The dim lighting from fringed wall sconces wasn't enough to guide our way, but coupled with the light from the city filtering through the windows of leaded glass, we could see just enough to maneuver by.

"I was thinking earlier that I wanted to come here again," I admitted. "This wasn't exactly what I had in mind."

"Again?"

"I worked here once. A waitress at a catered reception."

He paused, his attention on me fully. "Another clue that has a personal connection to you."

"Just a small one," I said, but he was right. "It has to be a co-incidence, though. I can't imagine I put that in my profile. It was just a one-shot deal."

"Maybe," he said, but I could tell he didn't fully believe it. "Doesn't matter right now. We need to get in and get out."

"Right. Where do you think we should look first?"

"Same place we were going to look in the station," he said. "Storage."

"Employee lockers, coat checks, anything else?"

"Let's start with the coat check. If that comes up empty, we can look for the lockers."

"We can split up," I said. "It'll go faster."

"Not a chance in hell," he said. And from the tone in his voice, I wasn't inclined to argue. "Where's the coat check?"

I was about to say that I didn't know when I saw it. "There," I said, pointing to a far corner. We headed in that direction and found a typical coat check booth, with a counter facing us and an oversized armoire behind.

While I looked for some sort of hinged gate to get me back behind the counter, Stryker simply hopped the thing, bouncing up, then over, like he was some Olympic gymnast.

"Nice," I said, impressed with both the vault and his ass.

In front of me, Stryker turned immediately to the armoire, leaving me to tackle the problem of how to get back there with him. Not being as agile, it took me longer to hop over, and as soon as I did, I noticed the cleverly concealed gate that opened into the back area. Figures.

"Find anything?" I whispered.

He shook his head. "There's not much in here, which makes sense considering it's July. A few raincoats, an umbrella tucked into a corner."

"Anything odd about anything?"

"Nothing I can see," he said.

"What about 'fifteen'? It's the bar's address, but maybe it's relevant here, too."

He pushed hangers aside one by one. "The hangers are labeled, but I don't see fifteen."

I sighed. I'd fantasized that we'd walk in, see a closet empty except for one item, and immediately pluck our prize from the darkness. No such luck.

I moved in closer and started going through the pockets of the coats that were there. Stryker helped, and when we finished, he opened the umbrella, inspecting it inside and out.

"Nothing."

"You know," I said, thinking aloud, "not everyone checks coats. Some people check purses, laptops, small animals . . ."

He gave me a weird look at that last one, but I just shrugged. An old boss of mine used to cart her miniature poodle everywhere. Most of the time, Bitsy dined with us at the table (oh, joy), but occasionally the mutt was forced to dine behind the scenes, babysat under the watchful eye of some poor hostess who'd been threatened within an inch of her life if anything should happen to the little darling.

I really didn't like that dog.

"Small animals aside," Stryker said, "you may have a point." He dug in his pocket and came up with a small penlight, which emitted a thin beam of light when he pressed a switch. He swung the beam under the counter, revealing some painted panels with slight indentations. I pressed my fingers into the notches and gave it a shot. Sure enough, the panels were sliding doors. I opened them all the way to reveal rows of gym locker–style baskets. All were empty.

All except one with a stamped metal tag: Number 15.

I swear, I almost cried, I was so relieved. "What is it?" I asked. There was definitely something in the basket, but in the minimal lighting, I couldn't really tell what.

Stryker reached in and tugged out a denim jacket.

I gave a startled little gasp. "Holy shit," I said. "That's my jacket!" My missing D&G jacket that had been a total splurge. "I thought it was gone forever." I snagged it out of his hands and put it on, relishing the familiar comfort of the soft denim.

"When did you lose it?" Stryker asked.

"Months ago," I said. "I'd worn it on a date with Todd, and—" I closed my mouth, suddenly realizing that I hadn't lost it at all. It had been stolen. And that meant that someone had been planning—and watching me—for months, too. As if I weren't already creeped out enough. . . .

"Think about that later," Stryker said. He was studying my

face, and I could tell he knew exactly where my thoughts had gone. "Right now, we're only concerned with the antidote."

He was absolutely right, and as I nodded, I patted myself down. Sure enough, I felt something small and hard in the jacket's left breast pocket. The pocket was closed with a metal snap, and I pried it open, then pulled out an ornate vial of liquid. Stryker shone the beam onto the vial, which, I realized, was really a small bottle of Very Irresistible Givenchy perfume. The distinctively beautiful graduated pink bottle had been defaced by someone printing DRINK ME along one flat surface in what they probably thought was a hysterical bit of closure. I was not amused. The liquid itself was a watery reddish color. Not the least bit appealing, and I eyed it with some trepidation.

"Mel." Stryker's voice was soft, but urgent.

"Right. Yes." A stopper had replaced the spray nozzle, and now I pulled it out, then lifted the vial to my lips. I paused, my eyes meeting his. "You'd do this if you were me, right? You'd drink the stuff?"

"Absolutely," he said, but there was a tiny bit of hesitation in his voice, and I wasn't consoled. He must have read my mind, because his entire body seemed to sag. "Shit, Mel. What choice do you have?"

Damn.

"Bottoms up," I said. I drank the contents, then tucked the vial back into my pocket.

A split second later, my head seemed to explode with light and sound. I was dead. I knew it. This was the absolute end.

I'd made the wrong decision.

I'd lost the game.

And, honestly, I was more pissed than scared.

The shot came from somewhere off to the left, and Stryker reacted immediately, grabbing Mel's arm and pulling her down to the floor with him. She yelped, her hands over her face, and he wasn't sure if she was terrified or confused. No time now for comfort, though. He pressed his palm to her back. "Don't move," he whispered as he shrugged the laptop case off his shoulder and onto the floor. He was back up almost immediately, still crouched behind the relative safety of the coat check counter.

The blast had echoed through the room, but Stryker didn't think they could count on anyone outside having heard and coming to investigate. The bar was too well insulated and too far off the beaten path at this time of night. No, they were on their own, and now he peered over the counter, his own gun at the ready.

There. A tall figure melding into the shadows, moving slowly toward them. A quick movement as Lynx fired again. Stryker hit the floor, but not before getting off a round of his own. Above him, the wood of the counter splintered. "Go," he hissed to Mel, urging her to crawl along the length of the alcove and then following her.

"Do you have a mirror?" he whispered when they were a few feet away.

"My bag." She nodded back the way they'd come. Stryker cursed softly, then moved slowly back to retrieve it. He could have made do without a mirror, but he didn't want the bag found in the morning, a glaring testament to their presence.

He brought it back, and she retrieved a small cosmetic mirror. He held it up so that it just peeked over the bar. Lynx was still approaching with care, his body hidden now by an ornate wooden beam. Stryker considered whether he could get off a good round but decided he couldn't. He'd wait for a clear shot. Lynx might not realize the alcove extended so far, which meant he'd be expecting Mel and Stryker about six feet from where they were currently crouched. A small advantage to be sure, but at the moment Stryker would take whatever advantage he could get.

He angled the mirror again, this time scoping out the hall that ran perpendicular to the hallway Lynx was currently moving down. Short and narrow, this hallway seemed to be primarily some sort of service route. It hit a dead end a few feet away, but there were two doors, one just across from their alcove and a few feet to their right.

Lynx was far enough along that he'd be able to see them. But he might not be expecting them. If they could get out and to that doorway . . .

They'd have to risk it.

There was no hinged panel in this part of the counter, which meant the only way out was over. "I'm going to lift you," he whispered. "There's a hall, then a door. Right about there." He pointed in the general direction. "I'll be right on your heels. Move fast and don't look back. Understand?"

She nodded, her eyes wide but determined.

"It'll be okay," he said, hoping he wasn't making promises he couldn't keep.

She pressed a soft kiss to his lips. "For luck."

"Ready?" He put his hands on her waist. "On three," he said, then counted down. On cue, she jumped, and he pushed, hoisting her up to the countertop with ease. As she rolled over and down, he pushed up and got off two covering shots, both coming at the same time Lynx's bullets hit the wall beside them.

One jump and Stryker was over as well. He rolled to the far side, getting off a shot as he did, then realizing that Mel was crouched on the far side, her back pressed against the wall. "Go on," he yelled.

"It's locked."

"Shit!" He whipped around and aimed at the lock, then got off three shots in quick succession. "Go!" She turned and went, racing through the door as he followed, pausing only once in the doorway to fire one shot back the way they'd come.

On the other side, he took her hand. As they ran, he glanced around, trying to get his bearings. They'd come back into the main room, and his attention was immediately drawn by the ornate bar and the magnificent stone fireplace. Neither one would make a decent hiding place. Once again, they'd been sitting ducks.

They rounded a corner, and he paused, pulling her behind

him as he peered back the way they'd come. So far, clear. "We need to get out of here. There has to be a back entrance. When you worked here, did you come in a service entrance?"

"Um, maybe. I don't remember." She turned, her gaze taking in the place, then pointed. "That way."

"You sure?"

"Hell no."

"Good enough," he said, and they moved quietly in the direction she'd pointed. They reached another set of locked doors, and Stryker cursed. He didn't have time to pick the lock, but he didn't want to call attention to them by firing, either. If there was an exit through those doors, though . . .

It was a risk they'd have to take. He stood back and fired. He pushed open the doors, tugged her through, and—

"Oh, shit," Mel said.

Stryker echoed the sentiment. This wasn't a service entrance—it was a balcony. They were two stories above street level, too high to safely jump, and Lynx would have heard the gunshot. Any minute, he'd burst through that door.

"Fire escape," she said. "There's got to be one, right?"

He nodded, and they raced to the stone rail closest to the wall, hoping to find the metal grid of an escape route. Nothing. Just a large refrigerated truck parked beneath them, probably delivering supplies to one of the restaurants in the station.

He turned, planning to cross the area and check for an escape route on the far side. He didn't get that far. The doors to the balcony were still open, and he could see the assassin's form through the leaded glass, backlit by the lights of the city.

There was no other way.

"Jump," he whispered.

"*What?*"

"That truck is probably at least twelve feet high. If we hit the roof, we should be able to manage without breaking anything."

"Stryker, I don't think I—"

"It's either the truck or him," he said.

She glanced toward the door, her teeth worrying on her lower lip, then she pulled herself up onto the rail and swung her feet over. He followed suit, taking her hand. He looked at her, she nodded, and together they jumped.

They landed with a clatter on the roof. If Lynx didn't know where they'd gone, he'd surely figure it out. "You okay?"

"I think so," she said.

"Then keep moving."

They kept low and ran toward the front of the truck, climbing down to the top of the cab, then sliding down the windshield and over the engine compartment. He hit the ground first, then held his hands up to help her down. The sharp crack of a bullet hitting metal sounded behind them, and he realized that Lynx had fired toward Mel, hitting the truck's hood and barely missing her head.

They didn't hesitate. Instead, they raced under the balcony, grateful for the cover, then eased through the open doorway. They were in some sort of service corridor, well below Lynx and The Campbell Apartment, but they weren't out of the woods yet.

Carefully, they crept through the passages, easing back and out of sight when a man in blue coveralls and pushing a dolly passed by on his way back the way they'd come. After a few minutes, they emerged though a metal door into the main concourse. A sign to the left announced the way to the S train, a subway train that shuttled between Grand Central and Times Square.

That would do nicely.

Stryker kept a close eye on their surroundings as they moved, the gun ready but hidden under his jacket. They made it onto the platform and raced onto the waiting train. He led them to seats facing back the way they'd come, and then he sat back, watching every face that appeared in the doorway.

No Lynx.

The doors closed and the train jerked, starting to pull away from the station. And then, there he was. That flash of dark hair and those precise, penetrating eyes. Like Stryker's, his gun was hidden. But Stryker knew it was there, under the assassin's jacket.

Stryker tensed, fearing that Lynx would see them through the subway car's window and fire across the platform. He didn't move, though. Just stood there, anger and defeat playing across his face as the train picked up speed and left the station, leaving the assassin behind.

For the moment, anyway, they were safe.

Beside him, Mel was still holding his hand, her grip so tight that his fingers were numb.

"It's okay," he said. "We're safe now."

"For how long, though?"

"I don't know." He wanted to tell her a soothing lie, but he owed her honesty.

She let go of his hand, and he swung his arm around her shoulder, pulling her close.

"Where to now?" she asked.

"From Times Square, we'll catch a cab to the Upper East Side. There's something I want to check out."

Chapter

42

Todd's apartment.

I couldn't believe it when Stryker told me he wanted to go back there.

I cringed at the thought and tried to sink back into the taxi's tattered upholstery. I didn't want to see the place again.

More, I didn't want the image of Todd's head—bloody and battered—filling my thoughts. I hugged myself, the warm sting of tears filling my eyes as I thought about Todd. I hadn't been in love with him, but somebody would have been. He was a good guy at heart, and he hadn't deserved to die. I mean, he gave me shoes, didn't he? If he were still alive, he'd go on. Marry a paralegal. Have three kids and a dog, and maybe even a hamster.

Some asshole had taken that away from him. An asshole who wanted me dead, and for no better reason than the fact that watching me die was the ultimate score in some sick mind-fuck of a game.

God.

And then I remembered Stryker's phone call and the latest information—that the car with the clue was registered in Todd's name. It didn't make sense.

I waited until we were almost there, then I sucked up my courage and turned to Stryker. "Why?" I demanded. "Why go back there?" I didn't really want to ask the question. Mostly because I didn't want to know the answer.

Stryker didn't answer. He just looked at me, his eyes filled with regret and pain.

Gooseflesh prickled on my arms. "You think Todd's behind all of this," I said. "You think he wants me dead."

He couldn't be right. Todd couldn't really be at the heart of all this.

Could he?

As I had the last time we'd come here together, I hesitated in the doorway, venturing in only when Stryker signaled for me to close the door. "I don't want anyone to know we're here," he said, and I had to agree wholeheartedly with that.

Stryker was at the bed, crawling around on his hands and knees, looking for God only knows what. I waited about forty seconds, then my curiosity got the better of me.

"What exactly are you looking for?"

He shook his head. "Not sure."

I frowned and started looking around myself, figuring I'd know it when I saw it. "Who do you think cleaned the place up?"

"Lynx," Stryker said. Then he looked up at me. "Or Todd."

I frowned, not liking the direction of Stryker's thoughts. "I saw blood. I saw . . ." I trailed off, closing my eyes as I sucked in a deep breath. "I saw *brains*. He can't . . . I mean, how could he . . . there's no way he could have survived."

Stryker didn't answer, but I could tell from his expression what he was thinking: Things can be faked, and death can be an illusion.

"No," I repeated, shaking my head. I moved to Todd's desk and started opening drawers at random. "He can't possibly—"

I clamped my hand over my mouth and took a step back.

"What?" Alarm filled Stryker's voice, but I couldn't answer. I could only stare down at the blotter on Todd's desk . . . and the code I saw there:

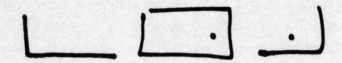

"He saw the message you received, right?" Stryker asked, his voice tight.

I nodded, mute, still trying to process what my eyes were seeing. "This is just gibberish," I said. "At least, it is if we're using the same code key."

"Maybe he was just doodling," Stryker suggested. "Could he have drawn this after you two got back here? After he saw the message?"

"I don't—" I cut myself off as understanding dawned. "No." I closed my eyes, wishing the answer could be different. "I would have seen. We were together the whole time."

It was possible, I supposed, that Todd had gotten up after I'd gone to sleep in the bathtub, ignored the fact that I was no longer beside him, and settled himself at his desk to draw pigpen codes . . . then spread bills and notes and photocopied pages of depositions over his blotter to partially hide what he'd been doing. Possible, but not probable.

"I'm sorry," Stryker said.

I just shook my head, feeling like my brain was moving through Jell-O. This didn't feel right. I *knew* Todd. Didn't I?

"Check the bureau," I said. "He keeps his passport in the back of the top right-hand drawer." I'd discovered that little tidbit last Christmas. Todd's Christmas bonus had been over thirty grand, and he'd danced around his apartment, waving his passport and promising me a trip to Paris. We'd never gone, of course. Lawyers who get thirty grand bonuses don't have the time to spend it.

I watched as Stryker rummaged around, pulling out various bits of clothing until I was certain that he'd removed a volume of material that simply would not fit in that drawer.

"Not here," he said. A muscle in Stryker's jaw twitched as he faced me. "He could be out there, planning on skipping the country when—"

"Search the rest," I said.

"Mel—"

"Do it."

And while he did the chest of drawers, I started searching the desk and the rest of the apartment. I was looking in the toilet tank when Stryker joined me. "Nothing," he said. "And I searched the kitchen area, too. It's not here, Mel. Face it. He's—"

I held up a hand, silencing him even as I sagged down into a nearby chair. I understood the ramifications. I hardly needed Stryker's blow-by-blow explanation of why he thought my ex-boyfriend was playing this deadly game with me.

No passport, no Todd, and no blood. It definitely didn't look good. All the little bits were falling into place. The only thing that was missing was why.

I asked the question aloud, hoping that Stryker would have a theory. Without a motive, I could still believe that it wasn't Todd behind this. Could still believe that my ex wasn't fucking with my mind . . . and my life.

Stryker didn't answer right away. Instead, he just looked at me with sad eyes.

"It doesn't make sense," I said, my words spilling out to fill the void. "He was there when I got the message. I saw his face. He was totally perplexed."

"People can act."

"Not Todd," I said, feeling surly. "And why would he? I mean, yes, we broke up, but I'm not that much of a prize. I mean, it's hardly like me leaving is going to prompt him to go postal on me."

The corner of Stryker's mouth turned up. "I don't know, Mel. I think you underestimate your appeal."

My cheeks burned at the backhanded compliment, but I wasn't inclined to be distracted. "I'm serious, Stryker. Todd doesn't even play online games."

"Maybe he started and didn't tell you."

I frowned at that but kept on. "But why kill me? And flee the country? That's what you're thinking, right? Because of the passport? Why do that? He's got a great career here. He's with a huge firm. He's saving money like crazy so he can buy a place."

I swept my hand around the apartment. "Not bad for a studio, but he could afford a lot more. He's saving every dime so he can buy into a co-op."

"That's what he told you?"

"Yeah." I frowned, something in Stryker's voice giving me pause. "Why?"

He pulled open the middle desk drawer and took out a yellow pad of paper and what looked like a credit card statement. I took the statement first, gasping when I saw the balance—over fifty thousand—and realized that the last payment reflected was less than the minimum. Keep that up, and Todd was never going to pay the thing off.

"He must've hit a rough patch," I said. Stryker was holding out the yellow pad. Reluctantly, I took it.

"Very rough," Stryker said, nodding at the pages I now held.

I glanced down, then closed my eyes, as if that could block the truth of what I was seeing: a list of creditors, each with a five-digit amount next to it. And the finance company for the Jaguar was listed right along with everything else.

Stryker waved the credit card statement I'd looked at earlier. "This is just the tip of the iceberg."

I grimaced. I'd had no idea Todd was in such bad financial shape.

"It gets worse," Stryker said.

I found that hard to believe, and I wasn't about to ask. I kept my mouth closed and just looked up, sure Stryker would tell me whether I wanted to hear it or not.

"Flip the pages," he said.

I did, at first finding nothing at all. Just blank yellow sheets. I riffled down toward the bottom of the pad, and a bit of black ink caught my attention. I slipped my finger in and marked the spot, then turned the top pages away. I was staring at a full page of doodles. Someone (presumably Todd) had taken a black felt tip and drawn typical doodle-type things. Mazes and concentric circles. Phone numbers turned into three dimensional designs. And there, among the fat, bold pen strokes, was something else. Something I really didn't want to see.

In one corner: PSW

And in another: MLP

I swallowed, numb.

"At least we know a little bit more about our enemy," Stryker said. He wasn't being unkind, just practical. Didn't matter. His words still cut me like a knife.

"No. This can't be right. He must have been framed," I whispered. "Someone left this stuff in his apartment to make us think . . . I mean, I just can't believe Todd did this."

"It's possible," Stryker said. "But—"

"You don't believe it."

"Honestly? I don't know what to believe. Someone's running this show, though. That much I know for certain."

"I want to get him," I said. My voice was low, and I hardly recognized myself. "Whoever's behind this, I want to nail his ass to the wall. You'll help me?" I said to Stryker.

"I'll do more than that," he said. "I'll hold him down while you kick the shit out of him."

And that, I thought, sounded like a pretty wonderful plan.

Chapter

44

Mel. Come on, Mel . . .

Something sticky. My hands and face were in something sticky, and Todd filled my head. I'd seen him, shaking hands with Lynx. Sitting behind a computer monitor in a dark room, the light from the monitor elongating his face and giving him an evil cast and a greenish pallor.

No. No, this couldn't be right.

Mel . . .

Sticky. Blood. Sticky blood . . .

"Mel!"

That time, I bolted upright, and a piece of pancake fell off my cheek. "What the . . . ?"

"Welcome back," Stryker said. He was sitting across the booth from me, nursing a cup of coffee.

"I . . . what? Where . . . ?" But I didn't finish the question, because I remembered. We'd left Todd's and gone around the corner to an all-night diner. We'd had coffee, then spent the night moving from diner to diner, all with the aim of losing anyone who might be following us. When we reached the fourth or fifth diner (I'd lost count) we ordered pancakes, then analyzed every minute of the last day in meticulous detail. When we were sure we hadn't missed anything, we'd dissolved into a silent funk. I don't know what Stryker was thinking about, but as for me, I'd been wondering what in my life was real and what was fake. I'd just been shot at, jumped off a balcony in a glorified James Bond maneuver, and had learned my ex might have betrayed me. I mean, come on. This wasn't my life. Had I suddenly turned into Sydney Bristow for real, only without the cool hair?

"Feel better after your nap?" Stryker said with a grin.

"Yes, thank you," I mumbled. I was absolutely mortified. I usually wore Bobbi Brown or Lancôme on my dates. Not maple syrup. Of course, we weren't actually dating (despite that glorious liaison in the shower), and I did have other priorities.

Besides, I already knew Stryker thought I was attractive. Surely pancake face wouldn't change that. . . .

I dipped my napkin in my water and tried to clean my face.

"Good," he said. "You obviously needed the rest."

I grimaced, but the truth was I did feel refreshed. Even more, I felt jubilant. I'd found the antidote with hours to spare. I was still running for my life, but at least I was no longer racing against an unknown toxin in my own blood.

At least, I didn't think I was.

"That really was the antidote, right?"

"I think so," Stryker said. "It wouldn't make sense to send you on a wild-goose chase and then give you sugar water."

"You're right," I said. "As much as anything in this nightmare makes sense."

"Or unless you weren't poisoned in the first place," he added.

I considered the point. We'd already entertained the possibility that the whole thing had been a bluff. "I guess I'll never know," I said.

"There's no point in dwelling on it," Stryker said, signaling for the check. "We need to keep moving. We need to figure out what the next clue is."

"I think I know," I said. I dug into the pocket of the jacket and pulled out the bottle the antidote had been in. "Do you know what this is?" I asked as I passed it to him.

"A pink bottle."

"You poor ignorant man," I chided. "It's so much more than that. This is the bottle for Very Irresistible Givenchy."

"Which is?"

"Only the most awesome perfume," I said. "But that's not really the point. Why put an antidote in a perfume bottle?"

"Because the bottle is the clue," he said.

I touched the tip of my nose. "Bingo."

He turned the bottle over in his hand. "Other than the DRINK ME, I don't see anything except the name of the perfume on this metal band." He handed the bottle back to me. "What do you think?"

"I think Givenchy's the clue."

"The brand?"

"Designer," I said. *"Brand* sounds like K-Mart."

"I stand corrected. So how is the *designer* the clue?"

"I have no idea," I admitted. "But Givenchy is my absolute favorite designer. Todd knew that. The game does, too."

"Your user name," he said. "GivenchyGirl."

With a start, I remembered something else. "Todd gave me a pair of Givenchy pumps," I said. "Right before this whole thing started."

Without bothering to wait for the check, Stryker stood up and tossed a fifty on the table to cover what was probably a twelve-dollar tab. "Come on," he said. "We're going back to your apartment."

Chapter

45

It took us thirty minutes to get down to my apartment. We took it slowly getting in, Stryker checking every nook and cranny in the building, then doing the same once we were safely inside.

When he was satisfied that we were alone, he shut the door and locked it. "Where are the shoes?"

I'd brought them back with me from our first trip to Todd's and had left them on a counter in the kitchen. I grabbed them now and carried them to the sofa. Stryker settled in next to me, and I handed him one of the shoes. We each examined our shoe, then traded and inspected the other just as carefully.

"Nothing," I said, disappointment washing over me. I'd been so sure.

"What about the box?" he asked.

"Oh! Good idea." I got up and went into the bedroom, finding the shoe box in the closet I shared with Jenn. I opened it up and poked through the tissue paper inside as I walked the short distance back to Stryker.

"Anything?" he asked.

"Not yet." We divided the tissue paper between us, carefully smoothing out each piece. As far as I could tell, the paper was simply that—paper. "I'll start peeling off the wrapping paper," I said.

Todd had given me a wrapped box, but the pieces had been wrapped separately, so I hadn't needed to rip through the wrapping paper to open my present. Now I took the lid and carefully peeled the tape free, revealing a box top labeled with the Givenchy logo and a large rectangle of pink wrapping paper. Other than that, though, I saw nothing.

"Nothing here," I said, glancing over at Stryker, who was doing the same thing with the bottom portion of the box. "You?"

"Nada."

"Well, shit."

"There's one more possibility," he said, looking pointedly at the shoes.

At first, I had no idea what he meant, and then the horrible, horrible truth hit me. "Oh, no," I said. "No way."

"Mel," he said gently. "We have to."

I nodded slowly. He was right, of course, but I just couldn't bear it. I took a deep breath, then passed both shoes to him, then moved toward the window. "I don't think I can watch."

"I'll do it," he said. "But stay away from the window."

I sighed, once again struck by the magnitude of what I'd been thrust into. Assassins lurking outside of windows, the destruction of my favorite pair of shoes. Nightmare-quality stuff. What, I had to wonder, would come next?

Chapter 46

"I'm sorry," Stryker said. We'd left my apartment and taken the subway uptown. Now we were walking along Madison, moving toward 63rd Street.

"It's okay," I said morosely. "We had to know for sure."

He'd taken the shoes apart bit by bit, and I swear he'd ripped *my* soul apart when he'd pulled out the sole. And when he'd tugged the heel free from the base, he might as well have kicked me in the gut.

My poor shoes. Destroyed for nothing. No clue. No nothing. Just a pile of destroyed leather. I almost cried just thinking about it.

After that, we'd decided that the clue had to be at the boutique.

"What time is it?" I asked as we hurried down the street.

"Right at ten," he said.

That was good news, at least. Givenchy is open from ten to six. At least we wouldn't have to break in.

"Any idea what we're looking for?" he asked.

"Not a clue," I admitted. "I'm kind of hoping we'll know it when we see it."

I love Madison Avenue. It's like another Fifth Avenue, only the tourists haven't discovered it en masse. As we rushed along, I peered into the windows of the various shops selling shoes, handbags and the most fabulous outfits. One store even had a display of V bags, including the much-coveted Sonata. I've always wanted a V bag, but they're not exactly in my budget.

Givenchy is located on the corner of 63rd and Madison, right next to Jimmy Choo, which, in my mind, makes it about the most perfect corner in all of Manhattan. The store is classy and spare, with stylishly trimmed windows capped by beige awnings marked with the store's name and logo. I paused deferentially and looked at the window display—shoes and purses suspended in midair surrounding a single mannequin. The mannequin was decked out in Givenchy evening wear, a simple silver chain with a medallion around her neck instead of the diamonds you'd expect with a dress as exquisite as that one. Everything in the window had an oversize pink tag on it, like a price tag, but with witty sayings instead, as if the window dresser had spent hours plowing through fortune cookies looking for the very best sayings.

"Look," Stryker said, his voice urgent.

I followed the angle of his finger, my gaze landing on the tacky silver necklace. "What—"

And then I saw it. The purple price tag tied onto the necklace. Not a pithy statement. No, this one had three simple initials: PSW.

"We need that necklace," Stryker said.

"No kidding," I said. "Is it for sale?"

"We'll find out."

He held the door open for me. I took a deep breath and stepped inside, leaving the hustle and bustle of Madison Avenue for the calm aura of Givenchy. The store was empty except for two saleswomen folding scarves at the counter. Immediately, one of them, a lithe brunette in a perfectly fitted gown, drifted over. Her gaze took us in from head to toe. I'd done my makeup on the subway, but there was only so much damage control I'd been able to do, and I firmly expected the woman's disapproval. Instead, she simply smiled and asked if she could help us. God, I love this store.

"There's a necklace on the mannequin in the window," Stryker said. "We'd like to see it."

"I'm sorry. I'm afraid those items aren't for sale. But if you'll follow me, I'll show you what we do have available. You're looking for necklaces in particular?"

"Could we just—" I began, but Stryker cut me off.

"Actually, we're more interested in shoes," he said. "For her."

I gaped at him, but he just smiled.

"Of course. What size?" she asked, turning to me.

"Um, eight."

"We're looking in particular for a red pump. The edge is wavy, like this," he said, indicating with his fingers.

"A scalloped edge, yes. I know the shoe." She gestured to a chair. "Please take a seat. I'll be right back."

She headed into the back, and I took Stryker's arm. "What are you doing?"

"Returning your shoes," he said. "And getting her out of the way." He cocked his head toward the window. "Now go get the necklace while I distract the other one."

He was buying me shoes! I couldn't believe it. I'd have my beautiful shoes back. Life was good (except for the obvious bad parts), and I hurried to the window and waited for my chance. It wasn't long in coming. Stryker asked the second saleswoman to show him a sports jacket, and while they were looking the other way, I stepped up onto the platform. The chain was fastened with a simple clasp, and it was no trick to get it off.

A passerby outside on the street gave me an odd look, but I just waved. Then I hopped out of the window and shoved the necklace in my pocket, along with the purple PSW sales tag. By the time the woman returned with my shoes, I was seated comfortably in one of the overstuffed chairs.

"You'll love this shoe," she said.

"I know."

I slipped off my Prada sneakers and socks, then slid my foot into the right pump, almost sighing with pleasure as the soft leather hugged the curves of my foot. I put the other one on, then took a brief turn around the store.

"How are they?" the woman asked.

"Perfect," I answered.

Stryker smiled indulgently at me. "We'll take them."

"Are you sure?"

"Positive." He nodded at my sneakers. "But just in case, you might want to put those back on."

I didn't have to ask what he meant. He meant in case we had to run for our lives. Regretfully, I took off the pumps.

He was right, of course. I couldn't run as well in the Givenchy. Lynx might catch me. Worse, I might break a heel.

>>>http://www.playsurvivewin.com<<<

PLAY.SURVIVE.WIN

PLEASE LOGIN
PLAYER USER NAME: *Lynx*
PLAYER PASSWORD: * * * * * * * *

      . . . *please wait*
      . . . *please wait*
      . . . *please wait*
    >>>Password approved<<<

>>>Read New Messages<<< >>>**Continue to Game**<<<

. . . please wait

WELCOME TO GAMING CENTER

>>>Retrieve Assignment<<< >>>**Report to Headquarters**<<<

WELCOME TO REPORTING CENTER

>>>Enter Journal Entry<<< >>>**Submit Viewable Report**<<<

PLAYER REPORT:
REPORT NO. A-0003
Filed By: Lynx
Subject: Temporary Setback
Report: Target located at Plaza and Campbell Apartment bars. Despite use of laser sight equipment, attempt failed due to interference by protector. Second attempt also failed. Due to laser sight equipment malfunction, 9mm standard sight Beretta utilized instead. Inferior lighting and poor conditions. Unable to obtain good shot.

The hunt proceeds.

>>>End Report<<<

Send Report to Opponent? >>Yes<< >>**No**<<

The Carlyle hotel. That was where her parents were, and that was where Lynx would go next.

It was a deliciously simple plan, and he felt no qualms carrying it out, particularly since the tracking software had been off-line since last night.

How else would he find the girl if he didn't draw her out? And how better to draw her out and throw her off balance than by providing her a personal tragedy?

Once he'd lost them at Grand Central, he'd been forced to comb through her profile for clues as to where she might go next, safe places she might visit, friends she might call. Her parents had seemed a long shot, living as they did in Texas. But God was smiling on him, because a few calls had revealed that her parents were traveling. Even more fortuitous, they were visiting their darling daughter.

He'd started with the five-star hotels, calling to see if they were checked in. He'd hit pay dirt with the second phone call.

Straightforward. Simple. Perfect.

He simply needed to get Melanie's attention. Get her in his sights and then take her out.

Oh, yes. This was undoubtedly the perfect plan.

By ten-twenty we were back on the street, shopping bag in tow, and heading up Madison toward 76th Street and The Carlyle hotel. As soon as we were about a block away, I pulled the necklace out of my pocket and looked at it. The chain was nondescript, just plain silver links, and the price tag was remarkable only in that it was large and purple and said PSW. Unfortunately, the medallion wasn't that interesting either. It was a small silver oval with the image on one side of an angel holding a sword and the words Pray For Me etched around the side. The back was smooth except for an inscription.

"What does it say?" Stryker asked when I relayed all of that to him.

"I don't know," I admitted. "It's very small, and I can't focus while we're walking."

"Then stop for a second," he said.

I shook my head. "No. It's almost ten-thirty. We need to get to the hotel. I can't risk Lynx finding my parents before we do." Now that Lynx had missed me twice, my fear for my parents' safety had ratcheted up. I'd tried calling them again earlier but hadn't caught them. I told myself everything was fine—they'd just been on the train coming back from Long Island—but I couldn't shake my nervousness.

"If anything happens to my parents . . ." I trailed off. My mom might drive me nuts, but I still loved her. And I sure as hell didn't want her racing through Manhattan with a madman on her heels.

"We'll get them out of New York," Stryker promised.

"I hope so. But if we can't think of something clever to convince them, then I'm telling them the truth."

I didn't want to, but I'd rather spill the whole story than see something happen to them.

Stryker nodded in agreement, then turned toward me as we paused at a corner, waiting for traffic to pass. "What about you?"

"Me?"

"We could just buy a plane ticket and get you the hell out of here."

I drew in a breath. So far, I hadn't allowed myself the luxury of thinking about running, but now that he'd voiced the possibility, I couldn't deny the appeal. A remote little Mexican beach and Stryker's twenty grand. Or, at least, what was left of it.

Stryker would give me the money, I was sure of that. Or, rather, I was as sure as I could be without asking him outright.

The thing was, I didn't want to run. I didn't want to live on a beach in Mexico. I wasn't the relaxing type. I can't remember the last time I took a vacation without having something else going on at the same time—writing a paper, preparing a presentation, catching up on tons of committee work.

A day at the beach would be fun.

Two days would be stressful.

Three days without my computer and my books and my friends would be nightmarish.

And a lifetime without all the conveniences and comforts I'd grown up with would be completely intolerable.

I suppose that sounds a bit ridiculous when balanced against the possibility of some nutcase whacking me as I rounded the corner from 59th onto Fifth Avenue, but this was *my life*. And I didn't want to leave it. I'd defied my parents in order to go to school in New York, and every day I survived here without any financial help from my mom and dad was a little victory.

Besides, I loved New York. It was fast-paced, exciting, and had the world's best shoes.

Most of all, it was home.

I wasn't about to let some psycho trash all that.

My life. *My* fight.

"Mel?"

"I'm not going anywhere," I said.

We hurried the last few blocks and reached the hotel at ten-thirty—a good thirty minutes before my parents were scheduled to arrive.

Manhattan has a lot of hotels, and The Carlyle is among my favorites. The possibility of a celebrity sighting there is high, though not as high as at The Waldorf=Astoria (where an encounter with Paris Hilton is practically guaranteed). But the thing I really love about The Carlyle is the smell. Silly, I know, but the hotel is so spotless that the scent of the magnificent flower arrangements seems to fill the air.

The rest of the hotel is pretty impressive, too, I had to admit as we approached the main entrance, marked by an ornate, art deco porte cochere. Beneath the overhang, two gold doors flanked a single revolving door. And sculpted trees were artfully placed on either side of the entrance.

A doorman held the door for us, and we stepped into the main lobby. The floor—a black marble, I think—was so polished that it reflected as well as a mirror. We hurried across the area, examining every face as we went. No one familiar. We took the elevator up to the thirty-sixth floor, found my parents' room, and pounded on the door.

Nothing.

"Well?" I said, gesturing toward the door.

Stryker grinned at me. "Are you suggesting I commit a felony?"

I rolled my eyes. "Just open it."

He pulled out the set of picks he'd used at The Campbell Apartment and went to work on the master key portion of the lock underneath the card key contraption, the part the maids and service people used.

I kept an eye out, trying to think of a plausible story if any of the guests or staff got curious about us. I shouldn't have worried; the corridor remained empty.

A few short moments later, and we were inside. The room was neat, with just a few of my parents' personal items scattered about. I checked the bathroom. My mom's makeup case wasn't there, confirming that she'd spent the night somewhere else.

I breathed a sigh of relief, finally able to acknowledge what had been haunting me: the fear that we'd open that door and find them laid out on the bed with bullet holes in their heads.

"We should get back downstairs," Stryker said. "Keep a lookout."

He was right, and we headed back down, then did a quick circle through the hotel. Breakfast was still being served in the Dumonet at The Carlyle restaurant. We stepped inside, and I looked around the room, taking in the expansive marble, along with the velvet-covered walls. Magnificent pieces of art filled the room, ranging from rich engravings to detailed hunting prints. There seemed to be treasure everywhere we turned.

The one thing we didn't see was my parents.

Our luck was the same in the Gallery, the Café Carlyle and the Bemelmans Bar. Fabulous art and tons of style, but I was too preoccupied with my missing parents to really notice. We explored the other nooks and crannies, then ended up back in the lobby. Once again, I dialed both their cell phones, and once again I got voice mail. I left another message to call me, but I wasn't expecting to hear back.

"What now?" I asked.

Stryker led me to a pomegranate-colored couch with its back to the wall and a wide view of the lobby. "Now we wait." He held out his hand. "Let's take a look at that necklace."

Chapter

49

Stryker peered at the necklace and the saint's medal suspended from it. Made of polished silver, the image was perfectly clear—a broad-winged angel holding a spear, his arm back as if to thrust the point home.

"Michael," he said. "The archangel."

"Oh," Mel said.

"It's a saint's medal," he clarified. "A lot of Catholics wear them. They pray to the saints to intercede with God."

She cocked her head, examining him in that perceptive way she had, as if there were no secret he could hide from her. "Are you Catholic?"

"Technically, yeah." He'd been raised Catholic, but he'd had a few issues with God after his mother died. "My background doesn't matter. Don't the clues always tie to the target?"

"Well, yeah, but I'm not Catholic. I'm—" She stopped, cutting her words off abruptly.

"What?"

"My profile. I did a paper a few years ago on ciphers and the Vatican. The Vatican was huge into cryptology back in the early 1800s, and I did a ton of research on it. I even presented the paper at some conference. I don't even remember where now. I probably would have mentioned it in the profile."

"Well, there's our connection." He flipped the medal over and squinted at the inscription. "Well, this means nothing to me."

"What's it say?"

He held it out for Mel to see.

$$y = a.cosh(x/a)$$

"Any idea what that is?" he asked.

"Sure," she said, not missing a beat. "It's the equation for a catenary curve. But what that has to do with anything, I really don't know."

"Uh-huh," he said. "And what's a catenary curve?"

"Well, I could tell you, but then I'd have to kill you."

He raised his brows, and she grinned. "Sorry. Just tossing your line back to you." She cleared her throat. "A catenary curve is the shape of a perfectly flexible chain suspended on its ends and acted upon by gravity."

"Great. Happy to know that. What does that have to do with an archangel? Or you, for that matter?"

"Beats the hell out of me," she said. "But we need to figure it out."

He nodded, momentarily forgetting about curves and saints as he once again scanned the faces in the lobby. They had a good view, but not a perfect one, and he wanted to double-check the rest of the hotel. He stood up, holding out his hand. "Time for one more walk-through," he said.

They made the circuit again and were standing near an obscenely large flower arrangement when Stryker heard Mel gasp. He glanced at her sharply, saw her terrified expression, and turned in the direction she was looking.

Lynx. Striding across the lobby to the elevator bank.

"He didn't see us," Stryker said.

"No," she said, her voice shaking with fear. "That woman. By the concierge desk. That's my mom."

Stryker turned sharply, saw the well-dressed blond woman commanding the concierge's full attention. Lynx didn't seem to notice, and Stryker assumed the assassin didn't know what the Prescotts looked like. But he'd bet money Lynx had their room number.

"I'm following him," Stryker said. "Go into the ladies' room. Your mom will meet you there."

"What—"

He pressed his fingers to her lips, then kissed her forehead. "Do you trust me?"

"Yes." She didn't even hesitate.

"Then go."

She nodded, hurrying in the other direction to the restroom. Across the lobby, the elevator dinged, and Lynx stepped on.

The doors slid shut, and the assassin disappeared. Not for long, though. Not if Stryker had anything to say about it.

He hurried in that direction, stopping only briefly at the concierge desk. "Mrs. Prescott?"

Her head snapped up. "Yes?"

"I have a message from your daughter. She asked to speak to you in the ladies' room. I think you should hurry. I think she's ill."

Chapter

50

The ladies' room was ornate and, thankfully, empty except for the attendant who sat on the little stool and handed out towels and various grooming products in exchange for tips.

The door banged open, and I was sure it would be someone else. With the way my luck had been going, it would have to be.

It was Mom.

"Melanie! Darling, are you all right?" She pressed a hand against my forehead. "That man said you were sick." She fingered my jacket, then examined my face. "Dear God, child. You look awful." She took a handful of my hair, held it up, then let it drop with a little *tsk-tsk*. I tell you, the woman has a real knack for fostering self-esteem.

I didn't bother with an answer, just took her wrist and tugged her into the handicapped stall with me. Fortunately, she wasn't expecting it, so she didn't fight me. I leaned around her and latched the stall, then parked myself in front of the door just in case she tried to bolt.

"*Melanie!* What the hell do you think you're doing?"

I put my finger to my lips. "Please, Mom. Please keep your voice down."

Her eyes widened and I cringed, expecting a blowup. But Mom surprised me. She nodded, then adjusted her skirt, making sure not to brush against anything in the stall. "What's going on, Melanie? Are you ill? *What is this about?*"

"I'm fine." And then, because that wasn't quite true, I amended with, "I'm not sick."

"Then what . . . ?"

"Listen Mom, I can't . . . I can't tell you what's going on."

"Melan—"

I held up my hand.

My mother's pencil-thin brows arched up, her matte foundation and powder caking a bit in the furrows of her forehead. No one interrupted my mom.

"Do you trust me, Mom?"

She blinked and took a step backwards. "What a question."

"That's not an answer."

"Of course I trust you, honey. I love you."

"I know. I know you love me, but sometimes . . ." I shook my head, mortified to realize tears were streaming down my face. No time. I just needed to say this. To take care of this. "You have to leave now. You and Daddy. Get out of the city. No bags, no luggage, no going back to your room, and no talking to anyone at all."

"Melanie? What are you—"

"Where's Daddy?"

"He wanted to self-park the car. You know how he is."

"The car? You drove?" Only my parents would drive to New York from Houston.

"Well, yes. We brought the Lexus."

"Leave it. Just leave it. Take a taxi to the airport and go home. I'll take care of the car."

"This is absurd. I'm not going to just—"

"*Mom.* Do it. For once in your life, do what I ask."

She pulled herself up to her full height, her fighting stance, and I dug my heels in. But then she reached out and stroked my cheek. "You're crying."

"It's important, Mom. Please, please, *please* leave."

She studied my face for a moment, and I held my breath. My mother had never once agreed with my decisions. The move to New York had been a mistake. My major absurd, my wardrobe frivolous, and my overall appearance sloppy. I didn't expect her to agree, but I had to try. And I couldn't tell her the reason because I know my mom; she'd call the police. No, she had to leave simply because I asked her to. Knowing my mom, that was asking a lot.

I sighed. She either left willingly, or I was going to get Stryker to remove my parents forcibly back to Texas.

With the pad of her thumb, she brushed a tear from my eye. "If you're in some sort of trouble, baby . . ."

I smiled. Trouble was an understatement. "I just need you to do this. No questions. I'll explain later. I promise." I looked at her, willing my eyes not to tear up anymore. "Please."

"Of course we will. If it's that important, we'll leave right now."

"It's that important."

"All right." She looked like she wanted to argue.

"Now," I said. "You have to leave now. Don't even check out. Just call from the road. Have them ship your things home. And after we leave this stall, don't say another word to me. Don't even look at me."

"I—"

"Mom. Please."

"Of course."

"Do you promise?"

She nodded.

"Say it out loud."

I thought she'd argue. Again, she surprised me. "I promise."

"I love you. Tell Daddy I love him, too."

"We love you, too, baby."

I managed a watery smile, then opened the stall and stepped out before pausing as something occurred to me. "Have you ever lied to me?"

Mom almost smiled. "No, baby. I haven't."

"Good," I said. "Don't start now."

I let Mom leave, waited two minutes, then followed. She was in the lobby when I got there, whispering something to my father. His face was creased, and he looked older than I remembered. I slipped back into the restroom and watched them from a crack in the door, afraid I'd never have the strength to keep my secret if I had to keep it from Daddy.

Their conversation lasted a few minutes longer, with my dad stalling and my mom encouraging. Finally, he kissed my mom's cheek, then brushed the pad of his thumb under her eye. My stomach twisted. I knew I was ripping them to pieces, but there wasn't a damn thing I could do about it. Not yet, anyway.

Finally, they headed to the front entrance. I slipped out of the restroom and followed, staying out of sight as I watched through the window. The doorman hailed a cab, and Mom and Daddy got in. And then they were gone. Thank God.

As soon as the cab pulled away, I moved back toward the sofa, still keeping a sharp eye out in case Lynx decided to make an appearance. I'd thought that Stryker would be back by now, and I was starting to get nervous.

I was just about to say screw it and head up to the room myself when the elevator doors slid open once again and Stryker strode toward me, his face all hard lines and angles.

I met him in the middle of the lobby and he took my arm, propelling me out the front door. "What happened?" I asked as we moved.

"He was gone by the time I got there. The door was kicked in and room was tossed, totally trashed. Presumably, he expected your parents to be there. Looks like he's losing his cool."

I think I nodded, but I'm not sure. Mostly, I was numb. My head was buzzing, and I was trying to hear words past the static. My parents were alive, but by how much?

"Do you think he's still here?"

"No. I think he bolted. But that doesn't mean he won't be back."

"Right," I said. "Let's get out of here."

We left the hotel and walked the few blocks to a Starbucks, where we could sit and regroup. We took a roundabout route, entering front doors and going out the back, Stryker looking over our shoulders the whole time. I might not be sure about a lot of things these days, but I was certain we weren't being followed.

I ordered us coffee while Stryker fired up the laptop. As I was waiting for the drinks, my cell phone rang, and I grabbed it. The caller ID showed Warren, my sometime study buddy. I considered letting voice mail take it, but I wanted to hear his voice. Any voice from my normal life, actually.

"Hey, Warren."

"Hey yourself. Where've you been? I called your apartment."

"I've been out," I said.

"Hot date?"

I laughed. "You could say that."

"Well, then forget it. I just wanted to see if you wanted to go in with me on a tutoring gig. Fifty bucks an hour. I thought you could use it."

I could, but there was no way I could say yes. "Let me see what happens with this guy. Can I let you know later this week?"

"All the slots might be filled by then," he said, "so no promises. You can try, but don't hold me to it."

"Trust me, Warren," I said. "I'm becoming pretty adept at living in the moment."

Warren started to ask me about my date—he wanted all the juicy details—but the drinks were ready, and I used that as an excuse to hang up. As soon as the dead air hit, I felt a wave of loneliness. I turned, searching for Stryker, a smile coming automatically when I saw him. I wasn't alone. And thank God for that.

When I got to the table with my latte and his coffee (plain, black, I mean, why even bother with Starbucks?), he already had a browser up.

"What are you doing?"

"The only thing I can. Since this math stuff isn't in my head, I'm plugging it all into Google. Maybe something useful will spit out."

"Worth a try." I scooted my chair next to his and peered at the screen over his shoulder. He called up www.google.com and typed "Catenary New York" into the search box. Pages and pages of hits came up, but nothing jumped out as being useful.

"Okay," Stryker said after we'd scrolled through a dozen pages. "I've got another idea."

This time he typed "Catenary Saint" into the search box.

"I thought you said he was the archangel."

"He's the patron saint of soldiers," Stryker explained. "If nothing pops up, I'll try *archangel,* but I figured this would get more hits."

He might have been right. The search returned pages and pages of results. I wasn't feeling particularly optimistic, but I started skimming again. A publishing website. An encyclopedia entry about the Gateway Arch, a biography of an architect.

I blinked, my eyes skimming back up the page. The Gateway Arch. *Of course!*

"That one," I said, tapping on the screen. "That's it." I threw my arms around him and leaned in, planting a kiss on his cheek. "You're brilliant. I should have thought of it, but I guess I'm too tired. Thank God for the Internet."

"Happy to be of service," Stryker said. "Do you want to clue me in on the answer?"

"Saint *Louis.*"

He stared at me blankly.

"The Saint Louis arch? The famous landmark? That's a prime example of a catenary curve. That's got to be our answer. *Saint* Louis. *Saint* Michael."

A slow smile lit his face, and I was struck again by how incredibly sexy the man was.

He reached over and stroked the back of my neck, then

stood up and started to rub my shoulders. "We make a good team," he said in a whiskey-rough voice. It was a good thing we were in Starbucks, because if not, we would have wasted a lot of time while I jumped the man.

"But what about it?" he asked, and suddenly I didn't feel so brilliant anymore. "We have two saint names now, but what do we do with them?"

"Pray?" I suggested.

"Besides that."

I shook my head. "I have no idea."

"Saint Louis. Saint Michael. Angels." I could feel him shake his head. "Other than the general idea of a church or religion, I don't have a clue," he said.

"Well," I replied helpfully. I took a sip of my latte, hoping the caffeine buzz would inspire me. Nope.

"Maybe we missed something," he said. "Some clue that we've just overlooked."

"Possible," I agreed. Right then, I was open to any and all suggestions. "Okay, let's think." I tugged the laptop toward me and pulled up a clean document, then started typing. Stryker sat down again, his head near mine, just close enough to distract as I made a list:

1. Pigpen message
2. HTML note about finding the antidote
3. The parking space. The car. Led to Harbor Lights Cruise.
4. Found. The watch. Led to
5. Restaurant/coat check/the bottle in the jacket pocket. Led to
6. Givenchy!! and saint medal

"Anything jump out at you?" I hoped so, because I wasn't seeing any patterns there.

"Sorry, no."

"Dammit," I said, fighting a rush of fatalism. "We've missed something. But I don't know what. I haven't got any idea what's key anymore." I ran my fingers through my hair and leaned back in the chair, scared, frustrated and angry with myself for not finding the answer.

"We'll get it," he said, taking my hand.

His sweetness just about melted me. "I told you I could do this," I whispered. "I stood right in front of you and told you that this was my thing and that I could figure out these codes and . . . *dammit.*" I spit out the last, and a nearby businessman looked up from his coffee and *Wall Street Journal,* startled. Well, sorry, buddy. But I was having a bad day.

"You will do it," Stryker said. "Not in your nature to fail, re-member?"

I made a face. "Maybe I'm about to learn the hard way."

"No way. We're still winning this thing. You're alive, aren't you?"

"Thanks to you."

He pressed a soft kiss to my lips, a kiss that I wished I could lose myself in. "We're a team, Mel. We'll figure this out. And we'll do it together."

Chapter 52

Stryker meant what he said. They *were* a team. A simple fact, but one that surprised him anyway. He hadn't truly been a member of a team since he'd left the Corps. More recently, he'd been working alone, shouldering full responsibility to protect his charges, be it a corporate executive or a briefcase filled with corporate secrets.

He'd expected the same when he'd gotten sucked in with Mel, but he'd had to face a hard reality. With this gig, he couldn't go it alone. Not only was Mel not the type to simply follow orders where her ass was on the line, but he also didn't have the skills to get her through this by himself. He needed her as much as she needed him. And in the end, they would get through this together. At the moment, though, he wasn't exactly sure how.

Beside him, Mel finished the last of her latte. "Thanks for

putting up with me," she said. "Now isn't that your cue to tell me to quit being morbid and whiny and to get to work?"

"Quit being morbid and whiny and get to work," he said, somehow managing to keep a straight face.

With a curt nod, she reached into her purse and pulled out the original message. She passed it to him. "See anything? A watermark? A tiny notation in a corner? A hint of something odd that doesn't seem to belong?"

He held the paper up to the light, but all he saw were the blocks and dots. "I think it's a grocery bag," he said. "But the paper's clean. There's not even a store name stamped on it. No manufacturer's mark. Nothing."

"Prestige Park," she said. "P.P. Peter Piper?"

"Picked a peck of pickled peppers."

"Very cute."

"Set it aside for now," he said. "Maybe something will click once we look at the other clues."

"The hyperlink. The message about the antidote. Were you able to trace it?"

"Nope. One of those free websites. I know a guy who knows a guy who could check the IP address of the uploading computer. Doesn't help."

She frowned. "But if you know the IP address, does that mean we know where his computer is?"

"Yes and no. Library computer. Manhattan." He watched the excitement on her face fade, and he wished he'd delivered better news. "I think it's a dead end."

"Guess so." She drew in a long breath. "So when did you learn all this?"

"Just a bit ago. My computer geek friend sent me a text message."

"Right." She frowned. "So if the IP address is useless, that leaves the message. It was long. There could be a dozen clues hidden in there." She navigated back to the bookmarked site. "Of course," she went on, "I don't have any clue what those other clues could be."

They were both silent, looking at the message, both equally uninspired.

"Okay," he said. "What's next?"

"The car."

"We went over it pretty thoroughly. Do you think we should take it to a mechanic and hook the system up to diagnostics?"

"No. I don't know." She started doodling on a napkin. "I just don't think the clues would require us to involve other people, you know? And it's not like we can run a car's diagnostics without getting a garage involved."

"Good point."

"Let's run through the whole list and decide. Who knows how much time we have before he finds us."

"Car and parking lot," he said.

"Right." She made a note. "After that, we got the watch."

"I'd say we already analyzed that clue to death."

She didn't argue, but she pulled the watch out and dangled it in front of her. "We haven't ripped the innards out yet. Should we?"

He considered the question, then nodded. "We probably should." He started to close up the laptop. "But not here. I think it's time to move on."

"Right," she said, shoving their papers into her tote and grabbing the shopping bag. He hooked the laptop case over his shoulder and headed for the door.

She moved ahead and was just about to open the door when he put his hand on her shoulder and tugged, effectively stopping her. She turned to him, her gaze quizzical, but he simply nodded across the street.

"We stayed too damn long."

Chapter 53

*O*h *shit, oh shit, oh shit.*

I scrambled backwards, stumbling over Stryker's feet as I tried to get away from the doorway before Lynx looked up and saw me. This time, there was no mistaking him. The man was right there, standing at the curb waiting for the light to change.

He looked up, our eyes met, and he smiled.

If Stryker hadn't been holding on to my arm, I swear I would have collapsed right then. My legs went numb, and I forgot how to run. Everything seemed to happen in slow motion. The light changing, Lynx coming, his hand slipping into his coat, the glint of metal as it emerged again.

"Go." Stryker yelled. He shoved me backwards, then grabbed onto me when I stumbled, tugging me with him as he raced back into Starbucks. "Back door?" he yelled to the barista. Her eyes went wide, but she nodded and pointed, and we raced in that direction.

I expected a bullet in my back, but none came, and when we burst through the back door into the alley, I paused long enough to catch my breath and utter one word: "Gun."

Stryker nodded. "I saw. I don't think he'll use it in public."

I glanced around. We weren't in public now. Other than the rats and roaches, we were the only ones in the alley.

Stryker read my thoughts. "Let's get the hell out of here."

I nodded, trotting alongside him as we scrambled down the alley toward the street, sideswiping piles of stinky garbage and alley cats, who'd come to do something about that rat population, I hoped. In just a few hours, my life had gone from Givenchy to garbage. Not exactly upwardly mobile, and I seriously hoped this wasn't a portent of things to come.

The street in front of us was blessedly busy, and we raced toward the taxis and cars, all moving at a typical Manhattan snail's pace.

"Taxi!" Stryker reached the street before I did, and his hand was out and up. A yellow cab pulled over, and Stryker motioned for me. Breathless, I raced the rest of the way, emerging onto the crowded sidewalk in time to hear a high-pitched whine and Stryker yelling, *"Down!"*

He threw himself onto me, and my elbow slammed against the concrete. I screamed in pain as Stryker rolled over, ending up in a crouch. I barely had time to register the movement before he had me under his arms and was tugging me into the waiting taxi.

As the car pulled across two lanes of traffic, I saw him. *Lynx.* Right there on the sidewalk, not ten yards away. His eyes seemed to burn a hole in me, and when his mouth moved to form exaggerated words, I shivered, because I understood exactly what he was saying: *"Next time."*

Chapter

54

It wasn't until we were in the taxi that I realized I'd been hit. Or, rather, Kate had.

A perfectly round bullet hole right in the side of my beautiful Kate Spade bag. Just looking at it made me queasy. Both because I'd end up consigning Kate to the trash, and also because I knew that a few more inches to the left, and the hole would have been in my belly.

Thanks to Stryker, though, I was whole, and I scooted over the bench seat toward him, wanting his strength to keep on protecting me, this time from the heebie-jeebies of such a near miss.

Stryker told the driver to take us to the Crowne Plaza, and as soon as we arrived and checked in, I tossed my jacket over the back of a chair, then peeled off my jeans, leaving me in nothing but a tank top and underwear. I'd like to say that my only motivation was comfort, but I'd be lying. We were in a hotel, we weren't racing the clock, and I wanted a second go-round with this man. I wanted it bad.

In the Plaza, I'd been just as desperate, but that had been a need for sex, for physical coupling. Stryker had been a bonus in that he was hot and sexy and totally turned me on, but I had to admit he hadn't been the point, even if he had been the inspiration. I'd just needed to get laid.

Now, though . . .

Well, now I wanted the man. I wanted him to hold me and kiss me and laugh with me. I wanted his hands on my body. I wanted his tongue in my mouth and his cock inside me. And I wanted it bad enough to toss subtlety to the wind.

Stryker had been watching my little striptease, and now he came over, tugging me down onto the bed and rolling me onto my stomach. He straddled me, his large hands working the kinks out of my shoulders.

I could feel his erection pressing against my rear, followed by his mouth pressed hot against my ear. I moaned, already desperate and ready.

He didn't say a word, and neither did I. He just touched me, stroking my shoulders, then he rolled me onto my back and cupped my breast underneath my shirt. Wildly, he pushed the material of my tank up, then closed his mouth over where his hand had been, his tongue flicking at my nipple.

His fingers snaked down, easing inside my panties. And as he explored me further, my body quivered with pleasure and I knew without a doubt that despite everything, this was going to be one fabulous afternoon.

Chapter

55

I woke up slowly, rolling over to curl up next to Stryker. Instead, I found an empty bed. Confused, I bolted up, looking around the now-dark room.

I found him standing in front of the window, the curtains open, the lights from Times Square glistening on his naked body. I propped myself up on an elbow and watched him, feeling sappy and sentimental and thoroughly sated. For now, at least, Stryker was all mine, and I liked that. I didn't know what would happen after the game—if I survived—and I didn't want to think about it. All I wanted was to live in the moment. To take all the pleasure and comfort Stryker was willing to give.

He shifted, the muscles in his back rippling as he turned to look at me, his somber expression morphing into a delighted smile at finding me awake. "Well, hello," he said. "Good nap?"

"How long did I sleep?"

"A few hours. I got a quick nap, too. We both needed it, but we need to get moving. I don't want to stay still."

I grinned. "Well, then, you shouldn't have exhausted me."

"The pleasure was all mine," he said.

"I'd debate that," I said, sliding out of bed and going to join him at the window. "I'm pretty sure a lot of the pleasure was mine."

He put his arms around me and pulled me close, and we stayed that way for a while, watching the traffic move below us and the lights of Times Square spread out all around us—the steam drifting lazily into the sky from the Cup Noodles sign; the neon extravaganza that marked the entrance to Toys "R" Us; the bright flashes of the NASDAQ sign. It was nice. Comfortable. But unfortunately, we couldn't stay like that.

"We need to get going," I said.

"That we do," he agreed. "Just do me one favor—put on some clothes. I'm not sure I'm up to fighting off all the admirers we'll meet on the street."

"Very funny," I said, but I moved to the chair and grabbed my clothes. As I tugged my jeans toward me, the jacket fell to the ground, and I bent over to pick it up.

"Wait," Stryker said, his voice so urgent that I froze.

"What?"

"The jacket," he said. "The vial was in the jacket."

I stood up, the jacket clutched to my chest. "Yeah . . ."

"Why?"

I started to say, "Why not?" but I kept my mouth shut as the import of what he said hit me. "Because it's part of the clue," I said. I felt totally and completely stupid. Since that jacket had belonged to me—and since the vial had so clearly led to a clue—I'd just assumed that the jacket meant nothing. That it was just a little dig, something meant to psych me out.

Clearly, I shouldn't have assumed.

I finished getting dressed, then spread the jacket out on the bed, my fingers going over every inch of it. Nothing. I turned it over and was about to repeat the process on the interior when I realized I didn't have to. I could see right away what the clue was: a care instructions tag that hadn't been there before.

The tag in the collar hadn't changed, but in one of the side seams there was now a plain white tag with ENIGMA printed on it. "That's it," I said to Stryker. "That's our clue."

Chapter

56

"**S**o I take it ENIGMA isn't a designer label?" Stryker asked. He paced in front of the window of our new hotel room, this one about two blocks from the first and equally dingy.

"This is a Dolce & Gabbana jacket," I said, showing him the real label. I pointed to the mysterious new label. "*This* one shouldn't say anything except Dry Clean Only or Machine Wash With Like Colors."

"Right. So the clue is 'Enigma.' What do we do with that?"

"I don't know," I admitted. "But it fits with the game. For one, the Enigma machine is one of my particular interests. It was an encryption machine made by the Germans. They used it in World War Two. Damn near unbreakable code."

"I'm familiar with the Enigma machine," he said.

"Sorry. I did a presentation on the Enigma machine a couple of years ago at a local high school. I guess I'm in teacher mode."

That had been fun, actually, and it was one of those moments that made me think I really was taking the right career path. The kids had been fascinated with both the machine and the story behind it. Not that I had a real machine. There is one at the NSA museum, but D.C. is a bit far to travel for a one-hour presentation. Even for the sake of academia.

"These clues aren't random," Stryker said, voicing what we already knew. "They touch at codes and ciphers because that's what you like."

True, and somehow hearing Stryker say it out loud made it less scary. Codes and ciphers *were* my thing. I loved them. Always had. And the fact that codes and ciphers were key meant that I was at least given a fighting chance to win the game.

And I fully intended to do that. I don't like to lose. And the idea of dying didn't sit too well either.

I'd been bordering on euphoria when we'd found the label in the jacket, but I was fast coming off my high. "So we know the code is an Enigma code or relates to the Enigma machine or has something to do with the word *enigma*. But we still don't know what exactly it is. If it's an Enigma code, where's the message?"

"Saint Michael Saint Louis," he suggested.

As guesses went, I had to admit it was pretty good. What I didn't think, though, was that it was right.

I shook my head. "Enigma codes are nonsensical. I've never heard of a code that was an actual word." I shrugged. "I mean, I could be wrong, but it doesn't feel right."

"The saint stuff must figure in somehow."

I nodded. I'm sure it did. I just didn't know how.

"So we're back to square one," he said. "What are we supposed to do with something that just says 'ENIGMA'?"

I didn't answer. I didn't have to. It was a rhetorical question. The answer was either right in front of our noses or we'd missed it entirely. Since I didn't see a damn thing under my nose, all I could do was sit back and wait for inspiration to hit.

I hoped one of us would have a moment of brilliance soon. I don't like waiting, and so far I'd been doing way too much of it for my taste.

Since I had no better idea, I sat down at the hotel desk and pulled out some stationery and a pen. At the top of a sheet, I wrote ENIGMA. Then I started rearranging the letters. I wasn't particularly good at anagrams—that was my friend Warren's bailiwick—but I figured with such a short word I had half a shot.

GAMINE Well, that was a word, but I didn't know what it meant.

IMAGEN Wasn't that Ron Howard's production company? No, that was Imagine. Probably not what I was looking for in either case.

GAIN ME Real words, but not exactly a crystal-clear message. Then again, I wasn't looking for crystal clear. Still, I had no flash of brilliance. I moved on.

GAME IN I frowned. That could mean something.

"We are in the game," Stryker said, startling me. I didn't realize he'd been reading over my shoulder.

"I know. We're about as in as you can be. But so what? How does that help?"

"It doesn't. It doesn't help one little bit."

I took my pen and scratched at the words until they were obliterated. "Fucking game."

Stryker didn't say anything—smart man—but he put his hand over mine. I closed my eyes and sighed.

"They're wearing me down," I said. "I'm scared and I can't think straight. This is what I do, what I love. Codes. Ciphers. And they're going to make it so that not only do I screw up because I'm just too damn tired, but in the end I'm going to end up hating something I love. No, correction. I won't hate it. You can't hate something when you're dead."

I sounded morose and whiny, and I hated myself for it. But I couldn't help it. I figured I had cause. And, honestly, all I wanted at that moment was for Stryker to put his arm around me and tell me it would be all right. That he'd figure everything out. That he'd take care of me.

I shivered a bit, the thought taking me by surprise. I'd never once wanted to be taken care of. I'd always been so independent, even moving to Manhattan against my parents' wishes. But that's what I wanted right now. So help me, that's what I wanted more than anything in the world.

And the irony? I couldn't even get what I wanted. *I* was the one with the talent for codes. *I* was the one who could solve the game to the end. Stryker (I hoped) could keep me alive while I did my job, but in the end it all came down to me.

I pictured myself finding the last clue and ending all of this. That would be a happy moment. At least I thought it would. "Stryker? Once the game's over, I should be safe, right?"

"That's the way it is online, isn't it?"

"Totally," I said. "Do you think Lynx will follow the rules?"

"So far he has. He could have slit your throat in front of Todd's."

"Nice," I said, swallowing. "But you're right. Once I've won, he's lost. So any prize he might get for winning is forfeited. There's no reason to keep after me, he'd just be risking every-thing."

"Besides," Stryker added, "he can probably sign up to play another game. Hunt someone else and try to win again." His voice was deadly serious, and I nodded. I'd thought the same thing myself about there being other games going on.

I was thinking about winning when my gaze landed on the jacket. I picked it up, turning it slowly in my hands, as if I could learn its secrets by osmosis.

"Maybe we aren't done with it," Stryker said. "Maybe the jacket has another clue."

I didn't have a better idea, so we spread the jacket out, each of us going over every inch, marking our progress with the tips of our fingers.

Nothing.

"Black light, maybe?"

"Black light?"

"Maybe there's something written that will only show up under a black light."

"Or with lemon juice?" I asked, raising a brow.

"Sorry," he said. "It's the only suggestion I have."

"We can try," I said, dubiously. "But where would we find a black light?"

"A nightclub. Novelty store. There's got to be one nearby." He nodded toward the window and Times Square below us.

"Okay," I agreed. "It's worth a shot." I started to get up, then thought of one last thing. "You know, the label was sewn in by someone else," I said.

"So maybe we should un-sew it," he said.

I wasn't sure "un-sew" was a word, but that was the general idea. "Give me your knife."

He handed it over without question, and I carefully pulled out the threads holding the new label in place. It came free, and I realized that about one-quarter inch of material had been sewn into the seam. And there, on that bit of material, was a message written in tiny, perfect script. *XKBFT THECF CHPTR YEDHH VQIPN G*

"What the fuck?"

"It's an Enigma code," I said. "It's got to be."

"Great," he said, "but what do we do with it? I thought the code was uncrackable."

I shrugged. "Well, no, not really."

"No?" He made a face and nodded at the jacket. "Go on, then. Get to it."

"Ah." I scowled at the code. "It's not really that easy. We need an Enigma machine."

"And where are we supposed to find an Enigma machine? Germany?"

"I was thinking more along the lines of Washington, D.C."

He nodded. "Okay. Let's go. Surely there's a commuter flight. It's late, but not that late."

I laughed. "Yeah, well, I think a phone call will work just as well. And it's faster."

"Who knew it could be that easy?" He passed me his cell phone. "Go for it."

I called and found out quickly enough that the National Cryptologic Museum was closed, which wasn't too surprising considering it was after dark. Undeterred, I called the NSA directly. Most likely, I'm now considered a terrorist threat. What I'm not is someone with access. After going through about eight thousand levels of after-hours staff, I finally found a person who was willing to not pass the buck. Instead, he told me directly that if I wanted to type something into the Enigma machine, I was going to have to haul my body down to the museum.

So much for my powers of persuasion. The ultimate irony, of course, being that working at the NSA is my fantasy. Though I should point out that I want a job in intelligence, not staffing the museum.

Stryker was watching me, his expression knowing. "Don't pass up an opportunity simply because you're afraid. There's very little in this life you can't go back and fix and change." He waved a hand around the room. "If we get this wrong, then yeah. You might have a problem. But get rejected for a job? Pick the wrong job? Babe, those are no-brainers."

"Thanks," I said, part of me wishing I'd kept my mouth shut on the cruise, and another part of me liking his support and encouragement. "We should probably concentrate on keeping me alive so that I can pick *any* job."

"Right. So what now?"

"Might as well give your method a shot," I said, nodding toward the laptop. "Maybe there's someplace in New York that has one on display."

We didn't find an Enigma machine on display. Instead, we found something better: an Enigma applet, right there on the Internet.

"Wow," I said, completely impressed. "Someone must have put some serious effort into this."

"Do you think it's accurate?"

I read the text accompanying the Java-based program. "It says it is."

I started inputting the list of letters we'd found on the jacket. As I watched the printout, my heart started to sink. This was not good.

SJPKL XEKKO LSUCS NOIZL PSVEI K

"Gibberish," Stryker said. "It's just a fucking load of gibberish."

I reloaded the applet and pointed above the keys on the little picture. "See these three letters? Those are moving rotors. Every time you type, they change, and a different electrical signal is sent. So you might type an *E* once and get a *G* as the coded version, then type another *E* and the second time it'll show up as a *Z.*"

"Right," said Stryker.

"Right," I repeated. "So the only way to decrypt the message is to know the *original* rotor setting."

He met my eyes. "Try PSW."

I bent back to the keyboard and readjusted the rotors. More gibberish.

"Dammit!" Stryker's hand struck the table.

"No, wait," I said. "I forgot about the plugboard." I pointed to the area at the bottom of the simulator. "Since we've got three letters, I can't plug them to each other. So I'm going to plug them to the first three spots. *P* to *A*, *S* to *B* and so on."

"Maybe we'll get lucky," Stryker said as I reset the machine.

I typed the coded message in again, and this time—thank

God—the answer made sense. Or, rather, the answer wasn't gibberish. At the moment, at least, it didn't make any sense at all to me.

YOUSE EKTHE HEAVE NNEXT TOHEL L

"Nice," Stryker said.

"The letters emerge in groups of five. It says 'You seek the heaven next to hell.'"

"Like I said, nice. What the hell does that mean?"

Stryker might not know, but the answer clicked with me right away. How could it not, considering the many hours I'd spent wandering the length of Fifth Avenue, lusting over the contents of the various stores? "St. Patrick's Cathedral," I said. "The clue is something at St. Patrick's."

He gaped at me. "What hat did you pull that out of?"

"Haven't you ever noticed? The cathedral's right across from 666 Fifth Avenue."

"And with the saint medal and the reference to St. Louis, a Catholic church makes sense."

"Let's go."

"Can't," he said. "They close up for the night. Vandals."

"Oh." I was antsy, wanting to go, to figure out the next clue. But while Stryker might be willing to break into a restaurant, I didn't think he'd be inclined to break into a church. "I guess we wait," I said.

"We can sleep," he said, his dark eyes burning into me with an intensity that made me warm and shivery. "Or . . . ?"

What can I say? I took the "or."

Chapter

57

As they walked into St. Patrick's the next morning, Stryker genuflected automatically, even though it had been years since he'd set foot inside a church. He hadn't been to Mass since his mother had gotten sick more than two years ago. As soon as he'd heard the news, he'd left the service, calling Riley to take him up on the offer of a job as long as Stryker could work from Jersey instead of D.C.

Riley had agreed, of course, and Stryker had gone home to Jersey City to be with his mother. He hadn't seen her in three years, and she'd lost weight and her skin had taken on a sallow, plastic quality. Her eyes had been the same, though. Sparkling with warmth and humor. And when she'd opened her arms wide and flashed that familiar smile, the sick woman in the doorway had once again become his mother.

He'd prayed that night one last time, begging God not to steal this vibrant woman from him.

God hadn't listened. And Stryker had stopped listening for God.

"Are you okay?" Mel had her hand on his shoulder, arching up on tiptoes to whisper in his ear. They were at the back of the cathedral, waiting for the priest to pass and the churchgoers to filter out now that Mass had ended.

He shook his head, as much to clear it as to tell her he didn't want to talk about it. She looked at him for a moment but didn't argue. Good. He wasn't up for arguing with her, and he'd been half afraid that she'd go all female on him, thinking that sleeping together gave her license to pick at his feelings. He didn't want to be picked. He just wanted to protect her. And, so help him, he wanted her in his bed again.

Beside him, she was gazing into the church with pure wonder. He understood the expression. The cathedral was stunning, like something transplanted out of Europe. Stone columns rising to a domed ceiling, stained glass everywhere, and so much detail that you had to believe it took masons centuries to complete the place. The place seemed to be made of arches, and he leaned over to whisper to Mel. "Are any of these arches the catenary thing? Like in St. Louis?"

"Could be," she said. She peered around. "Someone must know about the architecture of this place."

He tugged her sideways, then, easing them over to the Information desk. An elderly man with a ruddy face and piercing green eyes smiled at them. "Can I be of some help to you, then?" he asked, his Irish lilt seeming to fill the hall. Stryker couldn't help but smile.

"We were wondering if you knew about the architecture. Are any of these arches a catenary curve?"

"Ah, well, that I couldn't tell you. Mildred might know, but she's in Pittsburgh this week for her daughter's wedding."

"How about someone who could give us a tour?" Stryker asked. If they walked through the place, maybe Mel would see what they needed.

"I've been a member since I was in diapers and a volunteer since I lost my Sadie back in 'eighty-three. I think I ought to do just fine. Paddy O'Shea. The pleasure's mine." He peered at them through spectacles as he stepped out from behind the booth, signaling for the short, dark-haired woman beside him to staff the desk. "Anything in particular you're interested in? The stained glass? Cathedral history? I don't know arches from anything, but the rest I've got right up here." He tapped his temple as he walked past them into the nave. He started down the aisle toward the altar, not waiting for their answer and instead throwing out tidbits of information: the size of the cathedral, the year it was built, the architect, and enough other factual trivia to make Stryker's head swim.

"See that," he said, stopping and pointing to the baldachin over the main altar. "Solid bronze. Amazing, isn't it?"

"Are there any statues of the saints?"

"Well, sure." He peered at Matthew. "You're looking for Saint Michael."

Beside him, Mel gasped. "We are. How did you know?"

The old man cocked his thumb toward Stryker. "That boy's a soldier through and through. Couldn't slouch if his life depended on it. Must be looking for his patron, eh?"

Mel laughed, flashing a smile toward Stryker that tugged at his gut. He liked seeing her laugh. It erased the strain from her face and filled her with light. "You're right," she said, "but we're looking for St. Louis, too. Do you have them both here?"

"Well, of course we do. The St. Michael and St. Louis altar. Right there by the Lady Chapel."

"What did you say?" Mel whispered. "What altar?"

"It's called the St. Michael and St. Louis altar. Right beautiful it is, too. Would you like to see it?"

"Absolutely," Mel said. To Stryker, she added, "That has to be it. Everything fits. But what's the next clue?"

"Clue?" Paddy asked as he led them further into the cathedral.

"It's kind of a game," Stryker said as they followed. They'd turned to the left, moving up some stairs next to the main altar. They passed the organ, though it seemed more that they passed through it, with the organ on their right and the pipes on their left and the intricately carved wood surrounding them.

They moved down a passageway past a series of doors until Paddy signaled for them to stop. They were just to the left of the Lady Chapel, essentially behind the high altar. "There it is," Paddy said, indicating the white Carrara marble altar. It had a Gothic feel to it, with three towering, intricately carved spires over three niches. The middle spire rose the highest, marking the altar cross. The niches to the left and right contained statues of St. Louis and St. Michael, respectively. Behind the altar was a stained-glass window, through which a stream of light now passed, a warm purple with bits of dust dancing in the colors. A small altar rail surrounded the area, complete with red velvet kneelers, effectively keeping them from getting close enough to inspect the altar in more detail.

"A game, eh?" Paddy said, his voice low in deference to the altar and the nearby Lady Chapel. "You tell me what you're looking for, and maybe I can help you. Otherwise, can't see that I'm doing much good here."

"We're not—" Stryker began, but Mel cut him off.

"A scavenger hunt," she said, giving him an apologetic little shrug. "I know it sounds silly, but this altar is a clue. We're just not sure what the clue is."

"Ah, I see. A bit of the wild-goose chase, then."

"Something like that."

"So a clue led you to the altar, and now the altar will lead you to a prize?"

"Essentially."

"Well, I don't think there could be a message actually waiting for you here. Off limits, don't you know."

Stryker nodded. "It must be something about the altar. Something that points the way to something else."

"The direction the saints are facing, maybe?" Mel suggested, though without much enthusiasm.

"Oh, no, my dear. That's not it. The clue is obvious, though what you'll find when you'll follow it is a mystery to me. You'll come back and tell an old man?"

"If you can tell me what the clue is, I promise I'll tell you where it leads."

"Tiffany's, of course. What would have a better prize?"

"Tiffany's?" Mel asked, her face reflecting Stryker's confusion. "You mean Tiffany & Co. down the street? Diamonds and crystal and bridal registries Tiffany's?"

"That'll be the one. You'll be finding your next clue there. Mark my words."

"Okay, I'll bite," Stryker said. "What makes you so certain?"

"The altar, of course. The altar was built by Tiffany & Co."

"Mr. O'Shea, you're *my* patron saint." Mel took the man by the shoulders and kissed him on each cheek. "Thank you. Thank you, thank you, thank you."

"Well, now . . ." His already ruddy cheeks colored even more, and he shuffled a bit. "Unless you want more of a tour, I'd best be getting back to my post."

"We're fine," Stryker said. "Thanks again." As Paddy headed toward the front of the cathedral, Stryker turned to Mel. "Ready to go shopping?"

"On Fifth Avenue? I can't wait." Her eyes danced, and color lit her face as well. They'd figured out another clue, and they were on their way. He hoped her happiness lasted. The clues were getting harder and harder, and the stakes were still just as high.

She started to walk past him back toward the aisle, but he reached out a hand to stop her. "Wait. There's something I want to do."

He moved toward the shrine next to the Lady Chapel, then knelt and took a candle, dropping an offering into the little box. He lit the candle and bowed his head. He hadn't prayed in years, but it felt right to be there now asking for help from some power higher than himself, and the words came easily to his lips.

When he stood up, Mel was behind him, her face a wash of compassion. "Are you okay?"

"I was asking Mary to pray for you. To pray for your protection."

"Thanks, but wasn't that a waste of a prayer?"

He frowned. "What do you mean?"

"It's just that your prayer's already been answered," she said, taking his hand and flashing a smile that cut right through him. "I have you."

Chapter
58

St. Patrick's may be heaven on Fifth Avenue to some. To me, heaven was Fifth Avenue itself. More specifically, the shops that line Fifth Avenue.

Ironic, then, that as we moved down the avenue with all deliberate speed—passing all the stores I lust after on a regular basis—I couldn't have cared less.

All of them just passing me by. And me with a man carrying significant cash on his person. Really, I didn't care at all. (Well, had we passed Manolo, I might have cared a little, but fortunately it's not on the route, and I didn't have to suffer the agony of not going in.)

I'll confess to feeling a little OHMYGOD twinge as we rushed through the doors of Tiffany's. Most girls go there with their husbands or fiancés (or lovers or rich daddies). I was there to save my own life.

That sobered me up *tout de suite.*

The clerk who approached us wore her hair piled up, making her resemble Audrey Hepburn in *Breakfast at Tiffany's,* a little tidbit that I'm sure wasn't lost on her. "May I help you?"

Now that the question was out there, I realized I had no clue what to say. We'd made the trek up Fifth in silence, each lost in our own thoughts. I was so giddy about knowing where to go for the next clue that I hadn't given a thought as to how we'd recognize that clue in the first place.

Fortunately, Stryker wasn't as tongue-tied as me. "A friend called. He told us he'd bought a present for my girlfriend, and that we could pick it up here. Has anything been left for Melanie Prescott?"

Girlfriend? I turned the word over in my head and decided I liked it. Yeah, I think I liked it a lot.

As "Audrey Hepburn" headed back behind the counter to look for the mysterious package, I leaned toward Stryker. "Are you sure?" I whispered.

"Not at all. Got any other suggestions?"

"I've got nothing. I suppose there could be a message scribbled on the bathroom walls, but this place seems too posh. They'd probably paint over the message before I had time to find it." I made a face. "I hope you're right. If not, it's back to visit Paddy and see if he has any other helpful ideas."

Audrey reemerged carrying a clipboard. "We have several items waiting for pickup at the moment. What was your name again?" She looked at me, her pen poised to write.

"Melanie Prescott."

She flipped pages, her pen moving down the paper. "I'm sorry, that name's not on the list."

"Ah." Okay. Now what? "Um, he has a silly nickname for me. And I, um, can't imagine he'd actually give the name out to anyone. But maybe he'd use the initials? Is there a PSW?"

I held my breath, but I was certain it would be there. It had to be. If it wasn't, we were screwed, because I was fresh out of ideas.

Once again, she flipped through the list. A tiny little shake of the head, and I knew what the answer would be. "Sorry. Nothing like that on the list."

"Oh. Um . . ."

"Would he have put it under any other nicknames, sweetie?" Stryker asked. To the helpful "Miss Hepburn," he said, "Our friend Lynx is such a kidder."

She tapped the clipboard, ever efficient, but not nearly as patient. "Shall I check for that name?"

"Yes," Stryker said. "Please."

Once again, I held my breath. Once again, she shook her head.

I sighed. Obviously Stryker had wasted an intercession. He should have lit a candle and asked Mary to pray that we'd figure out this stupid clue.

I cocked my head, that ridiculous thought spurring another. "You know," I said, "Lynx might have left it in your name."

Stryker gave me a look that suggested he thought I'd lost my mind, but he went with it. "Possible. Try—"

"Michael," I said, effectively cutting him off. "Michael Louis."

Again with the pen down the page, and the whole thing was so familiar that I was half-cocked to walk away when she gave us the news.

"I've got a Louis Michaels," she said.

"Right," Stryker said, not missing a beat. "That's me."

"Hepburn's" brow furrowed as she peered at me. I shrugged. "You're working off a list. I figured last name first . . ."

I wasn't entirely sure she believed me, and my uncertainty morphed into full-blown negativity when she asked Stryker for his identification.

"Dammit, honey," I said. "I told you to bring your wallet." I shot her a look that I hoped suggested a female bonding moment. "He never listens to me." The corner of her mouth quirked, and I, encouraged, rushed on. "I understand you can't let us leave with it—we can come back tomorrow with his license—but could we at least take a peek?"

"Well, I don't know. That's not really—"

"I know it's awkward," I said, rushing on. "But we're seeing Lynx later this afternoon and I know he's going to ask if I like it."

"You'd really be helping us out of a jam," Stryker added.

She licked her lips, then glanced around the store, probably checking to see if her manager was watching. Finally she nodded. "Okay. A peek." I swear I wanted to kiss her, but I held back, figuring she'd only appreciate the gesture if it came from Stryker.

When she emerged again from the back room, she was carrying the trademark Tiffany's blue box, this one about the size of a shoe box. She opened it, fought her way past layers of packing material, and emerged with an engraved crystal plaque.

"How, um, nice," I said. "What is it?"

"I'm not sure," she said. "It's a bit big to be a paperweight."

So it was. The thing was about eight inches long, four inches wide and one inch thick. Solid crystal, with something etched on top. I leaned in for a closer look, Stryker right beside me. I heard his sharp intake of breath and knew that he'd realized the same thing I had. This was it. This was our clue.

"Oh, this is why," "Hepburn" said. She was looking at the paperwork. "A special order." She glanced down at the message and then up at me. "Does that mean something to you?"

"He likes to play games," I said. "Could I borrow a pencil and a sheet of paper?"

We might not be able to take the plaque with us, but at least we could take the message.

> *Secret roi urn,*
> *For Rebecca:*
> *552:2, 9:15, 36:6, 602:6, 635:67, 274:9, 800:67,*
> *642:54, 641:9, 148:53, 45:30, 51:7, 161:14.*

Chapter

59

"I'm sure glad we found that clue," Stryker said. "It's all so very clear to me now."

I shot him a look that was supposed to make him behave and aimed a finger toward the counter. We'd left Tiffany's with our clue and headed straight for the nearest Starbucks. Stryker might be suffering from a severe case of defeatism, but I was back in my element. Genuine codes. Not this pseudo-scavenger hunt over Manhattan Island, racing between esoteric clues. *This* was fun. Just like that very first pigpen code. If it weren't for that little downside of dying if I screwed up or Lynx found me, I'd actually be having a really good time.

Stryker returned with one latte and his boring cup of solid black coffee.

"So what do we know?" He leaned forward. "Actually, I

know what I know. Nothing. So the real question is, what do *you* know?"

"A bit more than that," I said. And, yeah, I was feeling a bit smug and pleased with myself. I scooted my chair around so he could see my notes right side up. "The 'secret roi urn' reference is a bit odd—"

"No shit."

"—so we'll leave that aside for the time being. This is the key," I said, pointing to the second line, For Rebecca. "And I mean that literally."

"Okay," he said. "I'll bite. What the hell are you talking about?"

"Do you read spy novels? Any Ken Follett?"

He shook his head.

"*Eye of the Needle? The Key to Rebecca?*"

"Sorry." Then, "Wait. The second one. Didn't that have something to do with a code and a book?"

"Exactly. Like Enigma, the system really was used during the war. A code was sent using a book as a key. In that case, Daphne du Maurier's *Rebecca.*"

"So we need a copy of the book?"

"No, no. The reference to *Rebecca* just tells us what kind of code we're dealing with. The key isn't that book. It's something else."

"What?"

I shrugged. He'd pretty much tuned into the heart of the matter.

He shifted in his seat, downed a slug of coffee, then shifted again. "Okay, back up here. You're sure the book we need isn't *Rebecca.* How do you know?"

"These numbers." I pointed to the first number in each pairing. "Those must be page numbers. But *Rebecca* doesn't have eight hundred pages. It must be something else."

"All right," he said. "What?"

I shook my head. "No clue."

He grunted. "So if these numbers are pages, what do these mean?" He tapped the numbers following the colons, one by one in succession.

"Not sure. Words or letters. We won't be positive until we figure out what the book is."

"Secret roi urn?"

I looked at him, tapping my pencil against my chin and nodding slowly. "No idea. Too bad Warren isn't here."

"Warren?"

"Used to be my study partner. He's a total anagram fanatic. The anagrams in *Silence of the Lambs* were too easy for him. He was totally bored. He'd figure this out in a heartbeat."

"No problem," Stryker said. "I can do that."

"Really?" I looked at him with respect. "I had no idea."

"Sure." He opened the laptop, and I sat there shaking my head, both amused and befuddled. But he was right. Less than two minutes later he'd pulled up an anagram generator on the Internet and had a whole list of words that could be made from *Secret roi urn.*

"We have to keep in mind that it might not be an anagram," I said as I scanned the list. Somehow words like *sorcerer unit* or *erect insuror* seemed less than useful. "Maybe it refers to a crypt. *Roi* means 'king,' right? So maybe dead royalty? Ashes in an urn?"

"Keep reading," Stryker said, his eyes never leaving the screen.

I did.

Crustier Nero
Trounce Riser

Oh yeah. These were helpful. *Not.* I kept my mouth shut and kept reading as Stryker scrolled through the list. It's amazing how many words and phrases (albeit nonsense words and phrases) *Secret roi urn* could produce.

Nicer trouser
(that one was amusing, at least)
Resurrection
(that one was at least a real word)
Escort Ruiner

The last one pretty much cracked me up, and I kept one hand on the back of Stryker's chair so as not to fall over in a fit of helpless giggles. (I know, I know. It wasn't *that* funny. But I think under the circumstances I was entitled to a little hysteria.) Escort Ruiner. Yeah, there's a *great* clue. We'll just go by every brothel and—)

I blinked, realizing with a start that I was an absolute and total idiot.

I must have made some sort of noise, too, because Stryker looked back over his shoulder at me. "What? What is it?"

"Resurrection." I said. "That's got to be it."

"Okay," he said. "I'll bite. Why?"

"Well, for one, it's the only really sensible word in the entire list."

He half nodded, but I didn't wait for him to say anything. "Plus, it fits one of the themes."

"Themes?"

"The religious clues. The saints, the cathedral, the altar."

"Okay." He nodded slowly, then added, "Yeah," with a much more vigorous nod. "That makes sense."

"So, if we're talking resurrection, we need a Bible, right? Does a Bible have at least eight hundred pages?"

"Sure," he frowned. "I think. It must—"

I stifled a laugh. "You're not sure."

He grimaced. "Don't rely on me. Let's find a Bible and look."

"Right." I paused. "Um, new problem."

"What?"

"The translation."

A grin played at the corner of his mouth. "English would be good."

"Thank you, Mr. Comedian. I mean there are about eight billion different translations of the Bible and even more editions. Unless we know which translation and which edition, the words or letters we need won't line up the same."

He shook his head slowly, and I tried again.

"You read Mark Twain in school, right?"

"Sure. *Huckleberry Finn.*"

"Right. And you bought some cheap paperback copy of the book, right?"

"Actually, my dad had a really nice leather-bound edition from some collector's set. I read that. Bent one page. Got read the riot act."

"Let's say you bent page one twenty-seven. If you went to a

bookstore and looked at page one twenty-seven of the paper-back, the words on the page wouldn't be the same, would they?"

He frowned. "I never thought about it, but I guess not."

"That's why in this type of code you always know the publisher, edition, all that kind of info." I gnawed on my lower lip, thinking. "Maybe *secret roi urn* tells us that."

"The resurrection version of the Bible?"

I shrugged. It certainly didn't sound familiar, but I was fresh out of ideas.

"Well, it could be—" He cut himself off, his brows pulling down into a V over his nose.

"What?"

"Not a Bible. The catechism."

"Ah . . . ," I said. I didn't want to sound stupid, but, "What's that?"

"It's like a reference book for Catholics. Very important to the faith."

"Oh." I nodded slowly. "Well, that makes sense. A lot of the clues have been pretty Catholic oriented. Does it have different editions?"

"I have no idea."

I sighed, exasperated. "Stryker, you're not listening to me. We have to know which edition or else we won't be looking at the right page, and we'll be reading the clues entirely wrong."

"Not page," he said. "Section."

He leaned back in his chair, looking perfectly content and absurdly proud of himself.

"Okay. I'll bite. What sections?"

"The catechism is broken down by sections. Or maybe it's paragraph numbers. I don't remember. The point is that there are at least eight hundred of these sections, probably a lot more. And every catechism is uniform. Doesn't matter how it's printed—it could be an audiobook—and the words and section numbers are all going to be exactly the same."

That had to be it. "You're brilliant," I said, leaning across the table and giving him a big hug. "So where do we find one of these things?"

"Where else?" he said. "Back at St. Patrick's."

"I've got a missal right here," Paddy said, reaching under the counter and pulling out a red leather-bound volume, then handing it to Stryker. "But I don't have a catechism on me, and we don't keep one at the Information desk."

Stryker passed the missal back. "Appreciate the help, but it's got to be a catechism."

"Oh, right. You're on a scavenger hunt. Hmmm." He stroked his chin. "Have you checked the gift shop? And if they don't have it, there's another shop outside. Just around the corner. Surely they'd have one."

"The gift shop's a great idea," Mel said. "Thanks so much."

She hurried off, and Stryker started to follow, tossing out a last-minute thank-you to Paddy for all his help.

"No problem, boy," he said as Stryker moved away. "You

must be winning your game so far. That other fellow hadn't even figured out what he needed to be looking for."

Stryker stopped dead, turning slowly back to face Paddy. "What other guy?"

"Tall fellow. Dark. Clean-cut looking, but I can't say I cared for the glint in his eyes."

Stryker's stomach roiled. Somehow, Lynx had learned about St. Pat's. But how? Had he tracked Stryker and Mel? Or was he interpreting the clues, too? Whatever the answer, Stryker didn't like it. The bastard was too damn close.

Beside him, Paddy leaned in, then lowered his voice, a bit conspiratorially. "I'm rooting for you and your lady friend to win."

"Did you tell this other guy about the altar?"

"Not me," he said. "But I'd told your whole story to Evelyn. She works the counter with me. She took a liking to the lad and, well, I think she's rooting for him and not you two."

"Tiffany's," Stryker said urgently. "Did she tell him about Tiffany's?"

"Yeah, son, I'm afraid she did."

Chapter 61

Stryker paced just inside the cathedral doors, his cell phone pressed to his ear. I sat off to the side, the catechism open in my lap and one ear cocked as I tried to decipher his half of the conversation. Not easy, and since I kept losing count, I finally gave up and just listened.

"Absolutely," Stryker said, his voice sounding perfectly calm and reasonable but his face reflecting a temper I hadn't yet witnessed. He turned in his pacing and our eyes met. I looked back down at the catechism. Section 552, two words out . . . there it was. *Peter.*

"No, no, really. It's not a problem. I'm just surprised, that's all." Another pause. "Exactly. He sent the thing, so why would he need to see it again?"

I snuck a peek and decided that Stryker looked calmer. Good. I didn't have to worry that he was going to start slugging passersby just for the hell of it.

Section 9, word 15. I flipped pages, found the section, and tapped out fifteen words with my fingertip. *Trent.*

Peter Trent.

Didn't mean a thing to me yet. I drew a breath and soldiered on.

A few feet in front of me, Stryker was wrapping up. "Right. No problem. And thanks again for all your help." Perfectly polite, perfectly calm. Then he snapped the phone closed. "Goddamn son of a *bitch.*"

"*Stryker!*" I said, pointedly looking around. We were, after all, still in the church. "I take it we have a problem?"

"She showed Lynx the plaque. Long story, he sweet-talked her, she mentioned the guy who bought it was named Lynx, apparently he has some sort of ID with that name on it, and so she showed it to him."

"Oh. Guess we shouldn't have used his name, huh?"

Stryker looked at his phone, hauled his arm back as if he were going to toss it, then sagged a bit as he obviously thought better of it.

"But wait a second," I said. "This could be good for us. His name really is Lynx? Can we check DMV records?"

He shook his head. "She said it wasn't official. Like a club identification card. He told her it was a nickname." He met my eyes. "If we had all the time in the world—"

"Right. I know." With time, maybe we could have turned the tables, hunted *him.* But time had been our enemy from the get-go, almost as much as Lynx himself.

I shook my head, determined not to dwell on our losses. All we had to rely on were my brains and Stryker's skill. I wasn't going to sap our strength by throwing bad vibes our way. "We're

just going to have to work with what we have." I held my note-
book up. "I'm actually making some progress on this."

"Good. I hope Lynx isn't sitting on a bench somewhere doing
the same thing. She said he copied it down letter by letter."

"I don't get it," I said. "Why does he even want the code? He
doesn't win anything by solving the codes. He only wins
by . . . well, by killing me." Now *there* was a lovely thought.

"But you're following the codes. If he solves the codes, he'll
find you."

I'll admit he had a point, but something didn't quite fit. "I
don't know," I said, thinking aloud. "That seems like a lot of
trouble. I mean, he hasn't had any problem finding us so far.
And at least two times, we weren't anywhere near a clue. We
were at the hotel once, and then we were at Starbucks. So how
did he find us?"

For a moment, Stryker's expression didn't shift at all. Then his
eyes flashed with inspiration. I expected him to clue me in, but he
said nothing. Instead, he moved slowly and deliberately out of the
cathedral and down the steps to the street, his arm extended to
hail a cab. When one pulled over, he turned to me. "In. Now."

"What? Where are we going?" But I wasn't really arguing. I'd
decided early on in this little adventure to trust Stryker. I wasn't
going to stop now.

"We need to keep moving."

I dutifully shoved all my papers and things into my bag,
then climbed in. He followed, his jaw tight and his entire body
more tense than I'd seen before.

"Stryker? What's going on?"

"He's tracking us."

I laughed. I couldn't help it. I had a sudden mental picture of Lynx as Elmer Fudd tracking Bugs Bunny. "You mean like a hunter? In Manhattan? You're joking."

"I mean like the military. With a GPS tracking device."

"Oh." Well, that was a horse of a different color. I turned the idea over in my head, deciding that I really didn't like the idea of being tracked. Nope. I didn't like it one little bit.

I shifted in my seat, trying desperately to make what Stryker said not be true. "Does that mean one of us has to have something with the GPS thingamabobbie in it?"

"Yup. That's exactly what it means. The question is what."

"Well, that's absurd."

He ignored the comment. "It's not the coat, because he found us before we found it."

He reached over and grabbed my bag, unceremoniously dumping my personal stuff all over the backseat. I'd shoved my new Givenchy shoes in my tote, too, and now they bounced to the floorboards.

"Hey!"

"It's got to be something one of us is carrying around. Something Lynx or the PSW powers that be could have loaded with a chip." He started poking through the debris.

"Do you mind?" I snatched a tampon and my birth control pills away and shoved them back inside.

He looked at the bag.

"Don't even ask," I said. No way was I watching him rip apart a tampon in a search for a microchip.

I thought the side of his mouth quirked, but I wasn't sure. "Cell phone?" he said.

"I've had it off since the last time I used it. It's running out of juice." I pulled it out and switched it back on, just in case there was a message. "It can't be the phone, anyway. He couldn't have put a chip in it. And in the movies, they can only do that triangulate location thing when the phone is on, which it hasn't been for a couple of hours." I know a lot about the spy business from movies.

"It might already have a chip. Some phones do now."

"Not this one. It's ancient. At least three years old."

"The original clue." He reached for the brown paper note, now pretty crumpled. He smoothed it on his thigh and held it up to the light.

I gaped. "You're kidding, right? How small can those tracker things be, anyway?"

"Pretty small. But as far as I know, not as thin as a paper fiber. I thought there might be a chip glued onto a corner. Something small and brown so that we just hadn't noticed it."

"Is there?"

"I don't see a damn thing."

He put the paper down and started fingering the rest of my stuff. I snatched up the CD just as he reached for it. "This, maybe?"

"I don't know . . ." He frowned. "I've never heard of a tracking chip in a CD, but I suppose it's theoretically possible. I hate to destroy it."

"I copied the file to the laptop," I said. "We should be safe."

"I'm still nervous about destroying the disc. What if there's something on there that didn't get copied? Something key?"

"Okay. That makes sense." There had to be a solution, though, and when I glanced out of the cab, I realized what it was. I tapped the Plexiglas, then leaned forward. "If you make your next left, you'll see a Kinko's. Could you pull up in front for a second?"

"Sure thing."

When the cab pulled over, I took my purse and the CD and ran inside. I have to confess I was feeling pretty clever, and I hummed a bit as I got back in the car with Stryker.

"What did you do?"

"Sent it by FedEx to Mr. and Mrs. Johnson at the Plaza. We never officially checked out, so I'm sure they'll hold it for a couple of days."

"Not bad," he said. "I can do you one better."

"Yeah?"

He held out his hand, now balled into a fist, then opened his fingers. The watch dropped down, dangling from its chain, the end of which Stryker still held on to.

I stared at him, my mouth hanging open. We'd never taken the gears and things out.

As I watched, he pried the back open with his knife, then used the same blade to force the interior gears out. I found a tissue in my tote, and we laid the pieces in my lap and poked through them.

"Nothing," I said.

"I know this is right," Stryker said. "It has to be. Lynx started shooting right after we found the watch. There's got to be a connection."

He held the watch in his hand, turning it this way and that before finally focusing on the ball at the top. About the size of a nice pearl, the gold ball topped the winding stem. Stryker looked at it, then me. Then he grinned and dropped the whole watch onto the floorboard of the taxi. He leaned over and smashed the blunt end of his pocketknife against it. The thin metal plating split apart. And there, among the remnants, was a tiny electronic chip.

"That son of a bitch," Stryker said slowly, knowing he should be furious, but somehow only able to feel relief.

"Stryker?" Mel had pulled her arm away, and now she was studying him from the other side of the cab. "Are you okay?"

"He was tracking us, all right," he said. He picked the chip up carefully, then laughed. "This is a GPS device. Tiny little thing, isn't it?"

Mel looked wary, but nodded. "And this is amusing because—"

"Because we found it before he found us."

"That's true," she said. Her forehead creased. "Um, shouldn't we get rid of it, though? I mean, is it still transmitting?"

"I sure as hell hope so," he said. "And I know just what to do with it."

He leaned forward to give the driver a new address, then settled back in the cab. "Time to send our friend Lynx on a bit of a goose chase."

Beside him, Mel smiled, clearly enjoying the joke as much as he did.

"It's too bad we didn't find it earlier, though. Now Lynx has the clue," he said.

"Maybe. But it only matters if he solves it."

"And you don't think he will."

"Not fast enough anyway."

"Have you solved it?" he asked.

"Almost," she said.

"Then don't let me keep you from finishing," he said. "We may have just won a battle, but I still have a feeling we're running out of time."

63

>>>http://www.playsurvivewin.com<<<

PLAY.SURVIVE.WIN

WELCOME TO REPORTING CENTER

PLAYER REPORT:
REPORT NO. A-0004
Filed By: Lynx
Subject: Game progression.
Report:
- Target tracked to Fifth Avenue area. Unable to fix location.
- Target departed without incident.

- Clue located, but uninterpretable.
- Tracking device too sporadic to be truly effective. A disadvantage, but not an insurmountable one.
- Assistance necessary; possible source of aid located. Persuasive tactics will be applied.

>>>End Report<<<

Send Report to Opponent? >>Yes<< >>_No_<<

The apartment lacked a quality. Walls that smelled of mildew. Laundry on the floor. Absolutely no window coverings. And the subtle stink of dishes left too long in the sink.

A lack of self-respect, Lynx thought. That's what it came down to. Warren Voight lacked class. He had brains, maybe. That remained to be seen. But class? Self-respect?

No.

Good. A man who lived like this—who didn't respect his apartment, his belongings or his surroundings—well, a man like that was easy to control.

All Lynx had to do was wait.

He dusted the couch with his hand, scattering a flurry of cracker crumbs. This wouldn't do. He picked his way to the linen closet, found one clean towel, then went back and draped it over the couch. He sat on it, settling in to wait.

He was prepared to wait all night, on that couch, facing the door. He had no choice, after all. No other options.

He'd tracked his quarry to the cathedral, but the sporadic nature of the GPS meant he'd gotten there just a bit too late. No matter. He'd used his own skills and followed the path cut by Stryker and the bitch. Right down the avenue to Tiffany's.

Yes, he'd simply done what he did best. Played the game. Played the charming friend. Pulled the information slowly and completely from that old hag at the church and the ripe little bitch at Tiffany's.

So easy.

The clue itself, however . . .

He opened the paper on which he'd written his notes, spreading it open on his knees. Secret roi urn? Rebecca? The series of numbers?

The references meant nothing to him, and as soon as he was back on Fifth Avenue he'd known that he had only one option. He was going to have to wait until the GPS system went back online. Unfortunate, and he might lose precious hours, but he had no choice. He'd mark her location, move in, and make the kill. He'd come too close too often not to succeed this time. In his heart, he'd already won this game. All he had to do was make it so in reality.

Fate, however, was not cooperating.

The system had come online. He'd pinpointed the location, rushed to the site, checking his laptop from the back of the taxi as he'd moved through the city. His quarry had never moved.

He wasn't familiar with the location. A hotel? A restaurant? Neither.

The software hadn't shown a pinpoint location, of course. That would have made the game too easy. But he'd known the vicinity, and he'd scoured the entire block.

Nothing.

And yet the computer had insisted they'd been there.

He'd almost missed it, actually. A note. Taped to a signpost.

Lynx.
Too late.
And now you're hunting blind.

And there, taped underneath the bold, black text, a tiny gray microchip. The GPS device.

He hadn't reacted. Hadn't caused a scene. He'd simply hailed a cab, gotten in, and let the taxi drive him through Central Park. He'd found the trees soothing. He'd needed to be soothed.

In the park, he'd found a solitary table near the boat house and called NYU. His story had been simple: He was checking references for a job. He'd spoken to one of Melanie's past professors, who'd referred him to a paper she'd written, which referenced another paper she'd written with Warren Voight.

And all accomplished in less than two hours.

He hadn't needed to panic. He'd been right not to lose his temper. He was back in the game. All he needed was someone to help him. And now he was here in her colleague's apartment, waiting for help to arrive.

Warren would help.

Of that Lynx was sure.

Chapter
64

Secret roi urn [Resurrection?]
For Rebecca:
Peter Trent holds the keys and is witness to your trials
and salvation.

"Good job," Stryker said, taking the paper I handed to him. "But I don't think you're through. You may have deciphered a code, but you haven't solved the clue. At least not that I can tell."

"Details, details, details." I couldn't help the light note in my voice. We'd lost Lynx (I thought) and we'd almost solved all the clues (I hoped). Sure, I still had to work out those pesky details—who *was* Peter Trent, anyway?—but we'd come this far. We'd manage, right?

"Okay," I said, giving in to a sudden fear that maybe Lynx

had figured out as much as I had. "Let's get busy. What the hell does this mean?"

We'd checked into a no-tell hotel on the Lower East Side. The kind with rooms advertised for "gentlemen" that have weekly, as well as hourly, rates. The place smelled funny, and there was no way I was sleeping on that mattress. But it did have a phone book, and Stryker was flipping through it.

"Three Peter Trents," he said. "And one P. Trent."

"So we just call them? What do we say?"

"You're the expert." He passed me his cell phone. "Have at it."

Reluctantly, I took the phone. This didn't feel right, but I wasn't about to accidentally overlook the resolution of the entire puzzle simply because I'd had a feeling. While the first number rang, I nodded toward his laptop. "Do me a favor. Do a search for *resurrection* and *New York*. Let me know if anything interesting pops up."

He fired a little salute in my direction and started typing.

I started spewing a line of bullshit to the guy who answered the phone. Did he know a Melanie Prescott? Did PSW mean anything to him? *Nada.*

I tried another tack. "Secret roi urn," I said, then closed my eyes and prayed he responded with something equally absurd, like a commentary on the rain in Spain.

Instead, he hung up on me.

No problem. I can handle rejection.

I dialed the next three numbers. Pretty much the same response, except for the guy who made a rude sexual suggestion about what he'd like to do with me in an urn.

I assumed that wasn't a coded response and moved on.

"Nothing," I said, reporting to Stryker. "Please tell me you've found something so I don't have to start calling Peter Trents in Brooklyn and Queens."

"Actually, I think I did."

"Really?"

"Hold on. I just pulled the page up." He typed some more, then lifted his hands in triumph before hooking his fingers behind his head. "Damn, I'm good."

I raised an eyebrow. "Did you run the search *I* asked for?"

"Hell, yeah. But it's all in the fingers." He let his chair fall forward as he waggled his fingers at me.

"You do have marvelous fingers," I said, my voice husky.

He laughed and pulled me into his lap so that I could see the computer screen, too. As I skimmed the page, I felt a little giddy, and it wasn't just from the feel of Stryker's arms around me. No wonder he was in such a good mood.

This was it.

This was the answer.

Chapter

65

"There!" I shouted, twisting back and pointing as Stryker missed the turn.

He slammed on the brakes, and the tiny Ford Aspire screeched to a halt. He kicked it in reverse, and I held my breath as we shot backwards to Highland.

He spun the wheel, we turned, and I started breathing again.

"You could have gotten us killed!" I said, but mostly just for show. Under the circumstances, I was getting used to almost being killed. A little reckless driving wasn't going to rock my world.

"So how far is the cemetery?" he asked.

I consulted the map but couldn't tell much of anything. Maps aren't my thing. All I knew was that we were on the south shore of Staten Island cruising on Highland, and we should be getting close. "Almost there," I said, sounding much more confident than I really felt.

We'd called Resurrection Cemetery from the city and spoken to a woman in the main office, who'd looked at the registry and confirmed that, yes, a Peter Trent was buried there. We weren't at all sure what we'd find at his grave. (I'll confess to being a tad creeped out. I mean, I certainly wasn't planning to dig the poor guy up.)

As soon as she'd confirmed our suspicions, we'd rented a car from Apple Rent-A-Car, and after a bit of a schlep, we were almost there.

Just when I was about to consult the map again, I saw the gates. I pointed, Stryker turned, and we were in.

"Where to now?"

I saw a sign pointing out the direction of the main office. "That way. Toward the older section."

"Right."

We pulled up in front of the little office moments later, and I ran in while Stryker left the car running. The woman I'd spoken to had a plot map ready for me, and she'd helpfully circled Peter Trent's grave.

Unfortunately, all her help was wasted on me. After twenty minutes of driving in circles (and passing the caretaker twice, the second time earning us a wave and a smirk), Stryker finally pulled over and snatched the plot map from my utterly incompetent fingers. "I warned you," I said.

He grunted, consulted the map, and managed to get us to the right place in less than five minutes. "I thought men were supposed to be the directionally challenged sex," he said.

I shrugged. "So I'm a trendsetter."

The cemetery was relatively new, not the spooky place I'd pictured at all. From where we were standing, I could hear boats passing and could see a bit of water beyond the hills and landscaping. The place was peaceful, soothing. The complete opposite of the way my life had been going the past couple of days.

The plots were neatly mowed, flowers abounded, and the landscaping was lush. A mix of flat grave markers and old-fashioned tombstones kept the place looking like a cemetery, but otherwise I was reminded of a nice park. If I hadn't been afraid of bad karma, I would have said that I'd like to be buried someplace like this. As it was, I kept my mouth shut.

Peter Trent's grave was marked with one of the tombstones, and we both walked solemnly to the marker.

PETER TRENT
LOVING HUSBAND AND FATHER
Born August 19, 1922
Died January 11, 1980
May He Rest In Peace

I looked at Stryker, and he shrugged, obviously having no more sense of why we were there than I did.

I turned in a circle, my arms out to the side, helpless.

"The message said he holds the keys," Stryker said.

"If that means we dig him up and pry a key ring out of his cold, dead hand, then I give up right now. *Not* happening."

For a second, I actually thought Stryker was going to argue, but he took a good look at my face and nodded. "Right. No grave robbing."

"Thank you." I pointed to the gravestone. "Under it, maybe?"

Stryker looked around, then up toward the sky.

"Under," I said.

"I'm looking for security cameras."

"Oh."

Apparently he didn't see any, because he eased against the headstone and started to rock it. At first it didn't move, but after a little work—and a little additional help from the Ford Aspire's handy tire iron—he managed to get it loose. He gently laid it flat on the grass while I looked around, hopping nervously, sure we were going to be arrested at any minute.

But there was no scream of sirens filling the skies and no cemetery attendants pointing accusing fingers our way. I still felt guilty, and I moved quickly to Stryker's side, wanting to find the clue and get the stone back in place as fast as possible.

Except there was no clue. Just black earth roughly the shape of a triangle. I bent down and clawed frantically at the dirt, certain I'd find a metal box, a key, something just under the surface. Nothing. Just a few grubs and spiders. Ick.

"It has to be here," I said, my fingers digging deeper into the dirt.

Stryker got down on his knees and joined me, both of us digging into the soft earth. We'd dug quite a hole before he sat back on his heels and pressed a gentle hand to my shoulder. "Give it up, Mel. Come on. Help me get the stone back in place."

My head screamed *no!* The clue had to be there. If it wasn't, we were screwed. But the rest of me ignored the protest. Instead, I nodded numbly, then climbed to my feet, holding the stone steady as Stryker seated it once again firmly in the dirt. In the end, it didn't look too bad. (Okay, Peter Trent's family wasn't going to be happy, but I figured the caretaker could clean it up. And it wasn't like we'd opened the grave.) My stomach clenched. Dear Lord, please don't let Stryker say we have to open the grave . . .

"What was the clue?—'Holds the keys . . .'"

"'. . . and is witness to your trials and salvation,'" I finished.

"Not exactly crystal clear, is it?"

As I shook my head, Stryker pulled out his phone.

"Who are you calling?"

"I'm not." He moved in front of the stone, held the phone at arm's length, and pushed a button. "Camera phone. We might need this later."

I made a face. "I was kind of hoping this was the last clue."

"Ditto."

"Okay, so the key part has us stumped," I said. "What about the witness part?"

"Something Trent saw before he died?"

"Great," I said. "We'll just have a little séance."

"Just a shot in the dark," Stryker said.

I moved over to the gravestone and stood right in front of it, careful not to lean on it in case Stryker hadn't completely stabilized it. "Come on, Peter. Tell us what you know . . ."

Peter stayed silent.

"Witness," I said. "Witness. Something he sees. What does a dead man see?"

"The sky?" Stryker said, his words finally kicking my brain into gear. "The trees? Passing airplanes?" He glanced at my face and shrugged. "Sorry. Best I can do."

"No, no," I said, rushing to kiss his cheek. "I think you're right on target."

I grabbed his hand and tugged him with me across the little path to the grave site directly opposite Peter Trent's. "He'd also see his neighbors."

We both looked down, silently reading the marker on this grave:

Thomas Reardon

"There's no birth or death date," Mel said.

Stryker didn't bother to answer. He pulled out the plot map, found the number and called the main office. The woman who answered identified herself as Cherise and asked if she could help him.

"As a matter of fact, you can. I'm just a little curious about plot C-456. Can you tell me anything about the man buried there?"

She asked him to hold, and he could hear her clicking keys at a computer. He drummed his fingers on his thigh while Mel paced in front of him.

"Are you there, sir?"

"I'm here."

"Actually, that site is empty. Our customer purchased it

and placed a memorial placard in honor of a friend or family member."

That was interesting. "All right," he said. "Who's the customer?"

"Archibald Grimaldi."

His surprise must have shown on his face, because Mel took a step closer, mouthing, "What?"

He held a hand out, indicating she should listen. "Do you know *when* Mr. Grimaldi bought the plot? Or when he purchased the marker?"

"I'm sorry, sir, I don't have exact information. But I can tell you that it was within the last two months."

"Two? Are you certain?"

"Yes, sir. I input the information in the computer myself, and I've only worked here for two months. Why?"

"Did you talk to Grimaldi yourself?"

"No, sir. Sir, is there a problem?"

Just that Grimaldi had been dead for well over two months. Why impersonate the man?

To Cherise, he said, "No. No problem. Thank you. You've been incredibly helpful."

As he was hanging up, Mel's phone rang. She listened, her face going white.

"What is it? What's happened?"

"That was my friend Sara. We used to study together." She licked her lips, a tear spilling down her face. "My friend Warren," she said. "He's dead."

"You don't know that it has to do with you," Stryker said, holding me close. "It could be coincidence."

I nodded against his chest, my tears dampening his shirt. "I know," I said. But I didn't believe it. I knew the truth. In my heart, I knew. And I think he did, too.

"Stryker . . ." I pushed back, drawing in a breath as I looked at him.

"I know." He took a strand of my hair and twisted it around a finger, his face as sad as I'd ever seen it.

"It's worse," I said. "Warren knows Todd. He'd trust him. If Todd asked him to decipher the thing, he'd give it his best shot."

"And if we're wrong about Todd, or if his little buddy Lynx did the dirty work, a gun can be pretty persuasive." He frowned, thinking. "*Could* Warren solve it?"

"I don't know. The anagram? In a heartbeat. The rest of it . . . ?" I trailed off with a shrug. "I just don't know."

"The anagram could be enough. All he has to do is realize that 'resurrection' is a cemetery."

"Warren would get that. Secret roi urn. Dead kings. Mausoleums. Cemeteries. It's not a huge leap."

Stryker took my hand, tugging me back toward the car. "Come on."

He didn't have to tell me twice. If Lynx knew the cemetery name, he'd be on his way. Which meant I wanted to get the hell out of there.

Chapter

68

We were on Highland when we passed him, a yellow taxi heading in the opposite direction. I saw his profile in the backseat and gasped, slinking down in my seat as I said a silent prayer.

Didn't work. The taxi slowed, made a U-turn, and started moving in our direction.

"Go!" I yelled, but Stryker had already floored the thing.

I turned in my seat, looking back, hoping that a taxi driver wouldn't be motivated to run lights or break the speed limit.

A ray of sun struck the barrel of a gun, and I kissed that hope good-bye. Lynx had a gun to the driver's head. As incentive went, that was pretty damn good.

Stryker turned off Highland, and we were in a residential area. "Do you know where we are?"

"No clue," he said. He weaved through neighborhoods and

careened across parking lots, putting the little Aspire through her paces. I held my breath, willing the taxi not to keep up. So far, the force of my will wasn't doing a hell of a lot of good.

Stryker made a few more turns, pushing the Aspire to her limits. The taxi stayed on our tail. Then Stryker cut across someone's lawn and down their neighbor's driveway to emerge on the street behind us. I saw the taxi start to follow, but it got caught up in the shrubbery—one of the benefits of driving a skinny little car.

About the time we were turning off the road, I saw the taxi hit the driveway. Stryker made two more quick turns, and the taxi was long gone.

We pulled over, camouflaged by the crush of cars in a grocery store parking lot, and waited. Nothing.

Home free. At least for now.

I leaned forward and kissed the dash. "Good car," I said. Then I planted a kiss on Stryker's lips. "And good driving."

"My pleasure." He gestured toward the backseat. "Fire up the laptop and see if you can find Thomas Reardon. Whoever he is, he's our next stop."

Thomas Reardon wasn't hard to locate. As it turned out, the man was a semi-celebrity, what with being Archibald Grimaldi's attorney and all. His office was on 42nd Street in a high-rise that faced the public library. Stryker snagged an illegal parking place, and we made our way inside, then found his name on the building directory. The fortieth floor. I followed Stryker to the elevator in silence. It was almost over. This was the end of the road, I was certain of it.

I just wasn't sure what waited for us in Thomas Reardon's office.

The reception area was as bright and cheerful as the receptionist herself, and despite being after five, the place was bustling with activity. "May I help you?"

"We'd like to see Thomas Reardon," I said.

"I'm sorry. Mr. Reardon is in a meeting. Could someone else help you?"

I looked at Stryker, who took a step forward. "Tell him it's Melanie Prescott."

"I really shouldn't—"

"Trust me," Stryker said. "He'll want to see her."

She made the call, her expression never shifting. "I'm sorry, he repeated that this simply isn't a good time."

"It's urgent," I said. "Tell him . . . tell him Peter Trent sent us."

"Ma'am, I'm sorry, but—"

"Please," I said. "If he won't see us, we'll make an appointment. I promise. But, *please.*"

She pursed perfectly glossed lips, then finally nodded. I held my breath. This time, the expression on the girl's face shifted from mild irritation to deferential respect. "Yes, sir. Of course, sir."

She stood up. "If you'll follow me."

She led us down a rather spartan hall lined on one side with cubicles and filing cabinets and on the other side with offices, most occupied by harried-looking attorney types. We rounded one corner, kept going, then stopped at the next corner.

The office we entered was huge. No bare white walls here. Everything was warm wood and soft lighting. There was a wet bar, as well as a sitting area complete with magazines and a couch. A full-size map of the world completely covered one wall, which was otherwise bare and not blocked by even a single piece of furniture. A huge desk rested in front of the window, a collection of framed photographs littering the desktop, along with piles of papers.

The office gave the impression of money and power, and I'll admit I felt a little awed.

"Can I get you anything while you wait?" the girl asked. "Mr. Reardon will be in as soon as he can break free."

"We're fine," I said.

As soon as she left, I moved to the window and peered down at the people below. Stryker moved beside me and held my hand. We stood silently. We were still there when Reardon walked in ten minutes later. Short and just a little pudgy, Thomas Reardon was gray around the temples and bald everywhere else. His suit was Armani, though, and what he lacked in looks, he made up for in bearing and an aura of controlled sophistication.

"Miss Prescott, I'm so sorry to keep you waiting."

I turned to face him. "Were you expecting me?"

"Not exactly," he said. He looked at Stryker. "And you are—"

"Don't bullshit me, Reardon," Stryker said. "You know exactly who I am."

Reardon took a step backwards, apparently not expecting aggression in his own office. "I'm sorry, sir, I assure you that I don't."

I laid a hand on Stryker's wrist, a silent command to wait. We'd figure it all out in due course. "This is Matthew Stryker," I said. "What did you mean by 'Not exactly'?"

He gestured to his couch. "Would you like to sit?"

"I'd rather stand."

"All right." He took a seat behind his desk. "This is a bit unusual, but I perform many services for my clients, including the retention of private information."

"I'm not following you."

"Vaults," he said. "I have some clients who would prefer not to utilize safe-deposit boxes."

"And Grimaldi was one of those?" I asked, entirely baffled as to what that had to do with me.

"Yes. The vaults are on my property, but accessible only by the clients."

"And . . ." Stryker looked less than patient.

"And when Archie died, he left several vaults still with contents."

"What?"

"I have no idea." He nodded at me. "That's where you come in."

"Me?"

"Archie arranged for the vaults to be claimed by the individuals designated by him, who would identify themselves in various ways."

"And one way was by saying that Peter Trent sent them."

"That's right."

"And that's all you know," Stryker said.

Reardon cocked his head and studied Stryker. "What else should I know?"

"The assassin, the target. The game."

Reardon leaned back in his chair. "PSW? I'm quite familiar with PSW. How does it—?"

"Goddamn it! We've been playing the fucking game across the streets of Manhattan. There's a killer out there stalking her. Our lives have been completely turned upside down, and you're telling me you have no idea what we're talking about?"

Reardon looked from me to Stryker and back to me again. I nodded. "I . . . I'm astounded. You're saying that you've been playing PSW? The game? In the real world? That makes no sense. It must be a hoax. A copycat. Someone playing off Archie's good name."

Stryker bent low and looked him straight in the eye. "If it's a copycat, then how did they know that everything ends with you?"

"I . . ." A look of complete befuddlement washed over Reardon's face. "I don't know."

Stryker studied him, then took a step back, nodding slowly. "All right," he said. "Let's just see the vault."

Reardon looked dubious for a moment, then he stood and moved toward the map. He laid his hand on Texas. A moment later, we heard a metal grinding noise, and the wall started to scroll upwards, like an old-fashioned home movie screen, revealing a bank of miniature vaults, each with an electronic panel displaying a row of zeroes.

"Holy shit," I whispered.

Stryker squeezed my hand, and I was certain his thoughts mimicked mine: Reardon had said he'd been given a list of "various" entry codes, "Peter Trent" being one. There were at least fifty vaults there. How many were Grimaldi's? And how many were prizes for the "various" players in the game?

"Here you go," Reardon said. "Miss Prescott's box is 8A."

"Open it," Stryker said.

"Oh, no," Reardon said. He looked right at me. "I understood that you would have the code."

Chapter

70

"**O**h," I said. "Right. The code."

I moved forward tentatively, as if the wall might close behind me, locking me forever in a small room with a wall full of vaults. I brushed my hand over the front of vault 8A, my fingertips dancing over the line of sixteen zeroes. I didn't enter any numbers.

"You do have the code, don't you?" Behind me, Reardon looked concerned, as if he wasn't prepared for this turn of events.

"Fuck the code," Stryker said. "Just open the thing, Reardon."

"I can't," the lawyer said. "I'm afraid I'm not privy to the entry codes."

"No, no, no," Stryker said. "That's bullshit. No way I'm going to believe that you—"

"It's okay," I said, interrupting. "We don't need Reardon. All we need is your phone."

That surprised him. "My phone?"

I held out my hand. "Give it here."

He handed it over without question, and I started pushing buttons until I found the stored pictures. I pulled up the picture of Peter Trent's grave. Tiny. I poked around some more, feeling slightly ill until I finally managed to locate the zoom feature. There. I could just make it out. . . .

I moved back to the vault and entered the sixteen digits. The door swung open, revealing a single manila envelope.

I took it, feeling salvation under my fingers.

"How?" Stryker asked.

"Peter Trent," I said. "He holds the key. 081919220-1111980. August 19, 1922. January 11, 1980. Good thing you took a picture."

"Good thing," he said.

We opened the envelope, and when we saw what was there, Stryker went immediately to Thomas Reardon's coffee table and fired up the laptop.

The envelope held two things: an access code to an offshore account and instructions for ending the game.

We took care of the game first, logging on, navigating to the Special Instructions page, and typing 817PQWXT8 in the appropriate box. The computer flashed and beeped and generally went through such machinations that I was certain we'd completely screwed up and fed the thing a virus.

When the pyrotechnics were over, the screen held one message:

CONGRATULATIONS, MELANIE PRESCOTT
YOU ARE NO LONGER A TARGET
PRESS "SEND" TO NOTIFY ALL PLAYERS OF THE GAME'S
CONCLUSION

Under the circumstances, the message seemed a bit dry, but I wasn't inclined to complain. I pressed Send, and the message dissolved, re-forming into a new one:

MESSAGE SENT
GAME OVER
HAVE A NICE DAY

Chapter

71

Lynx pulled the taxi up near Peter Trent's grave, slammed the car into park and got out. He still couldn't believe the asshole cabdriver had let them get away. A Buick that couldn't catch a Ford Aspire? What a load of crap.

He fingered his gun and aimed a wry look at the trunk. Well, that was one mistake that driver wouldn't make again. He just hoped the mistake hadn't been too costly. He could have had her. She'd been right there, so close—and so had his money.

But she'd slipped through his fingers, and now here he was, resorting to tracking her down. The woman at the main office had been quite agreeable, pointing out which grave Mel and Stryker had visited, and circling the spot on the map. Now Lynx was here. Figuring out another goddamn clue so he could find his quarry before she solved the next one.

He shivered slightly, unable to shake the feeling that time was running out.

He pushed the feeling aside. He wasn't inclined to morbidity, and he certainly wasn't inclined to self-doubt. He'd win. Of course he would. He always won. Always had, always would. There simply was no question. It was only a matter of how and when.

The when, he hoped, would be soon.

He walked around the grave, careful not to mar the footprints already on the soft ground. The tombstone was loose, and he said a silent curse. If there'd been something hidden under there . . .

No. The clue was still here. It had to be. Anything else was unacceptable.

But where?

He fingered the lighter in his pocket, turning its smooth casing over in his hand before pulling it out and lighting a cigarette. He took a step back and examined the ground. His grandfather had taught him about the hunt, and what Pa hadn't taught, Lynx had picked up on his own. Tracking was a skill he'd honed, and he put it to good use now, finding and following their footsteps. Across the path and to the grave immediately opposite.

Thomas Reardon.

The name meant nothing to Lynx, but he noted that they'd spent some time there, moving about but not leaving. When they had left, they'd gotten back in their car.

Thomas Reardon.

Somehow that name was important. The next clue? Someone to see? To meet?

He pulled out his PDA and logged onto the Internet, going immediately to a search engine. The browser closed, however, leaving a flashing email indicator.

Lynx frowned. He'd very specifically input the settings on his Internet options. When he was in another program, the only email that should take precedence was an email from the target in an active PSW game.

And the only currently active game was . . .

He opened the email. And read the message that wasn't from Melanie Prescott but was instead generated by the game itself. It was a message he hadn't expected to see.

Game Over.
The Target Has Survived.
Assassin Status: Revoked

No.
No. He shook his head.
No. It couldn't be.
NO. He hauled back and almost let his PDA go flying, but he caught himself just in time.

This was wrong. *Wrong.* He always won.

And this game really was no different at all.

Chapter 72

Had I not actually experienced it, I don't think that I'd believe that it is really possible to spend three entire days in bed doing absolutely nothing but having sex and eating.

I can honestly report, however, that it is. Completely possible and totally yummy. And let me just add that if you're going to survive a wild chase with a crazed assassin on your tail, celebrating victory afterwards with a totally hot Marine really is the only way to go.

Really.

At least until the buzz wears off and you start to fall into that girly-girl state: How do you tell if he's really into you? Is it just sex? Does he really care? Or is this all just a by-product of adrenaline and the ultraclose quarters you'd spent time in over the course of the aforementioned wild chase?

And that pretty much sums up my mental state when Stryker

got out of bed and started pulling on a pair of sweatpants we'd bought in the little gift shop located in the Plaza's lower level.

"So, um, you're really heading out?" He'd told me he'd need to leave soon to check on his house, find his way back into his life. The whole postadventure routine, I guessed.

He moved back to the bed and planted a bone-melting kiss on me. "You okay with that?"

"Sure." I waved the question away even as I pulled the sheet up higher around my chest. "Of course I am. I mean, you have a life, right?"

He gave me that typically male look, like he really didn't know what to say to me. Like I'd turned into a She-Beast and he had to handle me with care.

I sighed. I *was* being a She-Beast. We'd had a lovely time, but it wasn't like we had any sort of commitment.

Talk about a bummer.

His eyes narrowed. "I can stay. Or you can come with me. Or I can drop you at your apartment. You probably have things to take care of, too."

"No, no. I'm fine. Really."

"You're sure?"

"Oh, please . . ." I worked hard to keep my tone light and perky. "I'm alive. I'm sexually sated and physically rested. I'm at the Plaza. And I'm about to head out on the shopping excursion to end all shopping excursions."

He laughed. "I'm flattered you haven't gone shopping already."

I felt my cheeks warm. "What can I say? You hold more appeal."

"I'm not sure I believe that, but I'm flattered."

I grinned. "Really, Stryker. Life is good."

"But you're not going home?"

"Why should I? No one's home." I'd called Jenn to hear her voice and check on the baby. She'd sounded so happy that I hadn't had the heart to dump all over her. After she got back, we'd have drinks and I'd tell her one hell of a story.

"Besides," I continued, "it's not like I can't afford to stay here for a week or two. In case you forgot, I'm rich now." Twenty million rich, less the million I'd transferred to Stryker's account. Can you believe he only got an extra hundred grand for protecting me? A measly hundred! I was willing to split the twenty with him down the middle, but he wouldn't hear of it.

He took my hand. "If you get nervous—"

"I'm *fine*. Nothing's happened in days. The game's over. Lynx has probably skipped the country. Or else he's moved on to some other target." The idea made me queasy. I wanted to use my winnings to find and help other girls like me, but so far I hadn't figured out how. I was certain that other girls—possibly guys, too—were being forced to play this game, though. Somehow, I was going to figure out a way to find them and help them.

"The cops will find him," Stryker said. "And they'll nail Reardon, too."

I made a face, not nearly as certain. Neither of us had believed Reardon, but Stryker hadn't called him on it in the office because he figured it made more sense to lay low. We'd talked to a friend of his right after we'd left Reardon's office, stopping at the local FBI field office on our way to check me in to the Plaza. Stryker's theory was that somehow Archibald Grimaldi had set the whole thing up with Reardon. No one had expected he'd die, and now Reardon was running the PSW end with who knows how much help from the inside. It was a theory that made sense, especially since Jamie Tate had been sucked into the game well before Grimaldi had died.

The agent, Devlin Brady, had promised to investigate and keep the matter quiet. He and Stryker had talked about using the cyber unit and putting some surveillance on Reardon. Surprising to me, the FBI hadn't tried to seize the money. The way Devlin had explained it, there wasn't enough evidence to tie a bad guy to the transfer of funds. Reardon wasn't under arrest, Grimaldi was dead, and the money hadn't come from Lynx. Plus, he'd added confidentially, since the money was in an offshore account, it would be near impossible for the government to get it from me.

Fine with me. I figured I earned it.

Stryker planted a warm kiss on my lips. "If you need anything, you have my number. I'll call you later and see how you're doing."

"You don't have to," I said. "Really." It's not like we'd made any promises, and it *was* time to get back to our lives. I was feeling very mature. We'd had a lovely time. I'd wanted him, he'd wanted me, and we'd gotten our fill. And, yes, I *still* wanted him. But only if I was sure it was more than just a post-trauma relationship. I didn't want to be like Sandra Bullock and Keanu Reeves in *Speed*. They seemed so great together, and then it turned out to be just sex. I mean, look who she ended up with in *Speed 2*. . . .

Stryker just shook his head and kissed me again. "I'll call you," he said firmly.

And as the door closed behind him, I realized my cheeks hurt from smiling so broadly.

Chapter

73

Sex is great. Don't get me wrong. But to *really* celebrate, shopping is required. Intense shopping. Julia Roberts in *Pretty Woman*–type shopping.

I celebrated in a big way.

I started at Givenchy, of course, and spent so much money there that they offered to have my bags delivered to my hotel room. I sputtered a bit, saying that really wasn't necessary, but the saleswoman waved off my protests. I hit Jimmy Choo next, then moved from Madison over to Fifth Avenue, where I basically bought out the street. Gucci, Prada, Fendi, Bottecelli, Bruno Magli, Henri Bendel. Manolo, of course. By the time I hit Chanel, my feet ached and I complained of being overladen with bags. The manager called the Plaza for me and arranged for a car to drive my bags back to my room. This time, I knew the drill and graciously accepted the offer. As for me, I stayed and overladened myself all over again.

After one more limo ride for my bags (following a mass of purchases at Hermès, Dior, Tods and, finally, Bergdorf's!) I aimed myself toward Elizabeth Arden's. I'd always wanted to walk through that little red door, and there was something so sweet about doing exactly that.

This having a bank account thing really is all it's cracked up to be. It almost made my near-death experience worth it.

Almost.

When I climbed into a taxi five hours later I was completely relaxed, having been massaged, oiled, shampooed, manicured, exfoliated, primped and prodded.

I felt completely marvelous. Sex, spa and shopping. The three essentials of life.

I couldn't live like this forever (though I might have to give that one some more consideration), but after the past week, I think I deserved it for a while.

The sun was just starting to set as we pulled up in front of the Plaza. I got out, gave the driver a fabulous tip and headed to my room for an extravagant evening of room service, cable television, and a follow-up try-on-everything-I-bought session.

I'd been in the room a full five minutes before I saw the note. Brown paper on the desk, and as I walked closer, I realized that my hand had drifted to my throat.

A pigpen message.

I looked around, frantic, but there was no one in the room. I checked the bathroom and armoire. No one. I went back to the door, locked the bolt and put the chain on. Then I sat down at the desk and went to work.

Five minutes later I had my translation, and my fear had dissipated.

> *Couldn't stay away. I'm in room 412.*
> *I'd love the pleasure of your company. S*

I positively sagged in relief. Stryker had my second key, so of course he'd been able to get into my room to leave the note. I'll admit I was a little surprised he'd left a pigpen message, all things considered. But I'd never been good at figuring out the way a man's mind works. . . .

It took me about four and a half seconds to change into a sleeveless white Anna Sui top coupled with a flared Nanette Lepore skirt that hit just above my knees. I added a simple diamond drop necklace that I'd picked up at Tiffany's, then slipped into the Givenchy pumps that Stryker had bought me. I did a quick pirouette in front of the mirror, then dabbed on a bit more Bobbi Brown lip tint. When I stepped outside, I realized that 412 was the room right next door. How convenient.

The door had been propped open with an ice bucket, and I knocked as I pushed it open and stepped into the suite. (Much nicer than my room. Why hadn't I thought to ask for a suite?)

"Hello? Stryker? It's me . . ."

No answer. It occurred to me that I had no idea when he'd left the note, and he probably had gravely underestimated my shopping stamina. He probably had expected me back hours ago. Had he gone down to the bar? The restaurant?

The shower.

I hadn't heard it at first, but now I clearly heard the pounding of water coming from the bathroom. I headed that way, sashaying a little as I walked, more than willing to play the role of vixen.

"Hey, gorgeous," I sang as I moved into the steamy room. "Want company?"

Again, no answer, and I realized with a start that there wasn't anyone in there. Just an empty shower, spraying hot water into an empty stall.

From the main room, I heard a sharp click. The door closing.

"Stryker?"

No answer.

And that's when I realized. That's when I knew.

I was completely and totally screwed.

Chapter

74

I didn't wait to find out if I was wrong. Instead, I slammed the bathroom door shut and locked it. The lock was flimsy, though, and I knew it wasn't keeping Lynx out for any length of time. It wouldn't be any trick at all to aim a bullet at the doorknob, or even to just ram the door with his shoulder.

Basically, I was dead meat.

I looked around the bathroom, hoping for something heavy I could put in front of the door, or a window I could squeeze through. No such luck. I lunged in the direction of the phone, only to realize it had been ripped out of the wall. The window wasn't big enough for my head, much less my hips. And everything heavy—toilet, clawfoot tub, bidet—was bolted down.

Think, dammit, think!

I couldn't escape, which meant that all I could do was try to defend myself. I held my breath as I examined everything in the bathroom, Stryker's words echoing through my head—*Anything can be a weapon.*

Right. But what?

My eye caught the towel bar, and I frowned. Maybe . . .

I gave it a little tug, and sure enough, the ends came easily out of the brackets. I hefted it, testing its weight and firmness. Not a tire iron, but it would do. Or, rather, it was going to have to do.

So far, I hadn't heard any noise coming from the other room, and I wanted to cling to the tiny hope that maybe I was completely wrong and overreacting and would feel incredibly foolish in about five minutes when Stryker asked me what the hell I was doing holed up in the bathroom with a towel bar.

I could hope, but I wasn't laying odds.

And speaking of odds, I really wanted to increase mine. Unfortunately, my tools (i.e., the Plaza's well-stocked bathroom) were sadly lacking in the self-protection arena. I took one more glance around and saw the lavender-scented squirty soap next to the sink.

Not foolproof, but it just might work. . . .

Chapter 75

The doorknob rattled, and I bit my lip, afraid that if I didn't, I'd open my mouth and scream.

I stood off to one side but relatively near the door. I figured he'd expect me to be as far away as possible. I also figured he was pissed as hell and just wanted me out of the picture. That said, I expected him to come in with his gun drawn, sight me, and take me down.

I hoped that, by being this close to the door, I'd buy myself a few precious seconds.

I'd see soon enough if I was right.

The doorknob rattled again, this time with more persistence.

My heart picked up tempo, the beat so loud I was certain the guests in surrounding rooms would hear it and dial 911.

Silence.

No shaking of the knob. No heavy breathing. No click of a gun chamber being pulled back.

I waited, my body tense, my breath coming in shaky bursts.

Nothing.

I tightened my grip on the towel bar.

Nothing.

I shifted my stance for better leverage.

Noth—*crash!*

The door flew open, and Lynx stepped in, entering with his gun, his feet following. He turned, saw me, and I swung. At the same time that he fired, he put his foot down, landing in the slick surface of soap I'd spread on the floor. His feet shot out from under him, the gun discharging into the ceiling instead of my face.

I didn't even have time to congratulate myself. My towel bar was already on the move again, and I caught him about shoulder height. He bellowed and the gun went flying, sliding along the greased-up floor to rest under the clawfoot tub, way back by the wall.

I didn't try to get it. I just ran.

I followed the soapless path I'd left for myself, racing out into the room toward the safety of the door. Almost there. Almost there.

Almost—

His hands closed around my ankles, and I went flying to the floor. I twisted, kicking wildly as he tried to get a grip on my ankles or legs with his now slippery, soapy hands.

"Bitch! You fucking bitch!"

He was screaming wildly at me, one hand scrabbling for

purchase somewhere on my body, the other popping open a hunting knife.

I landed one good kick and got him in the face. As he howled in pain, I managed to get to my feet, knocking a coffee table over in the process and sending a lamp to shatter against the floor.

I ran toward the door faster than I'd ever moved before.

He'd bolted every lock, and my fingers slipped over the cool metal. He was up now, coming after me.

I got the first lock open.

If he caught me with that knife . . .

My fingers fumbled, but I got the chain off. I could see him out of the corner of my eye, coming at me, knife drawn.

I pulled the door open, and there was Stryker.

"Down!"

I hit the ground. He fired. And Lynx went down.

Stryker stepped around me and stood over Lynx's motionless form. He aimed his gun and fired one final shot into the bastard's head.

This time, it really was over.

Stryker held a hand out and helped me up. I took it gratefully, then folded myself into the strong comfort of his arms.

"Good timing," I said after an eternity had passed. "How did you know?"

"I didn't. I came back because I thought you deserved a sunset ride through the park in one of those horse-drawn carriages. I went in and . . ." He dangled the sheet of paper with the code. "It was on your desk."

I tilted my head back and flashed him a weak smile. "You interpreted it?"

He laughed and kissed my forehead. "Codes are your territory, remember? I just thought it was fucking strange. And when I heard the crash . . ."

I put my arms around his neck and kissed him. I remember thinking, when this whole thing started, that I needed a knight in shining armor. Thanks to Stryker, I had one.

Epilogue

It rained the day of Todd's funeral, which was appropriate, considering my mood. As the coffin was lowered into the ground, I took Stryker's hand, and we headed back toward the car he'd rented to drive me to the funeral and then to the airport.

"You okay?"

I shrugged. "I'm glad to know Todd wasn't involved. I just wish he were still alive."

"I know. I'm sorry."

They'd found Todd's body in the East River about a week ago. Apparently Thomas or Grimaldi or some other behind-the-scenes asshole had tossed his name into the game mix. Just a little red herring to keep things interesting.

I still felt a little numb from the now-certain news of his death. A little numb about everything, really.

"You sure you're up to this?" Stryker added.

I knew what he meant. "Yeah, I'm sure. Besides, a week with my mom will make me forget all my troubles. I'll have new troubles to deal with, or I'll be focused on her troubles. But it definitely won't be all about Melanie." I managed a little smile. "Besides, I promised them an explanation."

I knew more now, so I could tell a good story. I knew that the cops had found nothing in Lynx's computer that would identify the person pulling the strings. Neither Stryker's computer nor Jenn's laptop had been any help either. All had been confiscated and were now somewhere with the FBI.

We paused by the passenger side of the car, Stryker trying to keep the umbrella over my head while he opened the door.

"You don't have to drive me, you know." I knew what a burden an airport drive was. I was solidly in relationship territory. I wasn't, however, certain that Stryker was aware of that unspoken little rule. We'd seen each other almost every day since he'd shot Lynx, but were we in a relationship? I really wasn't sure. And I didn't have the heart to ask. I didn't want to be disappointed. "I can catch a cab," I added.

"I can drive you," he said, ushering me inside. "And I have something for you." He bent down and retrieved a packet of papers off the floorboards.

I took the packet and riffled through the pages, then looked up at him quizzically.

"Applications," he said. "I put the NSA application on top."

"I see that."

"You're good, Mel. Teach if you want, but don't limit your options. Not yet."

"Thanks," I said. The gesture almost moved me to tears, and

I didn't tell him that I'd already downloaded a ton of applications. They were in my suitcase, and I'd already planned to get busy on them while I was hanging out with my parents in Houston.

"We'd better get going," he said. But before he closed the door he added one last thing. "If it's all the same to you, I'll meet you after your flight back next week and drive you home. We can grab dinner on the way. Spend the evening together. The next morning, too."

"Sure thing," I said. I tried to sound casual, but as he walked around the car to the driver's side, I allowed myself fifteen seconds of thinking that this was a very, very good sign.

And as we sped through the rain and away from the cemetery, I couldn't help but think that it was time to put the past in the past, because I had a fine man and a fine future waiting for me.

Good-bye, Gap. Hello, Givenchy.

Up Close and Personal
with the Author

I've never been fond of interviews—I'm always afraid I'll stumble over my words or not say something witty or pithy enough to be remarkable. So when I found out that I had to interview myself about *The Givenchy Code*, I was, naturally, nervous. After all, who better than me knew that I had edited my school paper for over three years? That my college major started as journalism (before switching to film)? Clearly, I was a hard-hitting reporter. Would I be able to survive such an incisive, cutting interview, pitted as I would be against someone like myself?

You can imagine the state of my nerves when I sat down across the table from myself, praying that I'd be gentle in my interview technique. Here's how it went:

ME: Have you always wanted to be a writer?

ME: That's it? That's your hard-hitting question?

ME: Hey, give me a break. I'm just getting warmed up.

ME: Yeah, right. Probably can't think of anything more interesting.

ME: Are you going to answer the question, or what?

ME: The answer is yes. I've wanted to be a writer from the time I was tiny. I had a few detours wanting to be a veterinarian (allergic to dogs; ruled that out) and a Broadway musical theater diva (can't sing), but from the get-go I wanted to tell stories. More, I wanted to tell them on paper. I wrote long "novels" at the age of three, banging out nonsense on my dad's typewriter. Later, I started writing short stories, taking up an entire legal pad, front and back, with my handwritten scribbles that my mom would patiently type up for me. (I realize now just how patient my mom was, as the stories, while not horrible, weren't exactly fabulous. My handwriting, however, was). I wrote poems, I started and abandoned novels, I wrote screenplays. I pretty much piddled around with writing my whole life, never doing much with it, and going in fits and starts, with long stretches too filled with other things (specifically, law school and the subsequent pressures of a big-firm job) to allow for any leisure time to accommodate writing.

ME: So if you had no time to write, how'd you end up getting published? Ha! How's *that* for hard-hitting? Caught you, didn't I?

ME: You are *so* not Woodward or Bernstein! The fact is, there just came a point when writing became more important to me than not writing. When I knew that I wanted to be an author more than I wanted any other job. I pretty much gave up all my leisure activities, and my non-work time was consumed with writing.

ME: And now?

ME: Now I've reclaimed some of my leisure time. As of the summer of 2004, I'm writing full time!

ME: What was the job you gave up?

ME: I was an attorney.

ME: Ah.

ME: "Ah"? What's "ah" supposed to mean?

ME: Just that there seem to be a lot of attorneys out there writing books.

ME: What are you insinuating?

ME: (Innocently) Not a thing.

ME: (Glares suspiciously)

ME: OK, let's move on. How about the idea of the book? How did it come about?

ME: I've always loved treasure hunts. The idea of following a clue to another clue, and then to another. The first birthday party that I remember, my mom sent all us kids on a hunt. It was fabulous (My mom now tells me that from her end it was hell, but I guess that means she loves me!). When I was in high school, I actually sent some friends on a treasure hunt. Yeah, I know, it sounds geeky and weird, but I *was* geeky and weird, so there you go. I'd write out clues and if my friends interpreted them, they would be led to the next clue, and on and on until they found the final prize. Amazingly, no one suspected that it was me pulling the strings of this hunt.

ME: The book, Julie. I was asking about the book.

ME: Right. At any rate, I'd had this vague idea that a "Follow the clues" book would be fun. But the stakes needed to be really high. I wasn't pursuing the idea actively, just letting it simmer. And then one day, Melanie appeared in my head along with her story. A woman forced to solve codes in order to stay alive.

ME: The book is told in both first and third person. How did that come about?

ME: Actually, I tried to write the book entirely in Mel's point of view, but I just couldn't do it. Stryker wanted his fifteen minutes of fame, too. And so did Lynx. I originally wrote Stryker's first scene more or less as it is, then tried to translate it into first person from Mel's point of view. Didn't work. And so I finally realized that this particular story needed to be told from a mix of first and third person.

ME: Why not write Stryker's point of view in first person, too?

ME: I have absolutely no idea. All I can say is that it didn't "feel" right.

ME: How did the codes come about? Did you make them all up?

ME: Yup. And some of them were just serendipitous. OK, spoiler here, so don't read the rest of the answer if you haven't read the book. I included the equation for the catenary curve without any clear idea of where it was going. So I had a reference to St. Michael and to St. Louis. I knew I wanted the characters to go to St. Patrick Cathedral's because I *had* to include the reference to the 666 address. But I had no idea how to get them there. So I checked the Internet and Oh.My.Gosh, it turns out that there is a St. Michael and St. Louis altar in St. Patrick's Cathedral. I'd had no idea. It was like kismet.

ME: What about the 666 address? Why did you "have" to use it?

ME: OK, this is a really weird story. St. Pat's is on Fifth Avenue, and the first time I was in New York City, I was a sophomore in high school on a drama club trip. At the time, I was writing pretty bad poetry in my spare time. So we're walking around, and I see that from the cathedral's front steps, you can see a building that has prominently displayed the address 666, which, if you've seen *The Omen*, you know has scary implications. After the trip, I went home and wrote a poem about that juxtaposition. (And no, I won't include the poem here. Maybe, sometime, if I'm feeling like baring my teenage angst soul, I'll post it on my website.)

Fast-forward a few (very few, ahem) years to the writing of this book. I'm including NYC stuff, so, of course, I put in a reference to the 666 across from the cathedral. Then, after the book is turned in, but before I'd done revisions, I visited New York. I went to Fifth Avenue to check that location and . . . gasp! . . . no 666. I freaked. My editor assured me she didn't think I was nuts, even though she didn't remember the 666. I, of course, thought that I must be insane. Fortunately, the Internet came through again. I did a search and found other references to the odd congruence of church and address marker. The address is gone now (don't know why) but it *was* there, and if I can remember it, so can Melanie!

ME: Are we going to see more of Mel and Stryker?

ME: Absolutely. They show up again in *The Manolo Matrix*, though they aren't the main characters. Right now, *Manolo* is scheduled for March 2006 (but be sure to check my website in case that changes: www.juliekenner.com) and I'm working on the book right now!

ME: Okay, that about wraps this up. I'm thinking Pulitzer for my hard-hitting analysis.

ME: I'm thinking not . . .

They're sexy, smart, and strong . . .
they're the

NAUGHTY GIRLS OF DOWNTOWN PRESS!

Turn the page for excerpts
of the other Naughty Girls
of Downtown Press

AWAKEN ME DARKLY
Gena Showalter

DIRTY LITTLE SECRETS
Julie Leto

LETHAL
Shari Shattuck

Available from Downtown Press
Published by Pocket Books

Awaken Me Darkly

GENA SHOWALTER

First rule of fighting: Stay calm.

Second rule: Never let your emotions overtake you.

I'd broken both rules the moment I began following him.

Kyrin swept out of my way, and I flew past him. The storm had died, but the sun hid behind angry gray clouds, offering hazy visibility. Because of the sheen of ice at my feet, I had trouble stopping and turning.

Definitely not optimal conditions; however, I wouldn't back down.

"You do not want to fight me, Mia."

I whipped around. "Wanna bet on that too?" I sprang forward again, intending to kick out my leg and knock him flat this time, but he reached me first. He grappled me to the ground, pinned my shoulders to the ice, and imprisoned me with his body. Cold at my back, pure heat on top. Neither was acceptable to me.

"Still want to fight?" he asked.

"Fuck yes." I quickly landed a blow to his groin. Yeah, I intended to fight dirty. He doubled over, and I shot to my feet, slipped, then steadied.

Using his prone position to my advantage, I was able to land a blow to his left side and knock the deoxygenated air from his lung. He grunted in pain and sudden breathlessness.

I darted to his right and gave a booted strike. This time, he grabbed my ankle and toppled me to the ground. I lost my satisfaction, felt a moment of desperation. We struggled there, rolling on top of each other, fighting for dominance.

Physically, he had me at a disadvantage, and we both knew it. He could have attempted to smother me, but he didn't.

"It doesn't have to be this way," he panted.

Think, Mia, think.

I still had full use of my legs, and I made total use of them. I gave a scissor-lock squeeze around his midsection, forcing him to release my arms and focus on my legs. That's all I needed. With a four-finger jab to his trachea, his air supply was momentarily cut off in a whoosh, giving me the perfect opportunity to spring free.

My old combat instructor would have been proud.

I took stock of my options. I had to render him uncon-
scious if I hoped to win. He'd defeat me, otherwise. I would
have to be merciless, but stop short of killing him. I needed
his help, after all. His blood. I didn't want to spill a single
drop on this cold, hard ice.

"Concede, damn you," I growled, circling him like a ti-
gress locked on her prey.

"You first," he said, still on his knees.

"I am almost done playing with you," he said.

"Play with this." I launched a flying spin punt into his
side.

Quicker than I could blink, he advanced on me. He used
his weight to push into me, stumbling me backward. When
my body came into contact with his, the strength hidden beneath his clothing jolted me. He was made of solid muscle,
easily outweighing me by a hundred pounds, but he didn't
once use the power hidden in his fists to strike me down.
Why? I wondered, even as I punched him hard in the nose.
His head jerked to the side; he made no move to counter.
Why didn't he return attack? Why did he go out of his way
not to hurt me?

I circled him, but he surprised me by grabbing my jacket
and tugging. The ice at my feet aided him. Suddenly off balance, I tumbled into him, keeping a viselike grip. His warm
breath washed over my face as he leaned close.

"Now you will concede this victory to me," he ground out
low in his throat.

"When you haven't hit me once?" I said, a cocky edge to

my tone. I'd fought enough opponents to know Kyrin had had plenty of opportunities, but I wasn't going to admit *that* aloud.

His eyes darkened, revealing a hint of wickedness, and he leaned down until our lips brushed once, twice. Soft kisses, languid kisses. Innocent kisses.

Dirty Little Secrets

JULIE LETO

"I remember when you used to stroke me like that."

Marisela Morales punctuated her pickup line by blowing on the back of Francisco Vega's neck. She watched the soft downy strands on his nape spike and knew her luck had finally turned around.

His fingers, visible as she glanced over his shoulder, drew streaks through the condensation on his beer bottle. Up and down. Slow and straight. Lazy, but precise. He toyed with his *cerveza* the same way he'd once made love to her, and for a split second, a trickle of moist heat curled intimately between Marisela's thighs. For the moment, the part of her Frankie used to oh-so-easily manipulate was safe, encased beneath silky panties and skin-tight, hip-hugging jeans.

Tonight, she'd have him—but on her terms. The hunter had found her prey. Now, she just had to bring him in.

"I don't remember taking time for slow strokes when you and me got busy, *niña*."

Marisela sighed, teasing his neck with her hot breath one more time before she slid onto the bar stool next to his. She'd been trying to track the man down for nearly a week. Who knew Frankie would turn up at an old haunt? Since they'd parted ways, Club Electric, a white box on the outside, hot joint on the inside, had changed names, hands, and clientele a good dozen times. But a few things remained constant—the music, the raw atmosphere—and the availability of men like Frankie, who defined the word *caliente*.

Like the song said: *Hot, hot, hot.*

"We were young then," Marisela admitted with a shrug, loosening the holster strap that cradled the cherished 9mm Taurus Millennium she wore beneath her slick leather jacket. "Now, I'm all grown up."

Marisela wiggled her crimson fingernails at Theresa, the owner of the club. The way the older woman's face lit up, Marisela figured she was going to get more than a drink. *Damn.* Marisela loved Theresa as if she were her aunt, but now wasn't the time for . . .

"Oh, Marisela! *Mija,* how can I thank you for what you did?"

The sentiment was as loud as it was sincere. So she'd done

a nice thing for Theresa. The world didn't have to know. Good deeds could ruin her reputation.

And a simple thank-you wasn't enough for Theresa. She stepped up onto the shelf on the other side of the bar and practically launched herself into Marisela's arms. Rolling her eyes at Frankie, Marisela gave the owner a genuine squeeze. She deserved as much. She was a good listener, kept great secrets, and mixed the best *Cuba Libre* in town.

"*De nada,* Theresa," Marisela said, gently disentangling herself. She appreciated the woman's gratitude, but she had work to do.

"Anything for you. Anytime. For you, drinks are on the house from now on, okay? You and . . . your friend."

Even as she tried to be the courteous hostess, Theresa's voice faltered when her eyes met Frankie's. Marisela's ex hadn't been in the neighborhood for years. And in that time, he'd aged. His skin, naturally dark, now sported a rough texture, complete with a scar that traced just below his bottom lip. His jaw seemed sharper and his once perfect nose now shifted slightly to the right—likely the result of an untreated break. Even if he hadn't matured from a devilish boy to a clearly dangerous man, he likely wouldn't be recognized by anyone but Marisela and a few others who'd once known him well—the very "others" Marisela had made sure wouldn't come into Club Electric again, on Theresa's behalf.

"I never say no to free booze," Marisela answered. "*Gracias,* Theresa."

Theresa blew Marisela a kiss, patted her cheek, then

moved aside to work on her drink. To most people, a *Cuba Libre* was just rum and Coke with lime. To Marisela, it was a taste of heaven.

"What did you do for her?" Frankie asked, his voice even, as if he wasn't really curious.

Marisela knew better. She slid her arms on the bar, arching her back, working out the kinks in her spine while giving Frankie an unhampered view of her breasts. She didn't want him to waste his curiosity on what she'd done for Theresa; she wanted to pique his interest another way.

"Last week, *las Reinas* chose this bar as their new hangout. Not quite the clientele Theresa has in mind. Gangs aren't exactly good for business. I politely asked them to pick someplace else."

"Politely?" Frankie asked, his dark eyebrows bowed over his hypnotic eyes. "Last I remember, *las Reinas* didn't respond well to polite."

Marisela shrugged. She'd earned a great deal of respect from her former gang by choosing to bleed out. She'd used every fighting skill she'd ever learned, every survival instinct she'd ever experienced, to escape a lifelong bond to the gang. But she'd survived. Barely.

"They've learned some manners while you've been gone. Lots of things have changed. Like," she said, snagging his beer around the neck and taking a sip, "I don't settle for fast and furious no more."

Lethal

SHARI SHATTUCK

Through the silver rain dripping from the rim of my umbrella our eyes connected with a sharp magnetic click.

Boom.

I couldn't look away, didn't want to. He was gorgeously Japanese, tall and slim, about forty, dressed in a flawless black suit with a long overcoat. His straight dark hair had a deep glossiness that women would kill for, cut so that the front was long, meeting the shorter hair in the back, and moved over his brow in a sexy sweep as he walked with a smooth, sure, long-legged gait, with his black flashers fixed on my blue ones.

Ooh baby.

I entertained an arousing picture of him moving underneath me with that same grace, his hands firmly on my hips, mine pressed against his smooth bare chest, or sunk in that thick luxurious mane to give me a handhold, traction. If I hadn't been walking, I would have crossed my legs.

We were fifteen paces away and about to pass each other. Still his eyes held me, smiling a secret between us, and I felt that thrilling hook of a sexual jolt that I love so much, but that happens so rarely. I returned the smile knowingly and then continued past him and on into the open doorway of the bookstore, where I lowered my umbrella and shook off the rain.

I thought, He's watching me, waiting for me to turn. Arching my back just enough to accentuate my curves and opening my raincoat to reveal them, I turned flirtatiously and looked up.

But he was gone. Nasty little shock to my ego. Most likely he'd disappeared into one of the second-floor restaurants in the Little Tokyo Plaza in downtown L.A. Damn. Oh well. My dark green umbrella stood out from the several common black ones when I leaned it next to the door and turned to search for treasure in the Japanese-American bookstore.

I browsed in and out of the aisles for at least thirty minutes, picking out the biggest, most expensive picture books as well as some sexy paperback comics, selecting one with a sharp-eyed, dark-haired hero that reminded me of Evan. I flipped through a few pages and admired the artwork—the hero with a gun, the hero with a sexy half-naked blonde. Smiling to myself, I thought, It *is* us, and I anticipated showing it to him that evening. Turning another page I saw an illustration where the heroine stood over the body of a bad guy with a smoking gun, and I thought of how I had met Evan that way. Except I had been the one with the smoking gun.

Back on the street I continued on through the clean, sparsely populated shopping area. I wondered if it was the rain that made the place feel so deserted. As I crossed a concrete bridge over a subterranean shopping level, I leaned out a bit to try to see what was down there.

What was down there was a girl, a man, and an ugly confrontation.

A large man, in an ill-fitting suit and a baggy overcoat, had backed a pretty Asian girl up against a wall in an awkward niche behind the curved stairs. No one on the same level with them could have seen the two, hidden as they were by the wall.

The girl was turning her head away from the man as he pressed against her, talking to her fast and angrily. I froze and looked all around me. Nobody. I backed up a few steps to the top of the stairway, keeping my eyes on what was happening below me. Neither of them had seen me. The stairway curved slightly, and I would be out of sight for a few seconds. I started down the stairs as noisily as possible. Hoping that it would scare the man away.

I coughed. I cleared my throat. I stamped down the stairs with purpose. Instead of going the obvious, straight way into the shopping tunnel I turned right into the little nook, which reeked of urine, and coughed loudly again. But even a few feet away the man seemed oblivious. He was so focused on the girl and spewing his anger at her that he didn't even seem to hear me. The girl's eyes, however, shot to me, and there was a plea in them. *Don't leave me,* they begged.

The man noticed her glance and followed her gaze.

"Just keep going, it's none of your business," he snarled at me.

"See, it looks more like personal than business to me," I said. It was all I could think of.

"Keep walking, we're fine." He tried to smile. "Just a little disagreement, that's all. Isn't that right, sweetheart?" He shook the girl a little, prompting her to answer.

But I could see her answer as her eyes looked down between the two of them and then back up at me.

Instead I stepped in, almost casually, and smiled in what I hoped was a disarming and polite way.

"How about it 'sweetheart'?" I directed at the girl. "You think you two can work this out without counseling?"

"Take a fucking hike!" the man growled at me, raising the gun toward me, to scare me. It worked. The girl saw him aim at me, and with a scream, she grabbed at the weapon; I knew that was a mistake. With the umbrella in my left hand I swung down even as his arm came up, trying to point the gun and both their hands toward the ground, knowing it was hopeless, that his arm was far stronger than the flimsy aluminum and nylon. The man grabbed the girl by the hair with his other hand and threw her toward me. I heard the gun go off, felt a pressure against my stomach as the girl screamed and hit me, shoving me—books, umbrella, and all—to the ground. My left hand flew up, and the back of it smashed against the concrete wall. In my abdomen I felt a sharp, stabbing pain. I've been hit, I thought. Oh God, I've been shot.

"I don't see anything," she told me.

"Here," I gestured, pointing to where the pain was, low on my right side. Efficiently but gently, she pulled down the edge of my slacks, I was conscious of the rain, light now, falling on my bare skin.

"It's just a scratch," she said, "but it looks like a nasty bruise is coming up. Maybe some internal bleeding, we need to get you to a hospital."

"What?" I sputtered. "Where's the round?"

"I don't know," she said, shrugging, "maybe it bounced off you." She pulled the edges of my white mackintosh, now sadly limp and dingy, over me. Then she retrieved my dented umbrella and held it over my face.

Quite a crowd had gathered now, and I was disgusted to see several of them had video cameras running. What a world.

"By the way," said my capable nurse, "my name is Aya, Aya Aikosha."

"Nice to meet you, Aya. I'm Callaway Wilde."

"Thank you, Ms. Wilde." Her beautiful dark eyes searched mine. "That was very brave. Thank you."

"Oh, that." I dismissed it, for the second time that day thinking of the man who had tried to kill me a year ago and ended up dead on the sidewalk. "That was nothing." I waved a hand. "Call me Cally."

Good books are like shoes... You can never have too many.

Best of Friends
Cathy Kelly
Yes, you can have it all! Just be sure to share...

I'm With Cupid
Diane Stingley
What happens when Cupid wastes your arrow on a guy who isn't worthy of true like—let alone love?

Irish Girls Are Back in Town
Cecelia Ahern, Patricia Scanlan, Gemma O'Connor, and many more of your favorite Irish writers!
Painting the town green was just the beginning...

The Diva's Guide to Selling Your Soul
Kathleen O'Reilly
Sign on the dotted line—and get everything you *ever* wanted.

Exes and Ohs
Beth Kendrick
When new loves meet old flames, stand back and watch the fireworks.

Dixieland Sushi
Cara Lockwood
Love is always a culture shock.

Balancing in High Heels
Eileen Rendahl
It's called *falling* in love for a reason... and she's working without a net.

Cold Feet
Elise Juska, Tara McCarthy, Pamela Ribon, Heather Swain, and Lisa Tucker
Something old, something new, something borrowed—and a fast pair of running shoes.

Around the World in 80 Dates
Jennifer Cox
What if your heart's desire isn't in your own backyard? You go out and find him.

Try these Downtown Press bestsellers on for size!

American Girls About Town
Jennifer Weiner, Adriana Trigiani, Lauren Weisberger, and more!
Get ready to paint the town
red, white, and blue!

Luscious Lemon
Heather Swain
In life, there's always a twist!

Why Not?
Shari Low
She should have looked before she leapt.

Don't Even Think About It
Lauren Henderson
Three's company...Four's a crowd.

Too Good to Be True
Sheila O'Flanagan
Sometimes all love needs is a wing and a prayer.

In One Year and Out the Other
Cara Lockwood, Pamela Satran, and more
Out with the old, in with the new,
and on with the party!

Do You Come Here Often?
Alexandra Potter
Welcome back to Singleville: Population 1.

The Velvet Rope
Brenda L. Thomas
Life is a party. But be careful who you invite...

Hit Reply
Rocki St. Claire
What's worse than spam and scarier than getting a computer virus?
An Instant Message from the guy who got away...